Bloom

Bloom

BELLEBIRD JAMES

THE REAL VOYAGE OF DISCOVERY
CONSISTS NOT IN SEEKING
NEW LANDSCAPES,
BUT IN HAVING NEW EYES.

—MARCEL PROUST

For Poppy and Arlo

One

When Dad died, it rewired Mom's DNA and spat out an unrecognizable version. She was desperate to change, while I wanted everything to remain the same. That's why I'm shocked when she taps me on the shoulder while I'm at work planting in the forest behind the lake house. This is where we spent every summer; Dad is gone, but the lake and forest and everything about being here is an embodiment of him. A reminder.

I swing around to face Mom, and pull my earphones, cutting the soothing monotone voice of the podcast on restoring wildlife to urban areas.

Frown lines crinkle her forehead; they never used to, but now they're a permanent feature, and just like her pointy heels, slim-fitting white pencil skirt, and perfectly pressed blush-pink blouse, I don't know or understand this version of her that feels too delicate for the tangled overhanging branches and rugged forest floor paths.

"Hey, wanna dig in?" I say, holding up a sapling from the black tub next to me.

Before Dad died, she'd be in her cargo pants and tank top, smelling of sunblock, on her knees digging in plants with me.

"Oh, god no. Don't have time." And she stands there in silence, leaving me confused about why she's here. For three years, she's refused to talk about Dad or his plants or any of his environmental lawyering work, let alone *be* here.

Mom and Dad were both environmental lawyers, madly passionate about restoring wildlife, and it was so ingrained, such a part of us, I stupidly assumed that would remain the same. A version of her I assumed would never change.

"Everything okay?" I say.

She stands there stiffly, like she can't get away soon enough.

"I've got clothes ya can borrow, ha ha," I say, trying to lighten the mood. I rest the plant I'm holding in the hole I've just dug. "Got a spare uniform," I say, pulling my *Balducci Landscape Design* t-shirt away from my stomach. "We could swim after."

But she doesn't find it funny; a stupid joke. Mom's less than happy about the full-time summer job that Dad got me, as part-time paid assistant landscape designer for Mr. Balducci. And part-time unpaid volunteer tree planter to re-establish the forest around the lake, a project started by Dad and Mr. B.

"How can I help, Mom?" Whatever the reason she's here, it must be important.

"Izz, Jen from the office. Her daughter got her law acceptance letter today."

Nerves grip my insides. My desperate need to be accepted into law is the only thing that remains the same. And the only thing we talk about. It's the only thing we are both one hundred percent on the same page about.

"Have you checked?" Mom asks.

Like three hours ago. She says it like I don't know today is the first day that acceptance letters go out. That's why I'm here, buried in plants and dirt, because it's the only thing distracting me from the fact that if I don't get in, I have zero other plans.

"Not checked since this morning before work," I say.

"Well." Her hand rests on her hip.

I remove my gardening gloves as we walk through the forest, Mom on her tiptoes navigating the path to minimize the risk of dirt on her shoes, me plowing through in my steel-cap work boots, until we reach the parking lot and my work truck parked in front of the lake. The deep, forest-clad valley flanks the crystal blue lake water that floats for miles.

The reception is patchy in the forest and marginally better in the parking lot.

I don't bother trying to log on to the university portal. Out here, the website will time out before it loads.

I call admissions and hope Kate is on.

"Hello, Law Admissions; you're speaking with Kate. How may I help you?"

I wander to the bench seat on the lakefront and take in the view of the wooden jetty stretching far into the water. Mom follows and stands next to me.

"Hi, Kate, results come out today. Just wondering if you'd mind checking my status."

"Ah, Elizabeth, I thought I might hear from you today."

There's silence. Mom's stare is boring into me; my heart is banging against my chest, the beat filling my ears. I focus on the lake's edge, the sun and thin whisper of clouds reflected in the water.

"Umm, says pending," Kate says.

Inside, I'm unravelling.

I have gotten to know Kate, and I ask her a list of questions about the final date acceptance letters are sent out. It's safe to say she's patient—unlike Mom, who lets out a heavy sigh; I know she got the gist of the conversation.

Mom wanders to the weathered hut that sits on the lake's edge. She pauses in front of the veranda, the paint on the steps worn through to the wood. I know for certain she won't go inside.

"They'll tell me soon," I call.

Mom says nothing for a moment. Like she's contemplating or reminiscing.

"You'll find out soon enough." I hold in my worries and doubts, not daring to say, *What if I don't get in?* It's the only thing connecting me to the mom I knew and the dad I lost, and the only career I can see myself happy in for the next fifty years. I suck up the fear. Before, when I could trust, she'd wrap me in a warm, comforting hug and fill my mind with endless positivity about how things would work out. But that version of her died with Dad, and I'm too afraid to contemplate what will remain if this one last thread that's keeping us attached is cut. If I don't get in, she'll be a stranger.

She returns to her car. *Housing Co. Property Developers* is written in elegant script on the side panel of her BMW. Well, technically, Mike's. Less than six months after we buried Dad, Mom and property developer Mike began a whirlwind enemies-to-lovers romance. Mom, once a staunch environmental lawyer, worked for Dad, and together they despised Mike for butchering local forests to build subdivisions with cookie-cutter mansions. But somewhere along the line, hate turned into love, and he became consistent with Mom's theme of reinventing herself. She ditched law and began working for Mike. I'm the last in the family to continue Dad's legacy; I want to become an environmental lawyer and stay an environmental lawyer, because that's what's holding me together and it's the only thing that makes sense.

"It will be okay." She gives me her fake smile. Which cuts, because she's worried I won't get in, but not nearly as worried as I am.

Two

In the kitchen, I make toast and sit at the table. Mom dumps her bag on the chair next to me; she's wearing a fitted tank top and yoga pants. Mike, wearing a gym top and shorts, bursts into the kitchen. Sleepovers have a whole new meaning when they include your mom and her new boyfriend-slash-business partner. It's not that he's not nice. He's just not Dad. Though I like that he doesn't try to be.

Mom rests her hands around my shoulders, pulling me into an awkward backward hug. "We gotta go. See you tonight; text if you hear anything. No, wait, call me immediately."

Mike grabs his keys off the hook by the door and swings his arm around Mom's shoulders. "Ready? Wanna come, Izz? We're doing an outdoor yoga class at the botanical gardens. Sound like your kinda jam?"

"Oh, sounds cool, but—" I point to my cargo pants, then steel-cap boots, "planting up at Mrs. Wilson's today. Thanks, though." I chug the last of my coffee.

"Well, that sucks. Not much longer, and ya won't have to spend your Saturdays gardening." He says it like gardening is a bad thing. It's not. He just doesn't get it, but it's nice that he tries.

Eli walks into the kitchen wearing nothing but his mountain-biking shorts. "Sup."

The tan lines across his arms and around his neck form the outline of his mountain-biking t-shirt. Since he ditched law, he splits his time between living at home and roaming the country, chasing auditions and sleeping in his car. Much to Mom's horror.

"Do you ever wear clothes?"

"On special occasions." He smirks, which cuts because it makes him the spitting image of Dad.

"Not heard from Highmont yet?"

"No," I huff out, resting my elbows on the table and cupping my face in my hands. "Other people have heard, though."

Eli lifts the chocolate milk container from the fridge, flips the top, and guzzles it before placing the carton back in the refrigerator. "You've got this, Izz. Really." Wiping the chocolate milk dripping down his chin, he wraps his arms around me, ruffling my hair. "You'll get in, and if not Highmont, one other for sure." He rests his hands on my shoulders. "If that's what you really want." A sentiment he repeats all the time since quitting law school to follow his acting dreams. He smiles more now, even if he has zero actual plan. "I'm hitting the tracks. I'll give ya a lift to work when I'm back."

Eli drops me off outside work. Wooden letters hanging from the window spell *Balducci Landscape Design*; underneath, plants crowd the shop face. A green oasis amongst high-end fashion shops and the most popular cafés Rockridge offers.

Usually, I'm the first employee to arrive, and my job is to set up the display of plants outside the shop. And I've gotten good at making it chic. Today, someone's beaten me to it, and it's giving thrift-store vibes. I inspect the planter boxes outside filled with a haphazard eclectic mix of plants with zero color coordination or logical order. Crammed together are the marigolds, lavender, and vegetable seedlings, and sticky-taped to the window, a tacky neon orange sign in the shape of a star reads *Special!* It's annoyingly unpretty.

On the sidewalk, a wall of larger plants, bushy flaxes, and tall spindly pittosporums in no logical order separate the foot traffic from those sitting at tables drinking lattes.

Inside, I'm hit with the aroma of freshly baked bread. Behind the coffee machine, Mr. Balducci tips beans from an oversized bag into the grinder. He's not much taller than me and never without a faded black *Balducci Landscape Design* cap.

In his Italian accent, he says, "Morning, Izzy. Coffee for you?"

"Er, thank you." Glancing around, I note the shop's layout has changed. The café is no longer confined to a little corner; tables occupy most of the space, like landscape design is an afterthought. Pushed to the side are all the plants I thoughtfully laid out in aesthetic groups. My logical groupings to help customers visualize how their customized plantings might look are gone. Instead, there's a nauseatingly chaotic mix of natives and tropicals that could never coexist because they require different microclimates. Whoever did this is flexing their half-baked botanical skills. For fact I know it wasn't Mr. B.

"You like it, Izzy? Our newest employee, Nico, did it."

I'd temporarily ignored the fact that Mr. Balducci was hiring new staff, because I've been enjoying working solo.

Mr. Balducci points at the planted living wall behind him—a lush green backdrop. Overflowing pots filled with herbs, micro greens, and fancy lettuce spell the words *green café*.

"Err, it's amazing." I've yet to meet Nico. Does he know this is a landscape design company? It is stunning, but I'd love to say it's impractical. Though I'll admit, Mr. Balducci uses herbs and lettuce mixes to make his gourmet sandwiches and salads.

Mr. Balducci hands me a coffee. "Nico has café experience and suggested that updating and expanding the café might bring in more clients."

Has Mr. Balducci been frolicking through catnip? This change can't be a good thing, surely.

"And it's working." He wipes coffee bean dust off his black apron. His smile—an almost permanent fixture—widens, then drops. "Any news about law? Your Mom came in this morning. We'll miss you. Nico has come at a good time."

I picture Mom's fake smile falsely reassuring Mr. Balducci that it's practically guaranteed I'll get in. We both know she's saving face, avoiding the conversation about how, in fact, I might not get in.

I ignore his question, too embarrassed and tired to rehash the details of how it's not a guaranteed thing.

"I can work till the day I leave …" I glance around the café, "you know, to help—" I stop mid-sentence, before offering to change it all back to how it was.

Mr. Balducci's smile is bursting at the seams. He clearly believes expanding the café and this Nico person will be helpful. My hackles rise, like a cat that's discovered an imposter cat invading its territory. This new guy is trouble.

"Appreciate that, Izzy. I'll need all hands on deck with all the new contracts and now that I'll be lecturing at the community college." Mr. Balducci is a self-confessed workaholic who never turns down an opportunity to make money from his passions. Café, case in point.

"Seeing as the shop has been set up," I say, "I'll get to Mrs. Wilson's. Unless you would like me to, er, change anything?"

"Unnecessary. Nico is there already."

Oh, joy.

Mr. Balducci's focus slips past me as someone lines up for coffee.

I cut through the shop out the back of the parking lot. My favorite work truck is gone. Anyone who's been here more than five minutes knows that's my truck. I claimed it by hanging a fake potted plant from the mirror and adding *Izzy* across the pot. And I labelled the toolbox with my name in big fat capitals with four exclamation points. I didn't tell anyone per se, but exclamation points speak for themselves.

I load another truck with spare tools before leaving seven minutes late.

I drive out of town and wind up the steep forest-clad highway, the canopy of trees casting a shadow over the roadsides. At the peak, the road zigzags down with sweeping hairpin turns through the low-hanging fog until it flattens and thins into a straight highway. No matter the weather, it's pretty.

Once on the straight, I pull into Mrs. Wilson's driveway—a flat gravel road pitted with potholes and overhung by trees she refuses to cut. I offered to thin out the underplants to allow more sun in, and her response was that she liked the privacy, which I get.

I reach the lagoon. The newly dug-in natives surround the pergola, where Mrs. Wilson sits with her laptop. The bedding plants are sparse now, just babies, but soon they'll take off and give Mrs. Wilson privacy and shade when she writes. I don't beep or wave; we both like to work alone—it's the perfect system.

Mrs. Wilson's sprawling white character villa comes into view, with a wide veranda wrapped all the way around, surrounded by a cottage garden. I take a sharp right toward the double garage, and in my parking spot is my truck. I lurch to a stop. A tall, brown-haired guy with a not uncool botanical sleeve of tattoos lifts a spade from my toolbox and places it in a wheelbarrow. He waves and pops a friendly grin. I return a half-hearted smile and get out of the truck.

"Hey, you're the infamous Izzy." He holds out his hand. "Nico. It looks like ya stuck with me for a few weeks. Beautiful out here, right?"

"Yep, and yep," I say, shaking his hand, letting go as soon as is socially acceptable. "So that's my truck, and those are my tools." My tone is direct but friendly. I reach into my truck and grab the cactus hanging from the rear-view mirror. "See?" I point to my name written around the base of the pot.

His smile turns to a playful grimace. "A massive apology. I thought someone named the *cactus* Izzy. Made me smile." He's laughing now, and I'll admit it is funny. He's also annoying. And we are wasting time. Soon it will be a billion degrees and too hot to plant.

Returning to my open toolbox on the back, I close the lid, revealing the thick black letters that spell *Izzy*.

"No denying they're yours, noted, sorry. Ha ha, the yellow box and black letters make the lid look like a bumblebee." He's not wrong. Is he always this distractible? Oh my, I can see myself doing all the work today.

"Lovely," I say, which makes him smile, missing my sarcasm.

"From tomorrow, could you please use the spare truck and the spare tools?"

He rakes his hand through his hair. "Absolutely." Tattooed on his wrist are Roman numerals wrapped in a delicate fern frond unfurling up his arm and over his shoulder. *Cyathea dealbata*—at least he knows his ferns.

I grab a wheelbarrow from the open garage and one by one place the foreign tools from the spare truck into the barrow. I glance at Nico as he retrieves his water bottle from the back seat of my truck and skulls till it's empty. He's wearing black mountain-bike shorts, not the camo green cargo pants that are part of the Balducci Landscape Design uniform. Neither is the black-and-red plaid shirt tied around his waist. Or the black tank top. And going off his tan, he's in the sun a bit—not that his tanned-toned arms are useful in gardening, other than to indicate he's definitely fit and definitely healthy and should, in theory, be helpful hauling compost.

I grab the rolled-up printed plan for Mrs. Wilson's garden from the truck's back seat, unravel it, and hold it out toward him. "This is the plan, color coded where each plant goes." Pointing to the pool garden, I say, "You plant out the lavender," before directing my focus back to him.

"Nice—lavender, color-coded purple. That's quite the organization system you've got there." He smirks, which is mildly irritating. He strikes me as a non-planner, makes-it-up-as-he-goes kind of guy.

"The software works out the exact cubic feet of compost or plants needed, based on the exact measurements of the garden beds. Saves money and time. No over- or under-ordering supplies."

His smile drops as I flick through the pages of the detailed plans. All garden beds are color coded with corresponding, neatly written lists with the exact number of plants and cubic feet of compost or topsoil required for each area. I can't tell if he is in awe of the organization system or thinks I have lost my mind. Either way, his eyes, which are deep hazel with gold flecks—almost unnatural-looking—are conflicted.

"Oh, er, I just spoke with Mrs. Wilson and suggested changing it up a bit." A grimace now paints his face. "Ordered some stuff too."

"Wait, what? She's had the same plants in the same places for the last three years."

Nico grabs a crumpled piece of paper from his mountain-bike shorts and holds it out. It's a hand-drawn map of Mrs. Wilson's garden beds. He has to be kidding. This is not a garden organization system, it's a ten-year-old's plan. The only thing it's missing is the tree fort. He's labeled the garden sections with names of plants that are nothing like those Mrs. Wilson and I agreed on.

Nico taps at the garden sections. "Natives here, here, and here. Easy."

"I've spent hours drawing up the garden plan and ordered all the plants." The words fly out faster and ruder than I intend, and I walk off, toward Mrs. Wilson. Ordinarily I wouldn't interrupt her, but before I sucker punch this guy in the nose on account of being annoying, I should check things with her first.

When I'm almost at the lake, Nico yells, "Francesca said to go for it. I've already delivered the natives. I've laid them out in the garden beds where they're supposed to go. Ready for you to dig in?"

I pause, not wanting to interrupt Mrs. Wilson unnecessarily, and return to my truck.

My tone is stiff. "Her name is Mrs. Wilson. She's a private person."

"Honestly, she told me to call her Francesca," he says, running his words together. "We can return the stuff you've ordered, right? We can cancel the order. They've not delivered them yet." And with reassuring eyes, "It will all be okay." He's so calm and unruffled by my outburst it makes me more irritated. I'm internally screaming, *Be nice. The guy is delusional but clearly trying.*

Before I can say anything, he's on the phone with the suppliers and has cancelled my order.

"I'll start with the natives, and how about you start with the pool garden? And then I'll come to help you when I'm done," he says, all breezy-like, followed by that weird way he looks at me—it's like he's genuinely trying to be helpful. But I don't need or want his help. He's made the horrifying assumption I'm cool with his breeziness and random change in my plan. I'm not breezy, and I'm not cool. Enough said.

Nico lifts the handles of his barrow. "Better get started on those garden beds, right?" And he heads toward the cobblestone path that leads around the back of the homestead.

I grab my shovel and push through the pool gate. My nerves are unhinged; I am stuck working with this guy and don't have the security of my plan to follow. The pool water is a crisp aqua blue, which matches the clusters of oversized planter pots overflowing with zinnia flowers in every color. Boxed garden beds surround the pool.

Starting with the garden by the paved barbecue area, I stab my shovel into the soil and begin lifting and turning over the earth, readying the ground for natives and not lavender. In the distance, a pop-rock song blares, Nico singing along, his voice flat and crazy out of tune, making up the lyrics as he goes. He gets points for enthusiasm.

With the sun high overhead and not a lick of wind, sweat beads on my forehead, and my cargo pants and tee stick and scratch against my skin. Nico has already removed the old plants, weeds, and rocks from the garden beds, making my job much quicker than I'd planned. By lunchtime, I've turned over all the soil and planted all the natives he'd already laid out.

I follow the path around the back of the house to the pile of mulch by Mrs. Wilson's orchard, the multiple varieties of peach, plum, and nectarine trees laden with fruit. The music is blaring. I scoop mulch into my barrow when the music stops mid-song.

"It's delicious. Want one?"

And there's Nico, behind me, sitting in the shade under a tree, biting into a fuzzy peach. No shirt on, his tank top draped over a branch— probably where he plucked the stolen fruit from. I dig my spade into the mulch, lift the mound, and drop it into the wheelbarrow.

"I'm good. But thanks," and continue to dig. "We're not supposed to help ourselves to food from a client's garden. It's written in the contract we signed."

"She gave me the basket and said to help ourselves." His tone is upbeat. "She said there's no way she could eat it all."

When I face Nico, he lifts a basket filled with an assortment of fruit: peaches, nectarines, plums, and strawberries. And with a genuine smile he holds out the basket, gesturing for me to take some.

"We're not paid to lounge around half-naked, eating stolen fruit." The words rush out bitchier than I intended, and I immediately regret saying them. Something about him being half-naked makes me nervous, and while he's without a doubt disorganized, he's not awful.

And he has a point about the abundance of fruit. There are over fifty laden trees, and in my rush this morning, I forgot my lunch box and drink bottle. But I can't sit next to the not-unattractive Nico and eat stolen fruit when I was such a bitch about it. Anyway, the rules are the rules.

I'm heading back to the pool area when Nico runs past me, lifts his legs to his chest, and drops into the pool, water spraying my face. He glides along the bottom till he pops up at the other end. "Better!" He holds his breath, then dives back under.

Is this guy here to work and be helpful, or what? Does he know Mr. Balducci is paying him to work? Clearly, he makes up his own rules.

Nico bobbles around in the same spot with his head underwater, like an uncoordinated synchronized swimmer. A smirk sweeps my face. He's ridiculous. He sinks to the bottom of the pool and glides toward me with his hand stretched high, holding my keys to the truck. Nico's face bursts through the water. Droplets on his eyelashes.

Standing at the pool's edge, I grab the keys. "Thank you. They must have fallen out of my pocket."

"Welcome," he says with a wide, friendly, and welcoming smile that should be irritating. He takes a deep breath and sinks underwater.

I tip the wheelbarrow of mulch onto the garden bed and return to the mulch pile in the orchard to refill. When I return, Nico's gone.

Nico's voice rises from behind the pool fence. "I'll catch ya. I've got to get to my next job. See ya at five a.m. tomorrow."

"Wait, what?" I lean over the fence. Nico opens the driver's door of my truck and takes a seat. He tilts his head out the window.

"Can't be late for my first day slinging burritos." And he starts the engine.

There's only one place in town that serves real Mexican food, and I'm pleading to the food gods that's not Nicola's Cantina.

"Hang on, we don't start at five a.m. We start at nine …" But it's too late he's gone, and my truck ambles past the lagoon, where he beeps the horn and waves out the window to Mrs. Wilson.

My phone beeps.

Penny: *Yo girl, we still on for karaoke at Nicola's cantina tonight? Ya know ya want to?*

Me: *Yup. Mr. Balducci has hired someone to replace me, and guess who's training him? And he is ann oy ing.*

Penny: *Girl, ya'll be leaving soon to be a hotshot lawyer, lol.*

Me: *I haven't got in. I could be stuck with this guy.*

Penny: *Is he hot?*

Me: *haven't noticed.*

Penny: *I take that as Izzy's code, for he's both hot and annoying.*

Penny: *Every person Mr. Balducci gets you to work with, you give ridiculous names, Too Much Mulch Mitch, Overwater Olli and Talks Too Much Tatum. His name?*

I flounder, trying to think of the most appropriate name.

Me: *Nico Doesn't Need More Botanical Tattoos.*

Penny: *Nice. I knew it. He's hot.*

Me: *Nope. His annoyingness cancels all hotness.*

Penny: *Riiigghtt. So, are we on for tonight? P.S. you're gonna get into law.*

Me: *I hope so. I'm losing hope. FYI, get ready to thrash out some Beyonce.*

Penny: *I'll pick you up from Balducci's after work.*

Me: *Perfect.*

Three

At the back of Balducci Landscape Design, I return the spare truck next to mine, where Nico has left it in the wrong spot.

Penny's car is waiting on the side of the road. Pop punk blares from the tinny car speakers, and her legs stick out, resting on the open car door.

Peering into my truck window, and at my hanging cactus, Nico's drawn eyes, one on each spike and a mouth on the base of the pot.

Penny arrives next to me. "What are we looking at?"

"He graffitied my cactus, and I bet he thinks it's funny."

"Oooh, I see Izzy cactus had a makeover, she's cute, and I like this guy. His revenge is happy. Out of curiosity, what did you do?"

"Absolutely nothing."

Penny rolls her eyes, giving me her best *yeah you're full of it* look.

"He messed with my plan."

"I see," Penny says, busting out a laugh.

How we are best friends is a mystery to me. She's a loose cannon who bends the rules, and I follow them because it's comfortable and to live any other way is terrifying.

"Let's gap it." Penny is wearing a blue polo t-shirt, so she must have just finished up at her cleaning gig—job one. And tied around her waist is her most-hated item of clothing, a neon yellow high-vis polar fleece—job two, cool storage assistant at the supermarket. The full-arm floral sleeve tattoo is the only thing that resembles her. Since her dad left her mom, she moved from the house next door to mine, to a one-bedroom apartment. Penny busts her ass working two jobs to pay the bills. She got a higher GPA than me and was accepted into Highmont University's English department, though she'll never leave her mom.

I dump my bag on the back seat of Penny's car, between a sea of candy bags with expired stickers slapped on the front and Penny's laptop, covered in fanfic cut vinyl decals.

It takes three goes for Penny's car to start.

We drive through town, down the single street where sweeping driveways lead to cardboard-cutout mansions with the least imaginative use of green space. Most are luxury holiday homes that sit dormant during winter and pack out during summer, when the population of Rockridge swells.

Penny slows the car as we pass 370, the largest of the mansions and home to Scarlett Dove, Penny's favorite fanfic writer. The car lurches to a stop. Penny clutches the steering wheel while peering past me toward Scarlett's house. "She'll be at Fanfic Con. Eli's coming. You should come with."

The absolute highlight of Penny's year is when fanfic writers congregate and get their fic on. She and Eli go bananas for it.

"We could make a detour after and go check out Highmont Uni. Ya know, check out the law department."

"Would that be jinxing it? I've not been accepted."

"If by jinxing you mean fun? I know ya wanna. Over-preparedness and extreme organization is so your bag."

She's got a point. "Maybe."

Visiting the law school, getting my hopes up, and then not getting in would only make the letdown so much worse; I would have seen, for real, what I was missing out on.

"Don't know what I'm going to do if I don't get in."

"Collect cats and be one of those people. No, wait—plants. Plants are your thing. You'd collect plants and work for Mr. Balducci f o r e v e r with annoying tattoo guy."

Penny fires me a series of exaggerated winks. Which then turns to a solemn grimace. "Or you could be stuck working two soul-reviving dead-end jobs supporting your alcoholic mother. Living *my* best life."

She's the queen of using humor to deflect sadness; it's her super-power. When past trauma rips you one, sarcasm and humor are always an arrow in her quiver. It's easier than facing the reality. Because emotions are easier to ignore when you don't let yourself feel.

We continue down Boulevard Road until the mansions disappear, and we reach the oldest part of Rockridge, a wide sweeping road that winds through the valley, ending at the Wilburn Mountain Bike Trail. Here the trails rise steeply up and over the ridge and eventually meet up at the lake. Narrow, two-story wooden villas line the street, most in need of rebuilding, including mine.

We arrive at my house. Its top-story weatherboards are white, and the bottom story is a time-worn eggshell blue waiting to be painted— Dad ran out of time.

Penny parks next to Eli's rust-bucket brown station wagon, his mountain bike on the roof rack covered in mud.

Out of the car, I inspect the wire framing attached to the fence, pick up a jasmine tendril, and re-loop it, securing it on the frame.

Penny laughs. "And before you ask for the billionth time, I *can* smell the jasmine, and no, I cannot remember what variety it is." Penny points to the flower baskets hanging from the veranda roof. "They're cool, Izz. You finally got the watering system thing rigged up."

"But wait, there's more." Around the side of the house, I turn on the faucets, and water sprays into the baskets and all over Penny.

Penny squints one eye with the other closed. "Perfect, refreshing. I like it."

The door bursts open and Eli appears, with a towel wrapped around his lower half, and wet hair. Penny's eyes dart to his chest and then to her phone; a grin spreads across her face.

"Fanfic Con—we going?"

Eli grabs her elbow. "I was just about to text you that tickets went up for sale today." And he drags her inside. We move past the photos that line the hall: Mom and Dad together on the day they graduated law; another of Eli and me the day I graduated high school. They're so posed; none of us look like ourselves. My favorite is the candid photo of all of us in the forest behind the hut. Mom's actually smiling.

Penny and Eli climb the stairs and stand on the last one. I wait while they discuss the intricacies of Fanfic Con—how they'll have to sell pics of their feet to cover the cost of the tickets.

Penny cups the palms of her hands on the side of her face. "It's a F-ing nightmare."

Her deliberate over-dramatization makes Eli laugh.

I squeeze past Penny, pushing her into Eli. "I'm getting changed; can't go out like this."

"I better get changed too," Penny says. "Ya might need clothes to go out, Eli boy. Unless you're cool with going half-naked, whatevs. You do, you, boo."

Eli inhales a laugh, for Penny saying *you do you, boo*, using his own saying against him.

Eli moves to the doorway of his bedroom, which is next to mine. "We taking your car or mine?" he says, focused on Penny untying the arms of her worktop from around her waist.

"Mine. I'd like to get there without pushing a car," Penny says.

"Whhhaat," Eli yelps. "My car is in perfect working condition, it's iconic."

"Dude, I picked you up yesterday when the thing wouldn't bust a move—and get the freaking locks fixed. It's not cool having to climb through the trunk to get to the back seats."

I leave those two to argue about whether Eli's broken car doors are an added safety feature or not. The argument is moot because the front door doesn't lock; anyone could steal his car if they wanted to.

I take the mini watering can that rests on my desk and tip water into the plants crammed on my windowsill. I'm careful not to overwater. Too much love can be suffocating.

Rex, sitting on my desk, taking in the view of the forest-clad valleys, jumps to my feet, weaving his pudgy body between my legs. He lets out bird-like cat meeps and then digs his fangs into my ankle. Lifting him into my chest, his purr motor running, he smooches his face into the side of my neck before latching onto my hand with a death grip. Dad rescued him as a kitten from the lake parking lot, and he's never lost his wild streak. I both admire his attitude and fear his ruthless way of ensuring he gets what he wants.

Penny dumps her bag on my bed and pulls out her clothes to get changed into.

When I get out of the shower, she's dressed in black skinny jeans, a slinky fitted tank top, and hoop earrings. She's rummaging through my closet; pulls out my black Dr. Martens, slips them on. We've shared clothes for as long as I can remember, so much so that a lot of stuff I have, I'm not sure whose it originally was.

At my desk, I log on to the Highmont University portal. Framed, limited-edition signed Audrey Eagle botanical drawings are pinned to my wall. And below are plant guides and travel books in stacks.

Application: *Pending*.

I refresh my browser as if pending might miraculously change to accepted. I'm taken back to when I filled in my application and the one line I read in the fine print, *only forty percent of applicants are accepted*.

Penny appears behind me. She tugs my arm. "You'll get in. There's like two people max working on admissions, right?"

I paint on a fake smile. Highmont Law is the best school in the country, and Katie from the law admissions office told me they have a team meticulously assessing each applicant because getting in is so competitive. What if everything I did to get in isn't enough? What then?

When we're finally ready to leave, Penny giggles as Eli tries to tackle her out of the driver's seat. As we drive through town, Eli and Penny play car karaoke, a.k.a. who can sing a song without getting a lyric wrong.

Eli laughs. "Not even one of those lyrics was correct." And for some stupid reason, the terrible singing reminds me of Nico and his gardening karaoke.

We arrive at Nicola's Cantina, and Eli parks out front. Painted on the front window is a lady's head adorned with a crown of flowers from the jalapeno and habanero chili pepper plants.

The caption from her mouth reads *Dare to come inside; it's spicy.*

My phone beeps with a message from Mr. Balducci. Penny and Eli, already out of the car, press their faces on my window, their noses squashed against the glass.

"Come on, Izz," Eli says, playfully nudging Penny. "I'm starving."

Mr. Balducci: *Izzy, Nico will plant up at the lake with you tomorrow. It should take half the time. Then you can take the rest of the day off.*

I feel the burn from my eye roll. Mass planting takes a methodical routine without which you'd be there forever. With Nico, it's going to take triple the time.

Penny opens the car door and drags me out and through the bar, heavy with chatter. We pass the open kitchen, thick with wafts of meat grilling. Servers in long black aprons ferry laden trays of food and drinks to crowded tables. We lose sight of Eli, who's charged ahead through the crowd. When we catch up to him, I double-take at the guy he's speaking to. Towering nearly a head taller than Eli is Nico, holding a tray of empty plates, wearing a black tee that grips his shoulders. Eli fist pumps Nico's outstretched hand.

How and since when do they know each other?

"This is my sister, Izzy, and our friend Penny," Eli says.

Nico's smile hitches at the side. "Small world. Hey again, Izz, and nice to meet you, Penny."

I feel Nico's gaze on me as I watch the precise moment Penny notices the botanical tattoos covering Nico's arm. A smirk fills her cheeks. "Hey," she says. "Nice to meet you too."

Eli looks puzzled. His focus darts between Nico and me. "You two know each other?"

"We work together. Apparently." I strip any trace of bitchiness from my put-on smile. Which takes a ton of effort.

Nico catches my sarcasm this time, with the slightest breath out and the smallest eye roll I've ever seen. I stop myself from rewording my sentence, correcting my use of *work together.* I work, and Nico wastes time willy-nilly changing the plans.

Penny does an actual eye roll, although I can't tell who she's directing it at. If I can't read her mocking, it's more than likely targeted at my attitude.

Eli's attention darts between Nico and me with a smile that the discovery of this new piece of info is a good thing.

Nico's tone is tighter with an edge of playful sarcasm. "Yeah, I'm training Izzy. Cool, aye."

I snap my focus to him, this time with my *what the actual fuck?* eyebrows raising at his painted-on grin with ridiculously overwhite straight teeth. "Yeah, not even close." I push the words out in a breathy laugh.

Eli and Penny have a whole conversation playing out between their eyes, exchanging smirks, the way they do when something hits my nerves in a way they find amusing.

Eli thankfully changes the subject. "You work here, man? It's not uni break, is it?" Eli says to Nico. His face scrunches to one side as if he's questioning if he's missed something.

"Nah, no uni anymore, I ..." Nico stops before finishing.

In the kitchen behind him, the chef dings the bell on the counter, placing a plate of steaming nachos on a tray, before yelling, "Order."

"Suck, I gotta go, but good to see ya, man. We should catch up."

"And Izzy, I look forward to seeing you bright and early tomorrow."

"Oh, joy."

Penny nudges into me and grips my forearm, and pulls me in the direction of the outside courtyard. "Ha, Nico, eh, you two are hilarious."

Eli's face is contorted, trying not to bust out laughing. "Will be an interesting trip planting up the track tomorrow. Wish I could be a fly on the wall. No, wait, a bird in the tree watching it alllll play out."

"Ha," I huff out, "the guy has no clue what he's in for. He won't last a week, and then he will be gone because it's hard work, and he takes nothing seriously."

Eli looks confused again.

Penny laughs. "He didn't follow her plan at Mrs. Wilson's and graffitied her car cactus."

Eli fake gasps. "Not Izzy cactus. She's so cute. He's a nightmare."

We take our usual spot in the outside eating area. The rafters are strung with fairy lights, and rows of deep green giant potted plants separate the tables from one another. An urban floral oasis.

The server arrives and waits patiently while Penny and Eli agonize over what to order. From my view of the kitchen, I spot Nico, talking to a woman in running tights and a baby-pink cap. He holds out one of those portable payment machine things toward her, and as she swipes her card, she tips her head back, laughing like she's actually enjoying his humor.

Penny and Eli are still deciding what to eat—they've got this thing where they choose for each other. I don't need the menu; I order the same thing every single time. Beef burrito with sour cream, all the salad, fresh guacamole, and no chili. "Like zero spice, please," I say to the waitress, confirming my order. I always order the same thing because there's no risk—it's guaranteed to be good.

Penny closes her eyes and circles her finger in the air before placing it randomly on the menu. Opening her eyes and smirking at Eli and then the server, she says, "He'll have the raw fish ceviche with the hottest chili sauce, not on the side, like smothered all over."

Eli laughs and copies Penny, with his eyes closed and finger circling the air until it lands on the menu.

"And she'll have the esquites, or corn salad." Penny hates anything with corn. Popcorn included.

Despite our love of Mexican food—like, disgustingly obsessed—Eli is the only one of the three of us that can tolerate anything remotely spicy. Any hint of chili from the mildest can of chili beans has me reaching for the milk to drown the inferno in my mouth.

Tension creeps up my neck at Nico's earlier comment. Nico knows I'm training him.

He's new. He's not training me. A fact I'd love to remind him of tomorrow when he's struggling to get his half of the plants dug in before daylight ends. There's an efficient planting system, and then there's whatever Nico does.

In the main part of the bar, tucked in the corner, the machine plays the first karaoke song. Mexican food and karaoke are an odd combination, but somehow it works.

The server guides a group of people to the table next to us, blocking my view of the kitchen. Nico is now out of sight.

"Earth to Izzy." Penny chuckles, craning her neck to get a better view of inside the bar. "Nico's gone into the kitchen. You won't be able to see him."

Ignoring Penny's mocking, I ask Eli, "So how is it you know Nico?"

"He was my year at law."

Was at law. Hang on.

"That guy got into law?"

Eli's smile drops.

I'm hit with regretful whiplash. A lot of people apply all deserving of a place, but most don't make it in.

I want to ask for more details about why Nico left law, but Eli and Penny's exaggerated glances toward the kitchen, followed by, "Nope, still can't see him," stop me. They're enjoying how much Nico has got under my skin.

"He's a cool guy, Izz. You might actually have fun working with him," Eli says.

"I'll have more fun working without him."

Our food arrives. Before I take a mouthful of my burrito, I watch as Penny takes a minuscule spoonful of her corn salad. Her facials are everything. Eli pats her back as he exaggerates his pure delight over his food, letting out the odd *mmmm* and *ahhh,* and *this is delicious,* unfazed by the hottest chili sauce that Nicola's Mexican Cantina has listed on their menu.

"Hate you," Penny says to Eli.

I push my cup of water toward her, then take a bite of my burrito. The beef, tomatoes, lettuce, avocado, and that sauce are perfection. Though within seconds, my mouth is on fire, my eyes are watering, and I'm gasping for air.

Eli jumps to his feet. "What the hell?" His face is worried. He bangs my back with the palm of his hand.

I wave him away and grunt, "Not choking, spicy."

The commotion sends the panicked owner over. Without warning, he wraps his arms around my middle, ready to apply the Heimlich maneuver.

"No, she ordered zero spice, and it's spicy." Eli takes a bite of my burrito, and his eyes immediately tear up. "It's fuckin' spicy, dude. The sauces got mixed up, man. She's a hate-any-spice-at-all kind of person. She explicitly said no spice."

After apologizing profusely, the owner says, "I'll get a new order, and some drinks your way ASAP."

A minute later, a jug of horchata is on the table, and when I look up as the server pours me a glass, it's Nico's face staring back.

"Izzy, I'm so sorry. I got the sauces mixed." Genuine concern spreads on his face. Or at least it looks that way. Or he planted chili on purpose, and he excels at acting.

Tears stream down my cheeks, and my mouth is on fire. Sipping the milky, cool drink with hints of cinnamon and vanilla temporarily calms the inferno in my throat.

I run my finger along the floral patterns etched into the outside of the glass jug. Nico rests his hand on my shoulder, and bending down, he passes me a napkin. "Shit, I'm so sorry. The chef was slammed with orders and said just to add the sauces, and I did." He pauses. The weight of his fingers grips my shoulder gently, and he looks deeply into my eyes.

I can't tell if he's lying or not. "Did you add chili on purpose?" The words come out raspy. My mouth raw.

"Added the sauce, yes, but purposefully added the chili, no. I had no idea I got the orders mixed up."

When I look at Penny for moral support, she shrugs. She can't tell if he's lying either.

"Oh, hell, you think I did it on purpose?" he says.

"Because you did," I huff out, and I shift on my seat, forcing his hand off my shoulder, and the warmth from his fingers disappears.

"I wouldn't, I can't handle spicy food at all." He refills my glass with horchata and passes me the glass. "I really am sorry. It was a genuine mistake."

The guy at the next table impatiently waves his menu in the air to get Nico's attention. Nico glances at him. "I'll be there in just a sec." He returns his attention back to me. "I better go. Do you need me to get you anything?"

The way his soft gaze meets mine catches me off guard. I brush invisible crumbs off my lap, diverting my attention to my knees. I hate that I can't tell if he's lying or not. "I'm all good. Thank you for apologizing."

"Well then, next time, I'll make sure to add an amount of chili that won't threaten to cut your air supply off." He winks at me innocently, his eyes begging me to find it funny.

"Wait, what? So, you did?" But before I finish my sentence, he walks off toward the guy at the next table and takes his order. Irritation stitches tightly in my chest. If I didn't hate public displays of awkward conflict, I'd march over to him and, at least, say something that would bring him down from Nico's world where he thinks he's Mr. Wonderful. Though nothing witty or scathing comes to mind, and that only annoys me even more.

"He's joking." Penny laughs.

"Seriously, Izz," Eli says. "He wouldn't. He's messing with you."

"He planted the chili, I'm sure of it."

A few minutes later, Nico taps me on the shoulder. "Probs would be a good thing to have your number. You're picking me up on your way tomorrow, right?" Nico takes the seat next to me.

"I guess." I would refuse to pick him up if this wasn't a work thing. I relay each numeral of my phone number, then my phone beeps.

Nico: *This is Nico.*

My phone beeps again, this time with a message from Mom.

Mom: *Any news? You know my friend's daughter, two of her friends have just received their acceptance letters.*

I don't answer. I'm not about to find out here. It would be the best place to celebrate, but the worst place to cry.

Sitting comfortably next to me, Nico says, "If you guys want to stick around until we close, the staff have a karaoke sing-off with a few free drinks, if you're keen."

Penny bats Eli's arm. "Yeah, man, we're up for that." She grins at me. "You're going to stay, Izz, right? You promised a karaoke battle."

"I've got to get up for tree planting at five."

"Ha ha, ditto," Nico says. "Come on, it will be worth it, karaoke off some of that tense energy ..." and his voice trails off like he didn't quite realize the meaning of his words before they were ejected from his mouth with zero thought.

"You implying I'm tense?"

"Yes. And *lovely*, I'm sure." Nico grins, again like he assumes I'll think he's funny. Lovely is how you describe an elderly old lady. I would make a dig about how he shouldn't be karaoke-ing late when he has to plant at five in the morning. But that would only confirm his theory that I am, in fact, tense. Which I am not. Maybe he could do with being less chill.

"I was going to stay, but now I've changed my mind."

"Sure, sure," he says, in a disbelieving monotone. He doesn't believe that I would have stayed, that I can be fun. I would insist that I, in fact, can be fun if that statement said aloud wouldn't sound so lame.

I'm not about to tell him Mom's message is weighing heavily and tugging me home. That there's possibly an email in my inbox telling me if I have made it into law. And I won't take the risk of reading a rejection letter in front of him.

"Aren't you supposed to be working, or are you just here to gossip and look pretty?" And I tilt my head in the direction of the other server who is giving Nico the evils. And rightly so. In the time he's been here, she's taken all the orders and delivered all the food, solo. And he's chatted to a pretty blonde and played trickery on my burrito.

"So you think I'm pretty," Nico says, with an overdone toothy smile to really jam in his point.

"That's what you get from that?"

"I better get back to having fun while I work, because those two things can, in fact, co-exist." The server, who is now standing next to Nico, chucks an iPad into him, a not-so-subtle hint he should be taking food orders.

"We're slammed," she says.

"You gotta work to get paid, sweetheart," I say. He walks off toward a table of people waiting more than patiently for him to take their order. And I know that comment got to him; he flicks his head back, and the painted grimace says it all.

"I'll give you a lift home," Penny says.

"No. You two stay and hang out, do karaoke or whatever."

Penny chucks me her keys. "We'll get a cab home; you take the car, okay?"

Readying my bag, Nico follows me as I walk through the outdoor eating area and through the doors and into the main part of the restaurant. I turn on my heels, facing him, the packed bar forcing us to stand closer than I'd like.

"Let's not be hungover tomorrow. There's a lot of plants that need digging in."

He smirks. "Ha, I promise nothing. But you have a … lovely night."

A lovely night, what am I? Ninety?

Nico disappears into the kitchen, and before I make it outside, I text Penny: *That guy drives me crazy, and not in a good way.*

Penny: *I can tell, LOL.*

I'm relieved when I get home to find the house empty. Mom has left a note that she and Mike are seeing a movie. I love Mom's enthusiasm for me getting into law, and I know it's her way to be supportive. But it only adds to the pressure. I change into my pajamas and curl up with Rex in bed, then check my enrollment status. Pending. Still pending.

My phone beeps.

Nico: *Here's my address. I never gave it to you.*

And he's attached a video. Nico grips the handle of a margarita jug and pours a glass, taking a sip. In the distance, I vaguely make out Penny and Eli on stage singing karaoke.

Me to Nico: *Very responsible.*

Nico: *It's called fun. Try it sometime.*

Four

By five a.m. I'm packed and ready for a day of tree planting—with Nico.
I sit on the back porch sipping coffee. The sun's hazy golden rays filter
through the sycamore trees and over the boxed vegetable garden. It's a
ritual Dad and I followed before a long day of planting.

Penny: *hungover AF.*

Attached is a photo of Penny, panda-eyed and frizzy haired, wearing
her uniform for her cool storage gig at the supermarket, which starts at six.

Me: *How's the head?*

Penny: *Lol, killing me.*

Me: *Great night then?*

Penny: *Epic - Shoulda come, girl. Nico is rad AF, BTW.*

Penny: *Check ya Facebook.*

I click play on Penny's video loaded at two a.m.

Nico at Nicola's Cantina, gripping his microphone, singing "Happy"
by Pharrell Williams outrageously out of tune. It's impossible not to

laugh. He's hammered and I'm going to enjoy watching him struggle in the wilderness.

Me to Nico: *Morning. Just checking if you're ready to go?*

Really code for, if you're going to be hungover and less than helpful today, at least be ready when I pick you up.

Nico: *Morning Izz, I'm waiting for you.*

He's attached a selfie, of him sitting on a porch, a dog curled up asleep on his lap. In the distance, the sun rises over lush green paddocks dotted with grazing cows.

Me to Nico: *Bet that hangover is fun!! I'm leaving now.*

I realize we're both waiting for each other.

Nico: *See ya soon. P.S. in case you were wondering, I found this in the dictionary. FUN: Amusing, entertaining, or enjoyable…it was a fun evening.*

Ha. The nerve.

Me to Nico: Really. *LACKS FOCUS: inability to perform complicated tasks. Lacking physical or mental energy to concentrate, making careless mistakes.*

Nico: You're too fun ny. *I made breakfast for us. Ya know, to soak up the hangover. Serious question: Have you been hungover before?*

I pick up the work truck and head toward Nico's, following the main road out of town. I turn down a gravel driveway and pass through pasture paddocks. Sitting amongst the grazing cows is a dilapidated cottage, the roof rusted and the weatherboards patchy, revealing previous coats of paint. The drive winds farther inland, and just when I think I'm lost, I spot Nico's house: a modern, black two-story with floor-to-roof windows. Potted lush green natives surround two armchairs on the wide veranda.

I park next to a black van with *Nico's Mountain Bike Tours* written on one side. I recognize the van; it's often parked at the lake by the start of the trails.

Beeping the horn, I wait. Then wait for Nico some more.

Googling Nico's Mountain Bike Tours I come to a webpage. There's a photo of Nico resting on his bike at the top of Ridgeway Track, the view over Rockridge below. Beside Nico is a group of kids with beaming smiles and wearing full-face mountain-bike helmets.

Nico walks toward me with a backpack swung over his shoulder, balancing a bottle of Gatorade on top of a cake tin. He waves and grins, a ridiculously happy amount for a hungover person.

He opens the door and takes a seat. "Hey, hey, Izz. Thanks for picking me up."

"Mr. Balducci said I had to."

"Yeah, I'm not even a little bit sad about it. We're gonna have fun together."

"Well, look at you with all your delusional confidence."

"I try."

My focus shifts to his black t-shirt, with the same logo as on the front of his van as he rests his drink in the cup holder, then opens the cake tin, offering me a slice of home-cooked banana bread.

"Breakfast, help yourself."

"Thank you." I take a piece and bite off a mouthful. "Oh my god, it's amazing and still warm. You made this?" I say, devouring it. My voice comes out too pitchy.

Nico laughs. "Yup, you sound so surprised."

I put my hand over my mouth, so crumbs don't explode into his face. "Yes. I am in fact surprised that it's the best banana bread I've ever tasted, and you made it."

Nico hums to the music playing on the radio as I pull onto the highway. He pauses mid-song. "It's a crazy small world that I went to law with Eli, right?" He resumes humming, singing a few of the actual lyrics and drumming, using his fingers on the truck's dashboard. "Eli and Penny can't sing at all, but last night was fun."

I'm laughing before he finishes his sentence. "You were *all* terrible. Penny sent me video proof."

"Yeah, but what a night. Come next time. I hear you love to butcher Beyoncé. Penny showed me some vids too," Nico says, grinning.

Damn that girl.

"Gotta hand it to ya, you looked like you were less tense belting out 'Single Ladies,' almost like you were enjoying yourself. Interesting song choice BTW."

He twists the top off his Gatorade and skulls nearly the whole thing. Plugs his phone into the stereo and sings along to "Single Ladies" by Beyoncé. If I could I'd jam that banana cake into his mouth to make it stop. Better yet, leave him on the side of the road.

I turn into The Plantery, Mr. Balducci's wholesale plant-growing facility. The city council contracts Mr. Balducci to grow the seedlings to plant up the forest as part of the conservation regeneration plan that Dad helped set up and was extremely proud of.

The truck bounces over potholes, and we pass rows of young trees waiting till they're big enough to be transplanted to their forever homes. I park next to the office flanked by dome-shaped greenhouses, each one three times the size of my house. We leave the truck and head to the office. Meela, who I often talk to on the phone, sits at her desk.

"Hey, Izzy. Got all the plants stacked and ready for ya. I'll bring 'em out." And she disappears out back.

Nico wanders about the office space, checking out a map of Wilburn Trail pinned to the wall. Grayed out are areas managed by the city council and protected under the Conservation Act. Shaded green is land that isn't, including the land where the forest hut sits.

"Crazy how not all the land is protected," he says.

"Yeah, stupid, really." Dad used to complain it was the council's way of keeping land available for city expansion. But I don't mention that. It's too hard to mention Dad without getting choked up.

Nico glances at me. "It's only a matter of time."

"I hope the council isn't that stupid. That forest means too much to too many. Ethically, the forest should remain because it should remain—there doesn't need to be any other reason."

Nico's listening intently and nodding his head in agreement, which only encourages my ranting. "For years, volunteers have dedicated their free time, planting that forest to regenerate the biodiversity and preserve a place for our kids and their kids to enjoy." Memories of Dad flood back, making my voice catch, and I stop suddenly. "Woo, I'm ranting. I'll stop." Not everyone appreciates my long-winded opinion. The backs of my eyes sting. I don't want to cry in front of Nico.

Nico searches my face like he's registered the forest has caught a nerve. Usually, I hide missing Dad well, but the thought of Dad's forest being destroyed makes my emotions transparent.

"The trail network brings in a ton of cashed-up tourists to Rockridge. The council would be crazy to put the land up for redevelopment." He pauses. "My business and a ton of others would die without the tourists … Woo, sorry, now I'm ranting. The council has no plans, yet. So no need to worry, 'kay?" He says it like he's reassuring me more than himself. His complete understanding about the importance of the forest catches me off guard.

Meela shouts through the door, "Your saplings are stacked and ready to go!"

Outside, three racks bursting with plants sit on wheels. We get into a rhythm; I pass him a tray, he places it on the back of the truck.

We drive toward the lake. Within two minutes, Nico falls asleep, his head resting against the window. I keep the radio low so as not to wake him. The highway turns inland and zigzags up the tree-lined passes till we reach the ridge and a panoramic view over the forest-covered valleys and Rockridge Township.

Cars and campervans pack the parking lot. I find a spot in front of the lake. Kayakers are paddling out on the water; a bunch of kids jump in unison off the jetty.

Nico wakes. "Ha ha, wonder if those kids know there's eels down there."

"They weave through your legs," I say, "and that's why I'll never jump off the jetty again. Eli pushed me once." The memory makes me shudder.

Nico smirks, finding that fact amusing. "They don't bother you if you leave them alone. So you're telling me you never swim in the lake?"

"Oh, I kayak out to the pontoon and swim there, where the eels leave people alone."

Nico opens the cake tin, and I take another piece of banana bread. "It was my mom's recipe," he says. "I think this is the closest I've got to it tasting like hers."

We debate whether it's sacrilege to put chocolate chips in banana bread, until we agree to disagree. He's Team Chocolate while I'm Team Walnut. While we're lost in conversation, the truck's cab turns unbearably humid.

"Jeepers, we better get planting," I say. For someone that can be so annoying, Nico's surprisingly easy to talk to.

I drive to the lake hut and unlock the storage shed. Bikes, helmets, and a bike rack cram the entrance. A sign reading *Nico's Mountain Bike Tours* sits on the mass of stuff, making it impossible to reach the carry bags and forks needed to plant. Irritation etches up my spine.

"I just tidied this place a few days ago," I say, letting out a deep sigh.

"Woo, sorry. Mr. Balducci said I could stash stuff here." He grabs the helmets and bag of tools and places them on the grass beside the shed, returning for the bike rack. I grip one end, and we carry it outside, resting it against the side of the hut.

"Better, and really, I'm sorry for messing things up," Nico says.

"It's okay." It's not. I'm spending the rest of the day with him, and bitchiness will make things awkward. I grab a planting bag, clip the straps over my shoulder and the band around my waist until the two bags hang evenly off the side of my hips.

From the trunk of the truck, we fill our bags with plants, mine in neat rows, Nico's in no logical order. Just jammed in there, and he seems perfectly unbothered. Nico catches me staring at his disorganization, and a grin spreads on his face. "You want to reorganize them, don't you?"

"I really do." Laughter seeps out. I'm unsure why I find him catching me out so hilarious. His lack of organizational skills is unsettling.

The track winds around the edge of the lake before it turns inland. We climb above the tree line with zero shade from the sun. The planter bag's straps dig into my shoulders, and sweat beads down our foreheads. Nico pauses and slides off his t-shirt, shoving it in his plant bag. Bare-chested. Toned and brown. I definitely don't want to run my hand down his botanical tattoo because that would be unprofessional and highly inappropriate.

We reach the top ridge and rest our planter bags on the ground. Standing side by side on top of the picnic table set amongst wildflowers swaying in the breeze, we take in the panoramic view—the mountains in the far distance, rolling green valleys, and a black speck—Rockridge.

Dad and I would camp here to break up longer bike rides. And it's where we'd wait for the chopper to deliver plants. It's public land but it felt like we claimed ownership, like guardians. He'd tell me it was his favorite place, and it was only after he died I realized why. It was time spent with me.

"It's crazy how amazing this place is," Nico says.

I glance at him by my side.

"Yeah, it really is." My words catch.

Nico's questioning gaze is way too perceptive. Like he's unsure what's got me choked up, but he's picked up that something has. "You okay to carry on?"

Diverting my attention off him, I focus on the mountains. The missing is exhausting. I'm simultaneously done with it and stuck, unable to let the missing go.

"If you want to go, dump the plants, and I'll get them later," he says.

"No … thank you." I smile, the best-unfaked smile possible. "I'm all good." I purposely change the subject. "So how come you left law?"

His smile drops, and his gaze moves to the view. I realize at that moment both of us have things we're trying to avoid talking about.

"Do you remember about a year ago, the helicopter crash that happened up here?"

I do. It was horrific. A couple and their son, plus the pilot, were taking off over the lake, and the chopper went down. There was only one survivor.

And then it hits me. "Oh, I do."

The pain in his eyes. It's too close to home, and I fight the urge to tear up. It will make it harder for him. It's difficult to deal with the emotion that comes with telling people out loud.

"I was the one survivor. And I needed to quit law."

His eyes stay on the view. He didn't just lose a dad, but a mom too, and he was there to witness it.

"I'm so sorry you're living through that." It sounds morbid, but what's worse is someone not acknowledging what actually happened. It makes the struggle to put the pieces back together even harder.

Nico faces me. "Thank you. That's the most real response I've had. It's comforting."

"Welcome."

Nico runs his hand along the wood of the picnic table, over the grooves of the messages engraved into the wood.

"The messages people left are cute, huh?" I say. "I read them every time I come up here."

"Same," he says.

I hop off the table and inspect the seat. "This one's my favorite." I run my fingers over the etched words. *"You're in the wind, rain and earth, and the sun that shines. We will always be together."*

It's only when I read *XO Nico* that I regret reading the words out loud.

"My god, shit, I'm so sorry. Honest to god, I didn't know they were yours until right now."

"It's okay, really. It's nice to hear the words. Truly, it's okay."

"Oh, that's good." There's a moment of silence, and I wonder if he knows about Dad. It's only something I could reveal to someone who understands the darkness that gets left behind. He's been so open about what happened.

"I guess we should get these plants dug in," Nico says.

He jumps off the table, and we continue along the ridgeline for another half a mile or so. We reach the neat rows of saplings I planted overlooking the lake and forest, stretching for miles. There are gaps in the forest that Dad wanted to fill. Standing on the cliff's edge with Nico next to me, I suck in the breeze. It centers my focus. No words are necessary. He needs this place as much as I do.

On opposite sides of the path, we plant. I dig a hole, plant a plant, cover it with soil, shift three steps and repeat the process.

When I've run out of plants, I find Nico asleep in the tall sun-bleached grass, his plants not in uniform rows but haphazardly placed, as if they've naturally grown there.

Bending down, I gently tap his shoulder. His eyes still shut, he mutters, "Too comfortable. We should stay here."

He folds his arms across his chest, covering the text that reads *Nico's Mountain Bike Tours*.

"So why are you working so many jobs? Can't focus on one thing, eh?"

I regret the question as soon as the words fly out. Especially now knowing why he quit law.

I'm standing peering down at him, which is slightly awkward. His head rests in the grass. His hand covers his face while he blocks the sun.

"I need money to invest in more bikes, a new work van, tools. All my focus is on building my business because it makes me happy."

Nico stands. We carry our empty plant bags and wind our way back to the lake hut in a quarter of the time it took to climb up.

Back at the truck, the late afternoon sun dips behind the valley. The lake's water gently ripples around a dinghy tied to the jetty. Something captures my attention, floating in the water. "Is that an upturned rubbish bin?"

Nico stops packing his bike stuff in the truck. "Wait, what?"

We follow the jetty to the boat. In the distance an upturned trash bin has spilled, and rubbish drifts in all directions.

"I'm getting it," Nico says as he hops in the dingy. He hesitates, watching me. Waiting. It's not our boat. But if we don't get the trash now, by tomorrow it will have dispersed to every corner of an otherwise pristine lake.

"A-holes, whoever dumped their trash." Nico starts the boat's motor. It roars to life.

"I'll stay here in case the owner comes," I say. "Tell them what we're doing or something, so they don't think we're stealing their boat."

Nico speeds off, and I'm stitched inside. He clearly cares about this place as much as I do. I didn't just hear the anguish in Nico's voice. I felt it. Yet I couldn't move, or bring myself to break the rules.

After a few minutes, the boat's engine cuts, and I watch Nico in the distance. He takes his t-shirt off, dives into the water, swims to an upturned bin picking up rubbish as he goes. He dumps the trash in the boat before repeating the process.

I stand with my toes curled over the edge of the jetty, the air cool and the water lapping below. Maybe I should have gone.

After an hour, the boat's engine roars to life, and Nico returns with stacks of large, upturned plastic tubs. They are like those charter fishing crews use, filled with ice to keep their catch cold. An assortment of waste fills each one: broken buckets, torn nets, and discarded candy and Coke bottles.

"Got it," Nico says. He's smiling, at least.

"Let's get the trash into the truck," I say. We each carry a plastic tub crammed with waste, returning for more until we fill the back and there's no room.

Nico and I peer at the trash remaining in the boat, wondering where to put it. He rakes his hand through his hair. Our clothes are wet from hauling the water-soaked nets.

"We can put it in the shed and get it next time." Stinky trash messing up the storage shed doesn't sit well, but there's no other option. The public dumpster is already full after a day of tourists visiting the lake.

We haul the last of it into the storage shed in two trips. Nico stacks it neatly in one corner.

"Tidy," he says, with a satisfied smile.

"Appreciated. Thank you so much for collecting all the trash, it means heaps," I say. The back of my throat stings and I swallow hard. I appreciate what he's done more than he knows.

"Welcome."

There's a beat of awkward silence as we stand staring at each other. And I get the feeling he appreciates my connection with this place too.

Nico's tummy howls.

"Was that your stomach?" I ask.

"Ha ha, yup." He laughs.

"Come with me."

He follows me next door to the lake hut, set amongst the towering trees Dad and Mr. Balducci planted. The sweeping veranda takes in the full view of the lake. Bricks are missing from the lichen-covered chimney. It's weathered and old and the perfect setting for a fairy-tale movie.

Inside, I reach into the far corner of the cupboard and pull out a dry bag filled with dated chocolate bars. I hand him a Pinkie Pie bar.

"Woo, old-school, I like it. Haven't had one of these since I was a kid."

"They're like ten years old, so eat at your own risk."

Nico tears the wrapper off while I stash the dry bag back in the cupboard. While eating his Pinkie Pie, he checks out the glass jars filled with seeds that line the mantelpiece above the fireplace.

"For years, I've admired these." He puts one jar down and picks up another, inspecting the manuka seeds.

"My dad collected them," I bravely say.

"So cool." Sadness seeps into his eyes. And by that look alone I'm certain he knows about what happened to Dad.

"I'll plant them at some stage." In a small town, news travels fast, and everyone knows everyone, so it wouldn't take much for him to connect the dots that Dad is dead. As open as he's been with me about his parents' deaths, I'm not in the mood to talk about him.

"If you need any help to plant them, happy to, if it feels right." And then he quickly changes the subject.

As we walk back to the truck, he says, "Eli tells me you're waiting to find out about law."

"The wait is brutal," I say, getting into the driver's seat.

He grimaces. "Ooh, I remember."

"Some people I know have already got their acceptance email."

"I'm not going to say you'll definitely get in, I know the stats, but I really hope you do."

His up-front honesty is comforting. People assume I'm going to law, and that only adds weight to the worry I won't get in.

"Thanks, there are no guarantees."

When I get home, Mike is in the kitchen loading the dishwasher while Mom sits at the kitchen table in her dressing gown, drinking tea.

"Any law news, Izz?" No *Hi*. Straight into it.

Mike rests his hand on Mom's shoulder. "She just got home." He removes a plate of dinner from the oven and places it in the microwave.

Eli and I were skeptical of Mike at first—divorced with no kids, ten years older, but oddly, none of those factors has been a problem. It's weird that he seems to enjoy doing the stepdad thing.

The microwave beeps, and Mike places the dinner in front of me. "Thanks, looks yum."

Before Mom can talk about law again, I head to my room and eat dinner. I open my windows wide, and the curtains flick in the breeze.

My phone beeps.

Nico: *Thanks for a great day :) Not me googling where to find more Pinkie Pie chocolate bars.*

Me: *They're addictive, lol.*

My phone beeps again, and I can't help but smile; I'm assuming it will be a message from Nico. Instead, it's an email.

Message from Highmont University Law School.

Congratulations. We have accepted you into the Highmont University School of Law.

My nerves are live wires. I'm too shocked to scream with joy. The flood of relief buzzes through me. The extra tuition classes, the hours studying, ignoring the fact that people my age go out and have boyfriends—and I've done it. I can't get over the fact I'm officially a law student, and in six weeks, I'll be moving from Rockridge.

I screenshot my acceptance letter and message it to Penny and Eli with the caption *I'm reading this right, right?*

Eli bursts into my room.

"You're f-ing awesome. Mom's gonna freak."

I huff out, "She'll be relieved … and happy."

He rests on the bed next to me. "When are ya gonna tell her?" His grin's wide; he's as excited to see her reaction as I am.

I smirk and show Eli the text I've written but haven't yet sent: *I have news.*

"Wooo hooo," Eli says, slapping one hand on his thigh. "My bet is she will cry with happiness."

His comment catches me off guard. Something about the word *happiness* and how it lingers in the air. Without a doubt, we haven't seen Mom happy since before Dad died. From the moment she found out he was gone, the darkness swallowed her whole.

Mom hibernated in her room for months. Eli and I took shifts to make sure she ate and saw the sun daily. No matter how hard we tried, we couldn't bring back the person she was before. Getting into law might be enough to ignite a spark of the old version of her that celebrated the smallest of victories, with surprise afternoon teas and home baking and warm hugs, because it was impossible for her to hide how proud she was. Until Mike came along, I thought that part of her was dead and gone. So far, he's the only person who's lit even the tiniest spark, giving a glimpse of the person she used to be. As much as I'm grateful, it would be nice to feel I can add to her happiness rather than be a hurtful reminder of the person she lost. I'd do anything to change that.

"Send it," Eli says, grinning. "She'll know the news is law related."

I laugh. "I bet she takes six seconds to barge in and hug me before taking us out for ice cream, like she used to when we were kids."

"You're on. I pick. Eleven, she's outside doing yoga, ya know, an extra five seconds to make it inside. And to keep it interesting, I bet she screams with joy and confetti bursts from her head."

"You're ridiculous; confetti?"

"Yep," he says, laughing and playfully nudging me. "Just saying, the winner gets to crash on the floor of their sister's dorm while he searches for auditions."

"It's a hard bargain, but you're on."

I hold up my phone and show Eli the unsent text as he prepares his stopwatch. "On the count of three," he says, readying his finger over the start button.

"Three, two, one." And I hit send.

At precisely six seconds, Mom bursts through the door and launches into a spiel.

"Congratulations!" She rests beside me on the bed; I'm almost certain she'll wrap me in a bear hug. Instead, she opens the notes app on her phone. "We've got a lot to organize." Her tone is businesslike. She rattles off a to-do list, adding each thing to her phone notepad. Like I haven't thought of this stuff a million times before—there's a list pinned to my corkboard above my desk. I know what needs to be organized.

Eli looks as defeated by her emotionless response as I feel. "You win, six seconds," he says.

I search Mom's face as she speaks. The meaning of her words washes over me. No warm smile, no congratulatory hug, no squeal of joy. And definitely no confetti. No acknowledgment of what this means to me or that there's a reason to celebrate; it's like her ability to feel has died. The Mom we knew, she's officially dead and gone.

Mom's still adding to her list; sadness grips my chest. "I got the list sorted, Mom. Thank you."

Eli picks up on my change of mood and wraps me in a bear hug. "So proud of you; let's get ice cream." He switches his focus to Mom. "You know that place you and Dad would take us to as kids when we celebrated stuff?" Eli glares at Mom, waiting for her to get the hint. "We can line up with all the kids at the self-serve bar." He releases his hug and playfully nudges my side. "You'd have a height advantage now, ya know, to grab all the chunks of Pinkie Pie before the kids can."

Eli has a knack for diffusing emotionally awkward conversations with humor. I go along with it. I'm not about to have it out with Mom, and I saw the way she dipped her head when Eli mentioned Dad and the memory of what we once had. I can't go back to her being a hermit living in her room and the overwhelming, useless feeling that I can't make her feel better.

Mom stands as Mike appears at my door.

"Sorry, Mike and I have a meeting at the council, but how about …" Mom pauses, her focus on her phone, presumably looking at her work calendar, "how about next week we all go out for dinner?"

I wonder if she adds the occasion to her to-do list to check off. "Sure, Mom, sounds great."

Mike hovers at my door like he's unsure if he should come in or not.

"Mike," I say, "I got in."

He immediately starts singing, "Con … grat … u … la … tions … Iz … zy," booping the air with his fist, his voice flat and completely off tune. "Exciting news." And he plays the air guitar while singing, "Izzy is A-W-E-S-S-O-M-E," sounding out each letter like a robot. It's both cringe and adorable.

"Why, thank you, kind sir." It's hard not to laugh. "Dude, I hate to be the bearer of auto-corrected bad news, but *awesome* only has one S."

He starts over, this time spelling *awesome* correctly.

"You're quite something," I say, not fighting the laughter that's turned hysterical. "Thank you." And I mean it. It feels wrong that it's kind of a relief to have him around.

Eli leaves with promises of going for ice cream later. Mom and Mike head into town for their meeting. I'm in my room alone, with the signed Audrey Eagle illustrations that Dad gave me, of a coffee and vanilla plant.

I type out a text to Dad.

I got in.

I know he'd be proud.

I hit send. I know it's pointless because dead people don't check their messages, though it makes this moment both easier and harder.

Penny: *YO GURL! MASSIVE CONGRATS. FREAKING HAPPY FOR YOU!!!!!!!!!!!!!! I'm at work, and look who I just bumped into.*

And she's attached a photo of Nico in the frozen section of the supermarket, clutching a bag of mixed frozen berries and a carton of milk. The photo's captured him mid-laugh, the corner of his eyes crinkled with his wide smile.

Penny: *I'll call ya after work. I want all the deets.*

Penny: *P.S. Eli texted me I hear there's a DIY ice cream party happening. I like it, old school. I'll smuggle in some Pink vodka. P.P.S Nico is lovely (and hot).*

Me: *Yup.*

Penny: *Yup, to what?*

Me: *Pink vodka.*

Penny: *You hate pink vodka. Hot damn!*

Me: *:~0*

Mom barges into my room like no time has elapsed since rattling off her list. She picks up where she left off. "Apply for the student dorms, buy new clothes, clear out your room, resign from Mr. Balducci's …"

And she continues, but my mind's frozen on the fact I will have to resign from Mr. Balducci's. It's not like I didn't know it would have to happen. After Dad died, being at home trying to keep it together for Mom sucked the life out of me. Working at Mrs. Wilson's, at Mr. Balducci's shop, and for the forest regeneration project—it jammed the broken pieces of me back together. I would take it all with me to Highmont if I could.

"Did you hear me?" Mom says. I'm looking at Rex asleep on my desk, sandwiched between my plant ID books. I wish I could unhear her words. She makes me feel like I'm too small and too much at the same time.

"Got it, Mom, honest. There's zero chance I will forget."

Nico: *Massive congrats! Penny told me the good news. Whoop whoop.*

And there's a selfie of him pulling an exaggerated happy-goofy face. It's kind of adorable.

Me: *Thank you. I can't get over it! Soooo exciting.*

Six

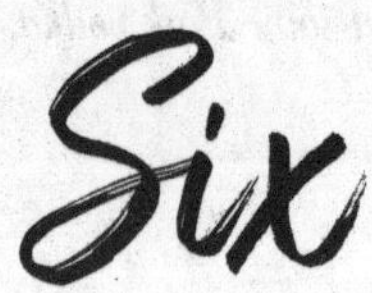

Mr. Balducci: *I'll need the spare truck. Can you please pick up Nico this morning?*

As Nico and I pull onto the highway toward Mrs. Wilson's, he turns the music up. "Meet Me Anyway" plays.

"I love this band," Nico says, singing along. He lifts his hoodie, showing me his black t-shirt with a couple lying in intricate white-stenciled botanicals. "They're pure art."

"I know, right? I have three of their t-shirts. The girly crop-top versions, though."

"The lead singer was a landscape designer," he says.

"No way. How did I not know this?"

Nico laughs, pulling his hoodie back down. "My buddy did the artwork, so I kinda got the inside goss. He's my second-favorite botanical artist, next to the legendary Audrey Eagle."

"Of course, goes without saying. I have two originals."

Drumming the truck dash with his fingers to the beat of the music, he says, "Whaaaat?" Pausing mid–drum solo, he adds, "That's insane. They're—"

"Limited edition," we say in unison, our voices pitched.

I'm about to invite him to come and have a look after work, but retract that thought on the account he might think that's weird. We are barely workmates, after all.

Driving through the quiet winding highway overhung with trees, we rank, in order of awesomeness, the best botanical artists, followed by a random debate on whether the art out front of Nicola's Cantina is an actual carnation or a made-up flower.

I giggle because Nico's argument is ridiculous, and he knows it. "Nowhere on the planet is there a carnation flower that is metallic purple," I say.

He grins. "Okay, you've got me there, but the shape and all its other bits—so carnation."

I tilt my head to the side, pretending to think, to make him wait for my answer. He laughs at me, which I find amusing and cute because he thinks I'm funny. "Ya got me with the accurate internal anatomy, but I still stand by my color argument."

"So, off to law for you soon, eh? Did you consider doing the landscape-design course that Mr. Balducci teaches? It sounds awesome … not that I don't think you'll nail law, but you'd kill it at landscape design."

The little I know about Nico is, he's an open book and it makes it too easy to be open with him.

"You're not the first person to ask, but no. I have wanted to be a lawyer for as long as I can remember, spent the entirety of high school working on getting a high enough GPA to get in, and doing every ridiculous extracurricular that would increase my chances."

"Yeah, I remember those days. Weird, looking back on it now."

There's something in his voice that makes me think he regrets it, that the time was wasted.

"You regret studying so hard to get into law?"

He pauses and glances out the window as we make the final descent down the valley and onto the flats with paddock after paddock of grazing cows.

"Yes and no." His focus is still out the window. The open, upfront honesty about him I thought was a given is gone, or at least feels guarded. It's a side of Nico I haven't seen.

"I was so overly committed to law I let important stuff pass me by. Like missing my mom's birthday—clean forgot—and not just once, for fuck's sake. Law wasn't for me, and life is too short to be doing stuff that doesn't set your heart on fire, especially when it comes at the expense of the things and people that matter."

And there's the raw honesty, like he's bleeding his heart out. I don't press him for more. Something about the way he won't look at me makes me think it's not something he wants to talk about further.

"Woo, sorry I'm being a downer," Nico says as we pull into Mrs. Wilson's drive. And he faces me and grins. "Law will be awesome. How excited are you right now, living the dream?"

At speed, I rattle off, "I'm so excited and nervous. It's going to be okay, right? Leaving everyone behind won't be easy. But law is everything I've wanted for so long. And it's not like I'm saying goodbye to the lake forest, Mrs. Wilson's, Mr. Balducci's, and my family forever. It's temporary. I'll come back a freakin' lawyer."

I carry on, forgetting to leave room for him to answer. "I know I'm about to enter a world of pain with twenty-four-seven study. I know academically I've got it covered—" I stop talking to catch my breath.

Nico grins, only fueling my excitement and rambling.

"Woo, that was a massive info dump," I say. "Nothing like someone you barely know bleeding their heart out at speed."

He chuckles.

"To sum up, getting into law is *everything*. Promise—I'm done." And I exaggerate a deep breath, which I'm glad he finds funny. "You left law to start your mountain-bike touring business?" I ask.

"Yup. I've been mad-passionate about mountain biking forever, been doing tours since I was sixteen. Funny how sometimes the best choice is right in front of you, but you don't see it until you experience what you don't want."

We pull up outside Mrs. Wilson's house, and Nico and I fetch a wheelbarrow from the open garage.

We're greeted by Mrs. Wilson. She's in her late forties but could pass for mid-thirties. Her long dark hair is tied in a messy but elegant bun, and not one hair is out of place. Fitted jeans, ripped at the knees. And an oversized t-shirt knotted at the waist.

Nico lifts a tray of plants off the back of the truck, placing them in the barrow.

"Nico, Anna said she can give you a lift back into town today."

"Oh yeah, she called last night. It was so great to talk to her."

"Awww, I love that you two are reconnecting," Mrs. Wilson says. She shifts her focus to me, as if to catch me up on the connection. "Nico and Anna were inseparable until Nico left for university."

Now it makes sense why Nico calls Mrs. Wilson by her first name. By the sound of things, they've known each other a while. I'm reminded of the first day Nico and I worked together and the garden plan I meticulously designed, and how Nico kindly informed me it wasn't what Mrs. Wilson wanted. I was so bitchy. Icy, even. And now I'm embarrassed.

Anna was Eli's year at school. She was popular because she didn't care about being popular. She was genuinely nice, sporty and caring, and it's no surprise she left Rockridge to study nursing at Highmont. I don't remember Nico, though, and I'm sure I would have, had he gone to the same high school.

I spend the morning in the vacant paddock behind Mrs. Wilson's homestead while Nico finishes the planting around the lagoon.

Using a can of spray paint, I mark out a path leading from the main house to the river and spray where the seating and flower beds might go.

When I began redeveloping Mrs. Wilson's garden, the derelict grounds hadn't been touched in twenty years. I've converted a wasteland into an oasis, and this is the last piece of the puzzle. Looking back at what I've transformed, I'm proud, but looking forward it's going to be hard to close the door and say goodbye.

I sit on the grass with my laptop, using the landscape-design program. I reorganize and adjust my measurements for the garden beds. Sometimes what looks good on paper doesn't always translate into reality. It's easier to plan when you're in the space.

The gentle river, tree-clad valleys, blue sky, and grazing cows refresh my mind, like rebooting your computer and downloading a new operating system. I was just okay before, but here I'm at peace.

A cow strolls over with doll eyes and enormous eyelashes. I stroke the soft hair between her eyes. Mrs. Wilson inherited the herd as calves when the place sold. She hand-raised them, vowing they'd never go to a slaughterhouse and would remain here for the rest of their days.

I adjust my landscape plan, including a new fence line to keep the cows separated from the new garden, and I add a feeding trough and a gate. I'm reminded of the comment Nico made earlier, about how he left law because he wanted to do things that set his heart on fire. But what if he left law because the grief over losing his parents made it too hard to leave Rockridge, and it has nothing to do with law at all? What if grief and guilt are holding him back?

After lunch, I work in the pool area. I dig my trowel into the soil, place the Chatham Island forget-me-not into the hole, and smooth over the soil, repeating the process until I run out of plants. Returning to the truck, I refill my wheelbarrow with more plants. In the distance, the roar of a motorbike soars up the drive before stopping at the lagoon.

Anna, in a black leather jacket, debikes, and takes her helmet off. Her long blonde hair flicks in the wind as she walks to the edge of the lagoon.

"Hey, Nico," Anna shouts across the water. Nico appears from behind a wildly overgrown flax bush, and rushes over, wrapping his arms around her, lifting her feet off the ground. It's a hug you give to someone you love, or if you're a couple in a romance movie. The corny kind where long-lost friends reconnect after realizing they loved each other all along.

I force my attention to filling my barrow with plants and, when it's full, wheel it back to the pool area, trying not to eavesdrop on their conversation. Glancing through the mass of jasmine growing up the pool fence, I see him slip his arm around Anna's shoulder. "It's so great to see you," he says.

Nico returns his wheelbarrow to the garage while Anna waits on the bike.

He leans over the fence. "See ya, Izz. I've got a shift at Nicola's Cantina." His arms rest on top of the fence, his smile wide.

"Bye," I say, wiping the hair stuck with sweat from the sides of my face, probably smearing the mud that's on my gardening gloves all over my cheeks.

Nico chuckles in the sweetest way; his focus darts around my face.

"There's stuff on my face, hey?"

"Yep."

He reaches his arm over the fence and gently brushes the dirt off the side of my cheeks, which I'm certain have turned a blotchy pink. An embarrassing nervous trait I inherited from Dad.

Waiting on her motorbike, Anna calls from down the drive, "Let's ride the rough road. It'll be fun, like old times. By the way, hi, Izz."

I wave politely.

Nico's attention diverts to Anna—like, all of it. They're kind of perfect for each other. Hot and smart and lovely.

"Yeah, sure, but can I drive?" Nico says, ditching our conversation to gather a helmet from inside Mrs. Wilson's garage.

Anna laughs. "I suppose."

She sits behind Nico, wrapping her arms around his waist and pulling herself into his back. The engine roars and Nico turns the bike around, waving as he rides off.

Me to Penny: *Do you remember Anna from school, Eli's year? Mrs. Wilson's daughter. Do you know if she has a boyfriend?*

Penny: *Lol, have you been drinking pink vodka, yo acting weird?*

Penny: *No clue about her relationship status. She's so nice tho. I don't know if you know this, but when your dad died, she was the one who set up the roster, so you guys had meals made and delivered to your house.*

It's like being sucker punched. The day Dad died rushes back; we were too grief-stricken to shop or cook—especially Mom. Those meals saved us. I assumed it was Mrs. Wilson.

Penny: *Why? Is this Nico related, by any chance?*

Me: *Just grateful for what Anna did.*

I return to digging in plants. The rough road leads to a view over the city—a popular spot for wedding proposals and loved-up couples. I drag the hose from the garage and spray water over the plants. Water pools onto the dry soil, disappearing as it sinks in.

Maybe Anna is just Nico's friend. A stunning, motorbike-riding, caring goddess-friend.

When I pull up at home, Mom's car isn't there. She takes her staff out for drinks with Mike on Friday nights.

I plonk my bag onto the kitchen table. The aroma of butter, garlic, shallots, and sage fills the kitchen. My stomach gurgles; distracted all day, I've barely eaten. Eli is wearing nothing but his mountain-bike shorts.

"Do you ever wear tops?" I ask.

"Nah. Want some?" He digs his fork into a pot, pulls out a neatly wound roll of spaghetti, and shoves them into his gob. "They're amazing," he says, his words muffled.

"Yup, share for sure," I say, sitting at the kitchen table.

He grabs a bowl, dumps half of his pasta into it, and continues to eat from the pot.

I stuff a full fork of pasta in my mouth. It's buttery-sage goodness, just the way Dad used to make it.

"So, Nico is cool," he says. "Small world, eh? I'm meeting him after work for a drink."

My cheeks heat up. "He's … chatty." Eli is an emotional soul. And I want to avoid a deep and meaningful conversation about my slightly hot, sometimes annoying, workmate.

"Chatty, eh?" He smirks, ruffling my hair like he used to when I was little. I duck away, pretending it's annoying. But secretly, sometimes, it's exactly what I need. I jam more pasta into my mouth. He knows what he's getting at. I know what he's getting at. We both know I'm not up for talking about boys with my brother. It's the brother-sister rule that was enforced after the embarrassing and failed attempts by Penny and Eli to set me up with their friends.

Eli says in a more serious tone, "He said you've got mad plant skills and he doesn't get the law thing. True that."

"That's easy for you two to say. You both dropped out." My voice is etched with purposeful, playful sarcasm.

"'Kay, 'kay, I take that back. I know it's a glow-up for you."

I laugh. *Glow-up* is Penny's term; she uses it all the time. "Yes, it's my *glow-up*." I emphasize the words because they feel like an understatement, and I enjoy mocking him. "I'm excited about law."

"Ya wanna come tonight? Nico's bringing a friend."

I wonder if the friend is Anna. "Er, I'm good. Thanks, though."

"Sure, sure. If you don't want to hang out with a guy that said you're amazing and is into the same weirdo stuff you're into, and is big-brother approved, then enjoy your night, alone, like the crazy plant lady you are." He's laughing and enjoying mocking me too much.

I ball up the tea towel on the table and chuck it toward his face, but it drops before it reaches him and falls flat on the ground.

"Maybe you could work on your throw."

"Ha ha, like you can talk. Hmmm, I'm going out with Penny tonight, my best friend, the girl you've secretly loved forever but won't admit it to yourself, hmmm."

Eli laughs. "I have absolutely no idea in the world what you are talking about."

"Sure, sure." I smirk.

Eli dumps the pasta pot in the sink. "Well, you'll be pleased. I'm gonna go put some clothes on." He heads out the door before darting his head back in. "We'll be at Nicola's Cantina, if you change your mind, 'kay?"

My phone beeps.

A Facebook request to be Nico's friend. Butterflies shoot through my body. He sends a photo from inside Nicola's Cantina—the back wall with a giant popping hyper-pink sunflower.

Nico: *Most definitely a sunflower …*

A laugh sneaks out.

Me: *But the color, lol.*

Nico: *LOL. Thought you'd like that, ha ha. A new variety we don't know about???*

Me: *On what planet?*

Nico: *A hyper-colored one, lol.*

Seven

I wake to a Facebook notification from Nico.

Nico's comment: *It's magic up there, eh?*

I play the time-lapse video Dad took when we camped in the forest behind the lake hut. The sun rises, shooting golden streams of light through the trees. The midday sun is a halo center sky; cicadas and birds are singing. And sunset—indigo moonlit trees with stars peeking through the forest canopy. It was a week before Dad passed, and the last night we spent alone.

I reply: *It's my happy place.*

Downstairs, Mom and Mike sit at the kitchen table sipping coffee. The way they look at me is odd.

"Izz, perfect timing," Mike says in an over-upbeat tone. "We have a proposition for you."

The word "we" hits differently now it no longer includes Dad. Credit to Mike, though. Without him, Mom would still be hibernating in her room.

"Mike and I are working on a luxury housing development complex, and we think we have the perfect job for you before you start uni." Her narrowed eyes and serious tone imply this is an FYI deal, not a choice. "We are applying for consent from the council to build a luxury apartment complex where the lake hut is."

I feel my actual face drop.

Any development of the lakefront land would destroy the hut and Dad's forest.

"You're kidding, right?" My tone is snappy. "You were an environmental lawyer, your husband was an environmental lawyer who dedicated his life to conservation, your daughter is studying to be an environmental lawyer, and your husband spent years working on conservation projects to re-establish that forest. Doesn't any of that mean anything to you?"

Mom ignores my rant, showing zero emotion as she describes the job.

"We will construct the complex in an eco-friendly manner, and your job will be community liaison coordinator, fostering a positive attitude with the public. It's a requirement for the project to get approval from the council."

Mom pours a coffee and places it in front of me.

I push it back toward her. "What about the forest and the hut?" I direct my attention to Mike.

"That old thing?" he asks in the joking tone he uses when confronted. "That space will house seven luxury eco-apartments."

"So you're saying you're going to tear down the forest and the lake hut."

"We're improving on what's already there. Think of it that way."

"Nothing needs to be improved. It's perfect as it is." The lump in my throat is making my voice hoarse.

"Change is a good thing," Mom says.

"You've got to be kidding me. Mom … Dad—" My throat stitches; it's all I can say without crying.

Mom darts her focus away. Deep down, she knows this is wrong. Like it's her messed-up way to rid herself of Dad, so it hurts less. But nothing can do that.

Holding back the need to yell, I say quietly, "Mom."

"Izzy, it's nothing to get sentimental about." She lifts a stack of plates out of the dishwasher and slides them into the pantry before returning for more. Like destroying the forest Dad loved has no effect on her.

"Apart from council approval, which is highly likely, it's the perfect practice for law. You'll be liaising with community groups to get their approval for the project."

To my core, I'm bursting with anger. My eyes tighten and glaze over. I'm afraid of what I could say next—that she's selfish and not the only one who lost Dad; if she loved him, she wouldn't do this.

"Izzy," she blurts, her tone steeped in anger. "We need this contract to pay your law tuition. There's no other way." She finally turns around from the sink.

Mike flicks the electric kettle on, the obnoxious overloud sound adding too much drama to my already rowdy mind. Out of my seat, I lean over the bench and switch it off.

Tears well. I'm facing Mom, but her focus darts to Mike. "I thought Dad had tuition covered. He said it was a done deal."

"That was before we had to live off one income and pay his debts from his business." She finally faces me, her expression cold and empty. "He was too nice, Izz. He did too much work for free, and I still owe money."

In a controlled, hushed voice, I say, "I can't believe you're doing this." I go to my room.

Curling around Rex, who's asleep on my bed, I'm mad at Mom but I didn't expect to be angry at Dad. He promised my uni tuition was sorted.

Me to Dad: *You promised you had fees covered, and the hut, the forest, dad, it's going to die.*

My finger hovers over Nico's name in messenger. How do I tell him his mountain-bike business could be threatened? I can't swipe from my mind images of giant construction vehicles decimating the winding, forest-clad trails to build straight, soulless, concrete access roads. No one is going to want to ride tracks like that, especially nature-loving bike tourists.

Below my window, car doors open, and Mom's voice rises from the driveway. "She'll come around. If she wants to become a lawyer, she has to. She's lucky the council will let me hire her without going through their formal hiring process." Bitter resentment lingers in her tone.

And Mike replies, "This is a lot for her. I wish there was another way."

The engine starts then fades, until the only sounds floating through the curtains are the early morning birds.

From my closet, I pull out a box labelled *Mountain Bike Gear*. I haven't ridden my bike since Dad died. I hug the stack of shorts and tees; the smell is a mix of washing powder, forest, and Dad.

I change and head downstairs to Dad's basement. A rush of cool air wafts up from the hundred-year-old steep staircase.

At the bottom of the stairs is Dad's workbench, his tools hung in neat rows on the wall next to our bikes. Around the corner, there's a double bed and a gallery of photos from Dad's adventures volunteering for the Conservation Corps. Replanting forests in Borneo, Ethiopia, Indonesia, and Thailand. My favorite image, though, is of Dad, Mr. Balducci, and me, aged six, planting the first seedlings to re-establish the forest around the lakefront.

I run my finger along Dad's bookshelf, which is filled with Lonely Planet travel guides, plant identification books, and jars of seeds Dad and I collected. My fingertip is dust-free; Mom has been down here too.

Holding up a jar to the window, the sunshine illuminates the mustard-yellow line down each ridge of the olive-green, hexagon-shaped seeds. The faded writing on the label is no longer legible. I rest on the bed, clutching the jar as if the seeds have weight. "*Izz, we should plant these out next.*" His voice plays over in my head like he's here.

On the wall next to our bikes hangs a map; shaded green are areas Dad and Mr. Balducci had finished planting, and left white are areas still to plant. Black pins mark the mountain-bike tracks we've completed. Ruthless Track still sits without a pin. According to Eli, if you have a heart attack and die in a chopper, you can't mark the track as complete. Black pins are only for tracks completed where everyone comes home alive.

My bike hangs next to where Dad's bike was. The derailer is bent. The seat is too low. And the tire is flat. I can't bring myself to ride or fix my bike. The smell of degreaser is too much. It echoes in the air, unearthing memories of Dad fixing chains while we talked about everything and nothing. Insignificant conversations then, but conversations I'd do anything for now. Dad's wall of tools blurs. I let the tears fall rather than force them away. His room is the only place I cry without fear of upsetting Mom, and where I don't pretend to be okay. That's the thing about grief. It has a habit of resurfacing, as though Dad dies over and over again.

I abandon the idea of biking the trails and opt for a walk. I text Eli.

Me: *Stole your car keys. Going for a walk at the lake. Are you okay? Have you heard about Mom and Mike's apartment plan? Come find me at the lake forest track if you need to. Love you. Izz.*

I park in front of the lake. Behind the hut, I sit on a log under the canopy of Dad's forest. Images of bulldozers felling the trees, and concrete mixers pouring foundations suffocate my mind.

The track winds through Dad's forest and around the lake's edge until it takes an abrupt turn inland. I walk up and over valleys until I reach the skid site on the ridge, where the trail flattens and links with others.

The song of cicadas rings through the dense overgrown canopy. Mountain bikers zoom past me down the thin technical downhill track.

Moments later, there's a curdled, "Ah, fuuuuuck," followed by a howl of pain. There's a steep drop-off just down from here. One wrong twitch of your handlebar, and you'll hit a wall of cliff rocks.

Around the corner, there's Nico, in a full-face black helmet, clutching his bloodied knee, whelping in pain. He looks like all the other mountain bikers, except for the bloodied fern tattoo on his arm.

"Hey, I got you," I say.

His eyes are steeped in pain. He gasps a labored breath. "Ahhhh."

I rest my backpack in front of him and retrieve the first aid kit from its top pocket. I grip the hand that's clutching his knee: "Take your hand off." Mud, stones, and threads from his torn shorts mix with blood oozing from the gash with jagged edges cut to the bone of his kneecap. I suck back the need to be sick and squeeze the saline over the cut, washing away debris. Nico winces in pain and jams his eyes shut, his face pale.

"You're going to be okay." I sound calm, but inside, my panicked nerves are shooting around in all directions, desperate to remember the first aid Dad taught me. His voice echoes, *"You'll want to practice lots because when you find someone in an emergency situation, shock makes you forget things."*

Nico is sitting upright; his body slumps and sways, his eyes half open, his focus on me, but it's vacant like no one is home. Gripping him close to my chest, I catch him before he falls, and lower his body to the ground. We're in the middle of a narrow steep track at the bottom of a five-foot drop-off, and above that, a tight blind corner. Soon another rider will hurtle down the track and crash into us. With a steep bank on either side, there's nowhere to go but down.

I cover Nico's knee with the largest plaster in my first aid kit, but it's far too small, not big enough to cover the wound. I wrap his knee in a bandage. Blood immediately soaks through. Ripping my t-shirt off, leaving me in my sports bra, I wind the tee around his knee, using the sleeves and my hair tie to secure it in place.

Gripping Nico's mangled bike, its wheel bent out of shape, I push it off the track and into the tree line, getting a glimpse of the view over the lake and surrounding forest.

I bend down behind Nico's head. "Sorry, this is going to hurt." I slide my arms under his back, hooking under his armpits, and drag him down the track toward Midpoint, to the only flat land, where there's cell reception.

I get into a rhythm, dragging his body until my arms shake and my shoulders give out. Then rest a second, re-secure my grip under his shoulders, begin again.

We reach the sign to Midpoint lookout. Dragging Nico off the track and through a forested shortcut, we reach the field of wildflowers and the panoramic view over the lake, forest, Rockridge, and the mountains beyond.

While I wait for my phone to pick up the reception, I lay Nico on his side by the trees, sheltered from the wind. He shudders and shivers. From my bag, I unwrap the silver emergency blanket, placing it over him and tucking it under his body.

My phone beeps with missed calls and messages from Mom. Ignoring them, I call emergency services.

"*Nine one one, what's your emergency?*"

The phone operator prompts me: "*Ambulance, police, or fire?*"

"We need a helicopter."

Nico tosses and turns, groaning. He is still wearing his helmet; there are cracks through one side.

I explain to the operator where we are, and by the time she finishes asking her agonizing medical questions, Nico has fainted.

"He's fainted," I say to the operator. I dump my phone on the ground and place my ear to his chest, relieved to feel it rising and falling.

"Ma'am, ma'am … ma'am?" the lady on the phone says.

"I'm here, I'm here." My voice is panicked; I just have to hold it together a little longer.

"A helicopter is on the way."

Nico comes round; he's shivering. I climb under the emergency blanket and huddle into his side, my hand gently resting on his chest. The wind whips around the trees. "I got you. It's going to be okay," I say. His arm rises from his side, and he holds my hand, linking his fingers with mine.

"Chopper?" he asks, his voice shaky, his eyes glazed and unfocused. He tilts his head to one side to avoid my face.

"I'm so sorry. It's the quickest way to get you to the hospital."

I hate that right now he's reliving the helicopter crash that killed his parents and nearly himself. Tears well. No matter how hard I try to stop them, they stream down my cheeks. I feel his pain, his loss, and the emptiness that comes with losing people you love.

Nico stares at me blankly through half-open eyes, like a weight is bearing down on his eyelids. Using the cuff of his sleeve, he wipes the tears from my cheek before his hand drops to his chest and his eyes snap shut. I hug him close, gulp down the tears, and try to ease out the wobble in my voice. "You're going to be okay."

The air vibrates with the whirr of a chopper approaching. Gently pulling my body away from Nico, I run to the picnic table and climb on top, waving my arms in the air. Closer now, the chopper approaches the cliff face in front of me, hovering in the cloudless blue sky before it flies over and lands. The blustery wind from the chopper's blades pushes the tall, sun-bleached grass and wildflowers in every direction.

The blades still spinning, a medic jumps out of the helicopter and, hunched over, runs to Nico.

In rapid succession, she asks me a bunch of questions about how I found him and how long he's been unconscious.

The medic inspects his head and neck; blood is still oozing from under his helmet.

"I didn't know if I should have left his helmet on or taken it off."

"You did the right thing."

Another medic arrives, and together they slide Nico onto a stretcher and place him in the chopper.

Inside the chopper, I sit opposite Nico while the medic checks his vitals and inserts an IV line. Nico comes to; the pained, unfocussed look in his eyes, and the way he tilts his face … I want to reach out and link my fingers with his, lie next to him and somehow take away all his thoughts.

"He's going to be okay, right? Does he know what's happening?"

The medic smiles, gently. "The drugs I've given him for the pain will knock him out a little. He's going to be okay."

The blades of the helicopter whirr once again, and we lift into the air and fly over the cliff, leaving the vastness of the lake and forest-clad valleys crisscrossed with sweeping trails behind, heading toward the hospital.

We arrive, and they take Nico away to operate on his knee.

After Nico's aunty arrives, Eli picks me up and takes me home. I immediately go to my room.

Mom opens my door, her face contorted. "I thought the chopper was for you!" That look she's giving me, the same as when Dad died, like the fear and worry have killed her inside, again.

"I'm fine, really," I say.

"That place is too dangerous," she says, wrapping her arms around me.

I want to wriggle out of her grip; I'm angry at her about the apartment complex, but considering she lost Dad to the forest, and for a moment thought she might lose me too, I can't add to the weight of her grief.

On my bed, there's a printed-out job description.

Community Forest Liaison Coordinator

Job description: Foster a positive relationship between the community and the proposed establishment of the apartment complex.

The salary is double what I'm getting at Mr. Balducci's and, added to the money I've saved, would cover my first semester of law fees.

I lie in bed for hours, too wired to sleep. The events of the day replay, over and over. Even though I know Nico is safe in the hospital and he's going to be okay, I can't stop thinking about him, hoping his leg isn't so damaged it will stop him from riding.

Mom comes in to check on me; I roll on my side and pretend to be asleep. When she leaves, my phone beeps.

Nico: *Just out of surgery. That forest sets my heart on fire, even if it broke my knee. I took this just before I crashed.*

Attached is a photo taken at sunrise from the ridge—the lake, and the forest bathed in the glow of the morning sun.

Me to Nico: *Stunning. I'm so glad you're okay.*

Nico: *I'm a little wired and woozy from the drugs but all will be loverly. Thank you, Izzy, for rescuing me.*

Heart emojis drift up the screen and I can't stop smiling.

Eight

While I'm watching Eli make pancakes in the kitchen, my phone beeps.

Nico: *So random Q: Is it weird that I am craving a Pinkie Pie? There's something magical about that fake strawberry-flavored marshmallow mixed with caramel.*

Me: *I know, right? Like nostalgia makes it taste better.*

Nico: *Exactly.*

Me: *How's the leg?*

There's a knock at the front door. It's Penny.

"What's with the knocking?"

"I wanted to make an entrance." And she pulls a pose, dressed in mountain-bike shorts, a tee, and sneakers. "Eh, eh." She doesn't look herself except for her winged eyeliner. Grinning, her focus shifts from me to Eli standing behind me.

"Look at youuu, nice. I made breakfast for us," he says.

We follow him into the kitchen. A stack of blueberry-and-banana pancakes sits on the table. He stabs a fork into the top two, plopping them on his plate, and pours over syrup.

"I'm pumped, Pens," Eli says, "got an epic track to take you on."

Penny's eyes go wide. "Epic?"

"Oh, don't worry. Easy tracks, a few minor hills. I'll be right there," Eli says, patting Penny on the back.

Penny's face relaxes. She's less sports-wise and more street-wise.

"You got this," I say. "It will be awesome." I never use the word *awesome*; weird.

"You're spritely today," Penny says. She leans into me and glances down at my phone at the precise moment a notification pings with a message from Nico. "Awesome, awesome," she whispers, a grin spreading across her face. "Spill the tea, girl," she says, playfully tapping my leg with her foot under the table.

"No tea, just checking how he is."

"Ri … ight." And she and Eli exchange smirks.

"I need to know if he … will be okay to work, ya know … so I can make a plan for more work if he's away." I'm rambling, but it's not untrue.

"Sure, sure." Penny and Eli say in unison, their eyes doing all the mocking.

Nico: *Leg is, er, swollen and dislocated. PSA, when they ask if you're happy to sleep in the geriatric ward because there's no space in general, say no. I woke to a lovely elderly man with dementia trying to get into my bed.*

Nico: *Though not all bad. We're playing chess. BTW, they're all sneaky cheaters. A.k.a. I suck.*

And a photo: Nico sitting in bed with a cast on his leg and a bunch of elderly patients crowded around playing cards with their thumbs up.

Me: *Lol.*

"There's a lot of grinning going on over here," Penny says, watching me take a picture of my breakfast of chocolate milk with a Pinkie Pie floating on top, before sending it to Nico.

Penny and Eli exchange smirks.

"We're friends. No big deal," I say casually, like texting him is no big deal. And absolutely doesn't give me heart bubbles every time he texts.

"Mm-hmm," Penny says.

"We should get going before it gets too hot," Eli says, jamming the last of his pancake into his mouth. "Oh, and I have something to show you on your bike." He grins playfully at Penny, placing his plate in the sink.

"Have fun," I shout as Eli and Penny head out the front door to the bikes. Penny squeals. "You got me a bell! It's the cutest."

Nico: *I'm legit jealous of that Pinkie Pie.*

He's attached a picture of his hospital cup of tea with a sad plain-Jane biscuit floating on top.

Nico: *Send help, lol. TEA? And GINGER biscuits.*

Nico: *On the upside, check out who I made friends with. The secretary of the Rockridge Botanical Society, the lovely Jan. She keeps hugging me.*

Nico: *But it's visiting hours now, and they're all gone, so it's just me and fat leg.*

And another picture. He's drawn on his cast over his knee—a cactus with a sad face.

In the pantry, I dig my hand deep in the back, retrieve the cookie tin, pop the lid, and pull out a bunch of Pinkie Pies before stashing them in my bag. I grab one of my cactus plants from my room—the one with a dome-shaped body covered in spikes, in a white pot with a knobby nose, two black dots for eyes, and a cute smile. I place the plant on the car's passenger seat, and it's not until I'm on the highway and take the turnoff toward Saint Peter's Hospital that doubt creeps in. I'm second-guessing my decision. Is it weird to visit your slightly annoying workmate in the hospital after you possibly saved their life? Or is it just weird that he was my annoying workmate and I'm wondering if I should have worn makeup and a nicer top? "You Make Me Feel Brand New" plays on the radio. The corniest of songs, but the lyrics are embarrassingly true.

I wind my way through the parking building and pull into a spot.

Ambulance sirens wail as I follow the signs to the gift shop. I flick through the cards. There's one with two hanging potted plants. The caption: *I adore hanging with you*. The ferns in the image are incorrect—not a species at all—but it's cute. I return the card and take a mental note of its position, even though I have no intention of giving it to him. I settle on an illustrated card covered in a mass of leaves. The text reads: *You're unbe-leaf-able*. It's funny. Grabbing a plain black gift bag, I place the plant, five Pinkie Pie chocolate bars from my handbag, and the card inside. While traipsing the hospital corridor looking for the geriatric ward, I rack my brain for what to write in the card.

Lost, I stop and check out the map outside the hospital café and locate the geriatric ward. Then, resting on the seat outside the café, I pull out the card and write.

Nico,

Get beet-a soon! Oh, kale, yeah!

Izz

I hope he likes it and write *Nico* in loopy handwriting on the front. From behind, someone says, "Izz."

I swing around, and there's Nico in a wheelchair being pushed by Anna in her nurse's uniform.

"What ya doing here?" His tone is upbeat.

"Nice to see you, Izzy," Anna says. I was silly to think he wouldn't have any visitors. "I just finished my shift and was taking Nico for a cup of tea. You're welcome to join us." She's lovely and perfect, impossible not to like. But does she know Nico doesn't like tea?

"Oh, I, er …" I stumble over my words, not wanting to interrupt them.

"Come with. We can go for a ride." And Nico pats the gap next to him on the oversized wheelchair, laughing. "Go on. One hot chocolate. If ya have the time, of course."

"Sure, why not?" I walk beside him, not taking up his offer to sit in the wheelchair, but not *not* wanting to.

"I'll get the drinks. What'll ya have, Izzy? It's on me—student nurse discount." And she waves her hospital ID stamped with the words *Student Nurse*. "It's one of the few perks of working twelve-hour shifts for zero dollars." Anna swivels the handles of the wheelchair toward me. "Here." She motions for me to take the grips.

"Let me guess, hot chocolate, right?" Nico says, smirking, and I love how it's kinda like our own inside joke.

I grin. "Yeah, thank you."

I push Nico to the farthest away table by a large window that overlooks the only clump of trees.

Nico repeats his question. "Whatcha doing here?"

I stumble over my words. "I, er, um …" Seeing him with Anna has me wondering if my intentions for being here are wrong.

He watches as I place the gift bag on the ground and, with my foot, scoot it under the table out of view.

I can be a friend. Friends, I chant to myself. "I popped in to see how you're getting on," I say, finally answering his question.

"Aw, that's so sweet, Izz," Nico says.

I peer over at Anna, paying for our drinks. She glances around the packed café, smiling at me when she spots where we are sitting. The fake pot plant resting on the table reminds me of the forest and my soon-to-be role in destroying it. The thought instantly makes me nauseous.

He pulls his phone from his pocket and leans close, which sends my nervous system into overdrive. He holds it up, showing me his booking calendar for his bike tours. "Three bike tour jobs booked with the botanical society. The lovely Jan is going to make it a regular thing—when my leg is better, of course. Just as well I invested in some e-bikes."

"That's so exciting. So happy for you."

His beaming smile drops into a downcast grimace. "Hopefully, the forest isn't slaughtered before then. Jan said the council has put forward a proposal to build an apartment complex at the lake."

He's watching me intently. I should tell him Mom is partly responsible and worse, I'm working for her, but I can't force the words out.

"It's okay, Izz," Nico says, his smile reassuring when it should be me apologizing. "We're setting up a community meeting to see if there's anything we can do to stop it. I said I knew the perfect person. We need you, Izz."

My body feels like it's free-falling through the hospital floors to the ground below.

"Yeah, of course. I'm in for sure." If only he knew I've now officially agreed to work both for and against the forest being cut.

Anna arrives with the drinks, places hot chocolates in front of Nico and me, and sits down. The tea bag tag dangles out the front of her cup. Lemon zinger. That girl needs no more zing; she's got it all going on.

"Oh, the forest thing. Count me in," Anna says, taking a sip of her tea.

Nico excitedly shows me photos of the new electric bikes he's invested in. He then retells the story of his first night staying in the geriatric ward, waking to find an elderly gentleman holding his hand.

"He thought I was his wife; called me June. I felt bad that he was confused and lonely, so I've not corrected him and now he brings me tea. Like five times a day."

"Aww, that's the sweetest thing," I say, trying not to laugh. It's sad and sweet at the same time, and I'm so glad Nico is there for him. His kindness grips me.

Anna yawns, letting out a tired sigh. She slips on her leather motorbike jacket and grabs her helmet from under the table. "I'll wheel ya back. Got to get home before I fall asleep."

"Oh, of course," Nico says.

"Or Izz could wheel you back if you're not ready?"

With a spoon, Nico digs out the marshmallows from his hot chocolate. "That cool, Izz? If you have time? I can introduce you to Jan.

You'll love her. That gal loves to jibber-jabber about plants and the environment, so you're in for a treat."

"Yeah, sounds great."

Anna stands. "Same time tomorrow, Nico?"

"Always keen for hot chocolates and an excuse to get out of the ward."

Anna laughs. "And I'll probably see you tomorrow, Izz, if you're working at Mom's."

"Yeah, I'll be there."

Anna waves as she lifts her bag over her shoulder and places her bike helmet under her arm.

"Thanks for everything, Anna," Nico says, waving as she leaves.

He immediately starts telling me about Jan, the lovely lady he's met from the Rockridge Botanical Society. As he speaks, the sun breaks through the gaps in the trees behind us, highlighting the gold flecks in his hazel eyes.

"Come meet her." He glances at his phone. "Visiting hours are nearly over."

A smile spreads across my face; his energy for life is contagious. Picking up the drinks, I run out of hands.

"Oh, I can take that stuff." He lifts the gift bag from the ground and places it on his lap. He holds out his hands to take the drinks, one in each hand. "At full speed," he orders, chuckling to himself.

A giggle leaps out. He's ridiculous.

I push him down the corridor.

"Oh, wrong way," he says.

I lurch, suddenly changing directions, and the gift bag on Nico's lap flops over and his card slides out onto the floor, name side up.

"Whaaaat? For me?" he says, unable to pick it up because he's holding two cups of hot liquid.

I pull to the side of the corridor. A pod of doctors speeds past, deep in discussion. I retrieve the card.

"Yeah. This is for you—everything in the bag, actually." I hand him the card and take the drinks. I continue to push the wheelchair while balancing the cups on the handles. He rips the envelope off the card, holds up my handwritten message, and his laughter fills the hallway. "It's the cutest. Thank you." He lifts the cactus in one hand and a Pinkie Pie in the other. "You're next level." Excitement rings in his voice. "I shall name the cactus Spike."

"Very original," I laugh.

"Yup, it's what I was going for."

It's shockingly easy to talk to Nico. He's the guy that gets along with everyone, including hot nurses who ride motorbikes. I just wish I knew what their deal was.

"We're here." He points to room sixty-seven.

Inside, there are six cubicles, all with the curtains shut.

Nico whispers, "It's one thirty-six. Visiting hours are over. It took six minutes for them to all fall asleep."

I push the wheelchair right up to his bed. "Need a hand?"

"Yeah."

I take the card, drinks, Pinkie Pies, and cactus, placing them on his bedside table—where there's the exact same card sitting open. Signed, *Love Anna.*

Nico grips my arm as he pulls himself out of the wheelchair, resting all his weight on his good leg. I swing my arm around his waist and feel the weight of him lean in as he swivels his lower half onto the bed before releasing his grip on me.

Pointing at the closed curtain next door, Nico whispers, "Jan is asleep." A soft snore comes from behind, and a cheeky grin sweeps his face. "Unbe-leaf-able."

And we both laugh because he's ridiculous.

"Seriously, though. Thank you," he says, darting his focus to the card and cactus. "It's so sweet of you. I—"

A nurse interrupts us. "I'm sorry, but visiting hours are over." Her smile is warm. "You're welcome to come back tomorrow. Nico, we are going to take you to radiology."

"I should get going. But feel better, 'kay?" There's an awkward beat of silence. Both of us smile. As I'm about to turn to leave, Nico holds out his arm, inviting me in to hug him. I lean into his body, my face pressed into his chest, and his arm wraps around my back. "Thanks heaps, for everything," he says hugging me tighter, and gently rests his head against mine, setting every nerve alight.

"Welcome," I whisper.

The nurse pushes Nico's wheelchair up to his bed, gripping the handles, and when we pull apart it feels rushed, forced, and I don't know how I got to this point so effortlessly.

"Bye," he says as another nurse arrives, and they ready him for wherever they're going.

Just as I reach the door, he calls out, "Izz! Er, if you want to …" His voice tapers off mid-sentence. "Come back another time and meet the lovely Jan from the botanical society."

Our eyes connect for a second before he answers the nurse's question about how much pain he's feeling.

"Yeah, I'd like that." And I leave, feeling like since the very first time we met, everything seems to contain more meaning.

When I get home, I pull up next to Mike's car. Mom grips the handles of two shopping bags from the trunk, which is full of stuff. I say nothing and pick up three shopping bags with *Cotton Co.* stamped on the side. We walk inside in silence. I feel her watch my every movement as I rest the bags on the kitchen bench, the tension from our earlier conversation weighing heavily.

"These are for you. Clothes for work." It's her way of trying to be nice while insisting I do what she asks, like a no-backsies kind of deal.

She pulls out a hideous floral shirt, followed by a pair of dress pants, both of which look a size too small. I'd be offended by her insistence on buying clothes in aspirational sizes, but I'm relieved there's no way they'll fit. If my school counselor taught me anything, it's that her need to reinvent herself and the people around her comes from her grief, not mine.

"They're too small. I'm an eight, not a six," I say politely. I know deep down buying me stuff is her messed up way of trying to clear the air between us.

"Just try them on. You're in desperate need of office-appropriate clothes."

Irritation creeps up my neck into my temples. She pulls out a second pair of the same pants but in navy blue, and three other blouses, all the same size, before pushing the pile into me.

"Thank you, but they're too small," I repeat calmly, but she's not listening.

"Just do it, and I'll be up in a second to look. I got you shoes too. You'll have to keep an open mind. It is an office you'll be working in, after all."

Code for *they're ugly*.

I haul myself up to my room and dump the pile on my bed. I slip the navy pants on. They pull across the tops of my thighs and cut me in the middle, and that's before I've tried to do them up. The material itches my skin; I think it must be some kind of polyester fire-ant blend.

I slip my comfortable jeans back on. I don't bother with the shirts.

Mom swings my door open. "Well?" Her arms are crossed.

"They're too small."

She huffs out a tired, disappointed sigh. "Return them. You're not coming into the office looking like that." She looks me up and down as I button my jeans, ripped at the knee, and pull on my Dr. Martens.

Mike pops his head in the door. "Did ya hear the great news, Izz? We got the first stage of the apartment complex development approved by the city council. Who's ready to celebrate?" And he jingles his keys. "Anyone up for a drive to the proposed site with a picnic?"

In that second, my body free-falls, leaving me hollow.

Mom intently focuses on me. "Isn't that great news, Izz? One step closer to you getting the money you need for law fees. All we need is the community liaison stuff approved, and I think we have it in the bag."

I divert my attention out the window. I can't stand looking at her. If she wasn't still hurting over Dad, and I didn't need the money, I'd be raging.

Mike jingles his keys again. "Come with us."

He's gotta learn to read the room. The tension between Mom and me has reached its peak. I don't want to feel angst toward her, but it's hard right now.

"No, I need to get some stuff organized for Mrs. Wilson's garden."

"You do too much unpaid work for that place and for Mr. Balducci," she snaps. "I'm sad we can't cover the cost of your fees. Money is tight. Appreciate this job, Izzy. You can't pay your law tuition without it." A mix of disappointment and sadness rings in Mom's tone.

Saying nothing, I busy myself folding the clothes she gave me and placing them back in the bags to be returned. She turns on her heel and leaves the room, and Mike follows obediently after her.

Nico sends a photo of Jan and him playing chess on his bed.

Nico: *She's keen to meet you and pumped about coming up with some ways we can save the forest. Wednesday, week after next, cool to meet up?*

I clutch my phone, staring at his message.

Me: *I'm in.*

Even though I shouldn't be.

Nine

Nico: *Check this out.*

Attached is a video of Nico using crutches to walk down the hallway of his house.

Me: *Nice, ya really picked up some speed.*

Nico: *A new record - six seconds…wild. Sucks my leg won't be better before you leave for uni and we can't work on Mrs. Wilsons river garden together.*

I'm going to miss his energy more than I thought was possible.

Me: *I'll need updates and progress photos for sure.*

Nico: *Of course.*

I couldn't resign completely from Mr. Balducci's; I committed to casual planting work at the forest. I did the math to see if I could keep some work for Mrs. Wilson, but given the ten-hour round trip from the university, and my insane law schedule, I couldn't find a realistic solution.

Pulling into Mrs. Wilson's, the sun's rising over the lagoon and the birds are mid-chorus. The reality that I will replace this view with a monochrome city is just sinking in.

Next to the lagoon on the roadside, I spot a black scrunched-up something. Pausing the truck, I pick up the damp black hoodie and hold it out. *Nico's Mountain Bike Tours* is printed on the front. Holding it up, with the view of the lake in the background, I snap a picture.

Me: *In case you're wondering where your hoodie went.*

Nico: *Never get sick of that view, eh? I've been missing that.*

Around the back of Mrs. Wilson's homestead, I drape Nico's hoodie over the pool fence to let it dry in the sun. I get to work laying mulch around the fruit trees, which takes me till lunch. Taking a break, I rest in the shade of a peach tree.

Me: *I can drop your hoodie off after work if you want it.*

Nico: *That would be awesome. Get my cast off today, woo hoo, hello moon boot, lol.*

The back door opens, and Anna walks out in a black bikini. She has a perfect curvaceous tummy and thighs. She's practically a Greek deity.

"Hey, Izz. I've got a spare swimsuit if you want to borrow?"

"No; thanks though. I want to finish up soon. I've got some stuff on this afternoon."

She walks to the pool gate, lifting Nico's hoodie. "Nico's?"

"Yeah."

"I'll drop it up to him. I'll be riding past on my way to work."

"Oh, yeah, I guess. Sure." Disappointment rings through me.

She rehangs his hoodie and dives into the pool in one perfect, gliding swoop. I pick a peach and, while taking a bite, snap a selfie and send it to Nico.

Nico: *They are the best peaches. Mrs. Wilson must have the bomb as gardener or something coz they're the sweeeeetest.*

Nico: *Are you taking a break? Eating stolen fruit, whaaaat.*

Me: *Think I'll go for a swim too.*

Nico: *Me and my crutches are on our way over. I bet you're hot.*

I re-read and re-read his message again. Does he mean what I think he means? How do I reply to that?

And in rapid-fire, Nico sends me a stream of messages one after the other.

Nico: *Because you're hot.*

Nico: *I mean, you're hot from working.*

Nico: *Not that you're not hot. What I meant was, it's crazy hot here and at Mrs. Wilsons, and I'd love a swim too, to cool down … because the air is humid. I promise I'm 100% not pervy, ok that's a lie, I'm almost certain I'm 99% non-pervy. I'm making this worse. Sorry. I'll stop.*

I sit there for ages thinking about how to reply. If he came over for a swim, I'd dive right in. And I'm one hundred percent pervy, but only for him. Thoughts of Anna have me guarded. So I write the most boring message because the truth is unwholesome and unfair on Anna if she's into him.

Me: *Lol. P.S. Anna will drop off your hoodie on her way to work.*

What I want to message is, how about you and I go for a swim, you pull me close, and I'll tingle all over when I feel your hands on my skin. I swipe the image from my mind; it's wrong on so many levels. I'm not the kind of girl who goes for someone who's potentially taken. We're friends. Friends.

Nico: *All good. Thanks – enjoy those peaches, I miss em.*

I pick peaches and place them in an unused plastic plant pot, lean over the pool fence, and hold up the pot of fruit. Anna is sunbathing on an inflatable mattress in the middle of the pool.

"For Nico," I say. "I'll put them by his hoodie."

"Aw, that's sweet. No worries."

I mound mulch around the flower garden outside the pool fence. And by two, I've run out.

Anna, dressed in her nurse's uniform, grabs Nico's hoodie and fruit. "Have a great day, Izz. The pool garden looks stunning! Mom is really going to miss you when you're gone. Your last day is Friday, hey?"

"Yeah, it is." No matter how often I tell myself, it doesn't feel real.

"I'm having a birthday party on Friday. You're more than welcome to come. Bring Penny or whoever."

"Sure, thanks."

"I've hired a karaoke machine."

Penny will need no convincing.

Wednesday after work, I text Penny.

Me: *I gotta shop and get work clothes. Come with?*

Penny: *Yup, meet ya at the mall.*

I pull into the underground parking lot, then into the only spot available in the farthest corner from the mall entrance.

Me: *Where you at?*

Penny: *WTAF. Looking at this.*

And she sends me a picture of the billboard outside the main entrance, advertising new lakeside apartments.

Me: *WTAF?*

When I find Penny, she's standing under the billboard. "Whatcha gonna do about that situation?" she says. Her arm thrusts into the air, pointing at the picture of the proposed subdivision next to Mom's and Mike's smug, smiling faces.

Penny glares at me. Then a pained smile spreads across her face, like she knows what I'm up against.

I get that sinking, out-of-body feeling, like gravity has disappeared and I'm free-falling. "I have to support Mom if I want to go to law, right? I ... *we* need the money. But the forest, Dad, and ... Nico." My voice tightens and constricts. "What the actual fuck am I going to do?" I am literally clueless.

"Uh-huh, girlfriend. You have options."

"Like?" I face her as we walk into the mall.

"Okay, ya got me there, but you're the smartest girl I know, er … you'll figure it out …" She pauses. "Because you always do … somehow."

I clutch the bag of work clothes Mom got me that I need to return. We head into Cotton Co. Out of all the clothing shops, Mom chose the most hideous. A mannequin wearing highlighter-yellow capris with some psychedelic print distracts Penny. The t-shirt with a chicken on the front reads *I'm a cool chick*.

Penny points at the mannequin, tilting her head from side to side. A confused grimace spreads across her face. "You do you, boo." She bashes her arm into my side. "Oh, girl, this shop, ain't it?" Then she backtracks. "Unless, of course, this vibe is totally up your street, in which case, my sincerest apologies." She laughs, which makes me laugh. Penny has a way of finding the funny in the mundane.

I take the clothes Mom got me and lay them on the counter with the receipt. The shop assistant peers down through her oversized, thick-rimmed, turquoise glasses.

"We don't do refunds, but I can give you a store credit, valid for a year."

I google the store's terms of service. "It says here that you are entitled to a refund if the clothes are in perfect condition, unworn other than to try, and the tags are still attached."

She adjusts her manager's badge as if it's scratching through her coral floral top.

"All the tags are attached, and the clothes are in new condition," I say.

"I see. Would you like to check if there is anything in the store that you might like?" The tightness in her eyes borders on giving me the evils. But the terms of service are the rules.

"No, but thank you. I'd like my money back, please."

Saying nothing, she returns the money in cash.

Penny makes a beeline for Factorie, a new clothing shop we adore. While I pause at the rack of neatly folded ripped jeans next to nineties rock t-shirts, Penny goes straight to the plaid shirts. "Ooooh, girlie, you got cash to burn. Let's get going-out clothes."

"If by 'going out' you mean clothes for the office." I'm kidding myself. There is zero appropriate office wear in here.

Nico: *What the fuck? Have you seen this?*

He's attached a photo of the same billboard we saw in front of the mall.

That free-falling feeling hits again.

Me: *It's depresssssssing. I'm not sure what to do.*

Penny peers over the phone. "O-M-G, it will wipe his business." She says it like she thinks that hasn't crossed my mind.

"I know," I say, the words flying out meaner than I expected. I correct myself. She means well. "Sorry, it's just …I know." The end of my sentence trails off as a whisper. He'll lose his dream.

"You gotta tell him about your new job? I mean, he's gotta know, right?"

"I will." Somehow.

Penny grips my shoulders. "Mm-hmm. Sorry, not saying that to be a bitch. I know this will make you overthink shit. Just sayin'. He might understand."

He won't understand. *I* don't understand.

And then it dawns on me—the photo he sent. He's here.

Penny holds up jeans and an emerald-green satin V-neck tank top. "They'd be perfect for going out."

"Speaking of going out, Anna invited us to her birthday party on Friday. I'm not sure I want to go, though."

"Oh, we gotta go. The last bash before you leave for uni, it'll be fun. Come on. Please?" She thrusts the jeans and top at me. "Try 'em on, add that popping deep-burgundy lipstick, and hot damn."

I follow Penny to the changing room, and we take stalls next to each other. As soon as the door shuts, I check to see if Nico has replied.

I slip on the jeans and tank top and glance in the mirror. I adore them both, but they're not office appropriate.

Penny's voice rises over the cubicle. "You don't want to go because of Nico, right?"

"Not exactly." It's more discovering Nico and Anna are *together* together. And it won't take long for Nico to figure out my connection with the apartment complex, and I dread seeing his face the moment he realizes I haven't been honest with him.

"Ya know," Penny says, "when I saw Nico at the supermarket, he told me you had an amazing vibe."

"He did not."

"True story. Maybe we could go to Anna's and just see how it goes."

My mind is stuck on what Penny said about telling Nico. Penny is right, maybe he will understand. Either way, being honest with him is the right thing to do.

"I'll go," I say.

Her cubicle door opens. "Show me."

When I'm out of the changing room, Penny eyes me up and down as we check ourselves out in the massive mirrors. The emerald-green top makes my eyes pop, and the V-neck stops at the perfect point, showing off the gold leaf necklace Dad gave me.

"Oh my god, love it. Perfect for Friday, just saying." Penny twists from side to side, checking out the black-and-white plaid shirt she's wearing. "Is it too similar to my others?"

I smirk. "You mean, is that black-and-white one the same as your white-and-black one?"

She laughs. "You make a valid point."

We return to our cubicles and get changed. I pay for the items, then beeline for the exit toward the parking lot, taking the long way but with fewer people.

Our phones beep simultaneously.

Eli: *I'm at the mall. Wanna get tacos?*

Penny gently drags me toward the food court, going on about what she'll order. I can't concentrate, my gaze settling on any tall male wearing a black hoodie.

We take the escalator up to the food court and wait in line at El Tacos. From behind, Eli pops his head between us, eyeing the guy at the cash register. "She'll have the extreme fire combo."

Penny laughs, playfully nudging him.

"What we having, sis? The usual very authentic Mexican chili fries with extra mayo on the side?"

Eli orders the spiciest tacos on the menu, with a thick vanilla milkshake to wash it down.

We take the only free table, which is by the escalator. Penny steals Eli's shake, straw between her lips, when she's distracted by something behind me, and her eyes widen as if they'll burst out of her head.

Nico appears next to me with his aunt Elena, who I met at the hospital after Nico's bike accident.

"Hey, funny seeing you guys here," Nico says.

Nerves catch my voice. "Oh, hey."

"Nice to see you again, Izzy," Elena says. Her olive skin, friendly hazel eyes, and wide smile are just like Nico's. She faces Nico. "I've got one quick errand to run. I'll come back in a bit, okay?"

"Yeah, all good." And he rests on the seat next to me, sliding his crutches under the table. "That banner, Izz? It's bullshit, right? They haven't even gotten community permission fully approved."

A knot is stuck in my chest. Eli and Penny exchange awkward glances.

"Yeah, it's the worst. The forest means so much to so many people."

Nico nods. "Well, good thing we're going to do something about it. There's a process to appeal the development. So glad you're going to help me lead this. With the lovely Jan too, of course." He glances up at Eli and Penny. "From the botanical society," he says to fill them in on a missing but essential detail.

Nico's aunty returns, clutching bags. "Ready?"

He focuses on me. "Better get me some new threads that can fit over this thing." He points to his swollen, bandaged knee in a moon boot. "I'll be seeing you all on Friday at Anna's birthday." He pauses and adds, "And at the botanical society meeting. I'll text ya the deets." Nico slides his crutches from under the table and, on one leg, glides down the escalator with his auntie.

Penny bashes my leg. At the same time, Eli says, "You gotta tell him."

"I know. I will."

Somehow.

Ten

Mom parks up outside work. Reading the notes app on her phone, she says, "Don't forget to contact your roommate for the student dorms. And sign your work contract so I can give it to the council." She continues to rattle off her list like she thinks I haven't considered any of these things.

"My new roommate is called Amelia, and we've already been texting. She seems cool. And I've signed the contract. It's in my drawer."

She rolls her eyes. "Why did you not tell me?"

Because we're not really talking, and I'll be destroying a forest.

She taps her phone, ticking the things I've completed off her list.

"I got this," I say.

"You start at the office on Monday, so wear your new clothes." She looks me up and down. I'm in my Balducci uniform: polo, cargo pants, and steel-cap boots. The disapproving looks started when she stopped working in environmental law and traded organic, ethically sourced clothing items for labeled business suits. To be fair, she looks stunning, but not as stunning as she used to. I miss the version of her without all the added extras.

Inside, Mr. Balducci is behind the coffee machine training a new barista. A line of people queue for coffee. Nico was also right about the café. Mr. Balducci has more clients than ever, and with the packed café, business is doing well.

"Morning, Izz," Mr. Balducci says over the hum of chatter and coffee beans grinding. "Mrs. Wilson just called. She'd like you to make some changes suggested by Nico to her garden plan."

"Ha ha, sure." Of course Nico suggested changes. He has a way of getting out of clients what they really want from their outdoor areas. It sucks that I won't be able to see the landscape plans I'm creating now through to the end. See the client's face when the transformation is complete.

Out the back, I log on to my work computer and check my emails from Mrs. Wilson and Nico, and immediately start updating her file.

Mrs. Wilson's plan is to establish a community fruit orchard using her existing fruit trees and adding groves of more. I trail through Nico's and Mrs. Wilson's emails. A line from Nico captures my attention: *You could grow fruit and offer it free to the community from a box at the front of your drive and at markets. And donate it to local schools.* I picture Nico's warm smile as he delivers fruit to classrooms, and hungry kids biting into Mrs. Wilson's peaches, sweet juice running down their chins. It's something Dad would have wholeheartedly supported. He would have loved Nico, and it feels weird that I wish Dad could meet him.

I overhear Mr. Balducci and Nico talking in the café.

"First day back," says Nico. "I'm excited. Bringing in my mountain-bike kids today."

When Nico started, he came up with the genius idea to collaborate with a kids' school holiday program. It's perfect, really. He teaches the kids mountain-biking skills and the importance of looking after the forests because, without the forests, there would be no tracks to ride.

I force my attention back to altering Mrs. Wilson's landscape plan when Nico taps me on the shoulder. The weight of his finger sends shooting stars down my spine.

"Cool, you're working on Mrs. Wilson's fruit project. I'm stoked she went for it."

"It's the sweetest idea." I smirk at my lame pun. But it is funny.

He laughs. "Phew, I'm relieved. Was about to apologize for messing with your plan."

Nico's holding his arm behind his back like he's hiding something. He places a box in front of me, the kind with a plastic window cut into the top.

"What's this?" I ask.

"A little something to say thank you for rescuing me." A warm smile sweeps his face. "Open it."

I lift the lid, and inside is a variegated hanging hearts plant. The edges of the heart-shaped leaves blush with rose pink. It's the sweetest gesture.

"Thank you, I love it."

"I knew you would," he says.

I lift the black pot out of the box and rest it on the edge of the desk. Tendrils of interconnecting heart-shaped leaves dangle down the side of my desk.

"I figured it would be an easy plant to keep in the dorms."

"It's so beautiful, and perfect."

There's an awkward beat of silence. I want to launch a hug on him to say thank you. But for some reason I'm stuck, frozen. And then when I finally decide a friendly hug to say thanks isn't overstepping the friends barrier, he's distracted by a message on his phone.

Nico replies, then quickly returns his phone to his pocket.

"Whatcha teaching the kids today?" I ask.

"It's cute. I can't ride yet, so we're doing a planting project."

A row of mature saplings, like mini Christmas trees, lines the back wall of Nico's workstation.

Six faces appear by Nico, dressed in mountain-bike gear minus the helmets.

"Team, this is Izz, landscape designer, and plant guru."

The kids' faces beam. A dark-haired boy with giant blue eyes steps closer to my desk. "Is she the lady that saved you when you hurt your leg?"

"She is," Nico says.

The boy glances at the computer screen. "Woo, that's a cool app. You can move all the boxes around like Minecraft?"

His interest warms me. "Yep."

"Could you build a secret garden maze?"

"For sure." I open a blank project page and shift from my seat. "Here, you can try."

After a minute of showing him the basics, he's built a maze out of pittosporums. The kid's a natural.

Standing next to Nico, I whisper, "Adorable."

"He's not the only one," he says, darting his focus from me to his group of kids, who are checking out the tool rack.

I feel my cheeks blush.

"We're going to plant these," he says, holding up one of the potted saplings. He rests the plant on his desk and passes a plant tag to each kid. "Write your name and attach it to the tree like this." In capital letters, he writes *NICO* and secures the tag around the tree trunk. "Then we'll go plant them, and when we're riding, you'll be able to check on them."

Nico unravels a map of the forest and rests it on his desk. "We'll plant the saplings in the treeless gray sections, linking the forest fragments together."

It's impossible to focus on Mrs. Wilson's plan.

I grab a jar of Dad's seeds from my drawer and pass them to Nico.

"Your dad's," he says, a startled look on his face.

"Yeah."

Neither of us looks away. Nico smiles. "Thank you, we will take the best care of them."

"Can I call mine Pokémon?" one of the other kids says.

Nico smirks.

"You can name them whatever you like," I say.

"They will take a little while to grow, but you can leave them here, and I can look after them as long as you promise to come and check in on them and give them water and food."

"Like a burger," one kid says.

"Yeah, Izz, are you feeding them burgers?" Nico says.

I point to the worm compost box, just visible out the open back door. "Worm poo."

The kids break out in laughter.

"Come with me," I say, and they follow me to the worm box. I lift the first layer, showing vegetable scrapings, then lift each layer, revealing more and more worms. "They're tiger worms. They eat the vegetable scraps, and we use their poo as plant fertilizer."

"Worm poo." The kids laugh, daring each other to dip their fingers in and touch the worms.

"Oh jeepers, sorry, I'm taking over," I say to Nico. "Got a bit carried away." Their enthusiasm for something I care deeply about gets me a bit caught up.

"Ha ha, not as bad as me taking over Mrs. Wilson's garden plan."

"We make a great team, and it's been the best working with you," I say, too nervous to see his reaction to my comment, and shocked that I let the words fall out so easily. I pass a seedling pot to each kid, and using their fingers, they dig a small hole in the soil and plant one of Dad's seeds.

"Oh, before I forget." From his backpack, he pulls out a new Izzy cactus. It's exactly the same as the one that hangs from the mirror in my work truck, though clean, without Nico's graffitied smile face. He passes it to me. Our fingers glide past each other in the exchange, sending butterflies en masse to my stomach. "Sincere apologies for defacing Izzy cactus."

The kids are watching our exchange, their heads turning from me to Nico as we speak.

"Thank you." His gesture is adorable. Original Izzy cactus has grown on me and makes me smile with her lopsided, exaggerated grin. It reminds me of him.

The kids finish planting, and I return to working on Mrs. Wilson's garden plan.

Next to me, Nico says, "Thanks heaps, for hanging out with us."

"Anytime."

"Well, that's us, guys. We're done, and also running late." He turns to me. "The lovely Anna is helping me teach the kids some first aid."

Her name catches a pang of unwanted jealousy.

When I get home from work, I place the hanging hearts plant Nico gave me on my windowsill.

I'm lying in bed, about to turn my light off.

Nico: *FYI, tiger worm poo was the highlight of the kids' day, go figure.*

And he's attached a photo of the kids standing next to their labelled saplings they've planted on the edge of Dad's forest. And also a photo of Anna, with one of the boys wrapping her arm in a sling. I'm flooded with a rush of sadness I can't shake. And it hits me. My feelings for Nico have crossed the friendship line, and now I want someone I can't have. It's a glimpse of how Penny must feel—she's watched Eli go out with girl after girl, loving him from a distance.

Me: *They're adorable. I had the best time with them.*

Nico: *Can't wait till your dad's seedlings are big enough to plant. Could plant them at the summit. That would be an overnight camping trip, though.*

Me: *I'd love that.*

Nico: *Woo, I'm beat. Who knew kids can be so fun and exhausting? They're a constant whirlwind of questions. Nighty Night.*

Me: *Night.*

Eleven

I get changed for the last time into my cargo pants, t-shirt, and steel-cap boots. Usually, motivation to get to work is not an issue. Knowing I'll never work at Mrs. Wilson's again makes it hit differently. If I start, it will end.

Nico: *Happy last day. P.S. Check under the seat by the lagoon.*

Me: *??*

Nico: *You'll see.*

No one is home when I reach Mrs. Wilson's. It's a perfect late-summer morning; the sun is just rising. I pause the truck by the lagoon, once hidden behind overgrown trees and weeds. A sad wasteland turned into an idyllic wonderland.

I park the truck for the last time by Mrs. Wilson's homestead.

Posted to the front door is a note:

Izzy,

You are an absolute gem. I wish you well and know you will be successful in whatever you do.

Love, Mrs. Wilson

P.S. It's your last day, so don't work too hard. Water the seedlings and collect the fallen fruit, that's all.

I would have liked to have thanked her in person, and it cuts a little that she's not here in person to say goodbye.

At the lagoon, I switch the tap on the hose connected to a water tank secluded in the bush, then shift the pipes from the sprinkler system around, so it reaches all the newly dug-in plants.

I run my hand under the bench seat along the grooves of the wood and pull out an envelope. On the front are two hand-drawn mini cactuses with the cutest smiley faces, with prickles coming out at odd angles from their heads. The sweetness of Nico is next level. From the envelope, I pull out a card on which is an aloe vera plant with a speech bubble saying *Aloe, how are you?* And a thyme plant with a speech bubble saying *Long thyme no see.* Inside the card is a pack of heritage cape daisy seeds— my favorite—and a note that reads:

Izzy,

It's so sad to see you go. Happy last day :)

Go to the orchard.

I wander about the rows of fruit trees. Sunlight reflects off gold stars stuck to each peach. Written on each star is a word. Peeling off the stars, I stick them on the back of the envelope, rearranging the words. They read: *I'm going to miss you, look up.*

A cane basket hangs from the highest branch, camouflaged the color of the wood. Sliding it off the branch, I find inside a single homemade chocolate cupcake with chunks of a Pinkie Pie jammed in the middle. A note reads *Something yum for your break. Go to the woodshed.*

Inside the woodshed, a small rectangular box rests on the neat rows of newly cut wood Nico has stacked. I slide the lid off. There's a pair of pruning shears, and engraved on the metal blade: *You're unbe-leaf-able.* A note reads *I know your old ones suck, and just like your love of plants, these will last a lifetime. Go to the mailbox.*

I stroll past the lake and switch the sprinkler system off. There's nothing left for me to do. But so much I want to do.

After parking the truck by the mailbox, I lift the red door, and inside there's another envelope. A note in Nico's handwriting, with the address of Nicola's Cantina:

Now it's thyme to party.

Nico

P.S. I'm pretty fly for a fungi.

I'm choked up now, and push back tears, at Nico's sweetness and how working on Mrs. Wilson's garden held me together when Dad died, and amplified a passion for something I didn't know would become so deeply intertwined with the person I am.

The last line:

P.P.S. Plant puns are the beets. Hope they plant a smile.

I laugh out loud to no one, just me, about to get on a lonely highway and leave behind a job that to my core feels like home. Yet, I'm still smiling, and that's because of him.

I thrust the note to my chest and pull my phone from my pocket.

Me: *OMG, you're too mulch.*

Nico: *Lol, welcome. You leaving is a big dill.*

At six o'clock, Penny bursts through the front door. Dinner isn't till eight, but she takes literal hours to get ready. Standing in my room, she flicks through the hangers in my closet and holds up my new jeans and tank top.

"Yeah, baby. Ya get to wear the new gears. Bet ya glad you don't have to wear that get-up anymore," she says, focusing on my cargos and Mr. Balducci's uniform on the bed.

"I don't know, kinda love 'em. I'll take them with me to uni."

Penny grins. "You do you, boo." She strips off and stands in her new jeans and bra. "Which top?" She holds up one in each hand.

I focus instead on rereading the notes Nico gave me. "The right one."

Penny sighs. "Come on, ya didn't even look. What's with all the cards?"

I shove the notes in my drawer by my bed and put my full attention on Penny. "Try on the other," I say, to take the attention off what's in my drawer. She'll overhype it, and I don't want to add any more meaning to another person I must let go of when I leave.

"What do you think?" Penny twirls in her perfectly fitted jeans and low-cut white slinky blouse.

"Stunning."

Penny heads into the bathroom and begins dotting concealer under her eyes. I slip on my new jeans and satin emerald-green tank top, steal Penny's black strappy high-heeled shoes, and glare at my reflection in the mirror. I don't look like me or feel like me, but I like what I see.

From the bathroom she says, "I got raspberry vodkas. The height of sophistication. Aaaaand they match my lipstick." She pouts, then presses her lips together, evening out the thick layer of gloss. She glances at my feet. "They're cute and hot, girl. Wear 'em."

"Not the most practical things, but yeah, I like them too."

Standing side by side, we finish applying our makeup. I wing out my eyeliner, deepen the smokiness of my eyeshadow, and apply a gloss over my scarlet lipstick.

We park outside Nicola's Cantina. Painted on the window, there's a lady with flowers and jewels adorning her head and a speech bubble from her mouth: *Dare to be brave.* It's spicy inside. The unrealistic hyper-colored flowers remind me of Nico. I snap a pic and attach it to a message.

Me to Nico: *Daisy slash rose slash dystopian flowers?? Haha.*

Nico: *Cool, you're here.*

Inside, a band is playing, and I follow Penny and Eli through the bar to the outside courtyard. Fairy lights are strung through the roof rafters, giving a starry-night vibe, and large potted plants divide the space into private nooks.

"Hey, hey. Look who it is!" Nico says, sitting at a table in the far corner. "Surprise." His focus snaps to my feet and back to my face.

"Hey," I say, facing him and then Mr. Balducci and Mrs. Wilson. "You guys are so sweet."

Nico pats the space next to him.

Sitting next to him, his leg is pressed against mine. The waitress comes over with a tray of drinks and places a margarita in front of me and everyone else squeezed around the table.

Mrs. Wilson clears her throat with an elegant *hmm.* "Here's to Izzy, a talented landscape designer. Thank you for your hard work bringing my gardens back to life. I wish you well with law school."

All eyes focus on me. Holding back tears, I say, "Thank you," my words catching. I take a sip of my drink, the glass rim coated in salt, and the salty-and-sweet booze immediately goes to my head.

Mr. Balducci says, in his thick Italian accent, "Izz, you are like a daughter to me, and it's been a privilege and pleasure to work with a young person as talented as you. There's always a place for you at Balducci Landscape Design."

"Wow, thank you. It's been the best." That's an understatement.

I've learned the hard way that goodbyes aren't my thing. Since Dad died, farewells hold more weight and leave me questioning. *What if this is the last time I see this person?* I've been here less than two minutes, and it's taking everything to hold back the tears.

"You guys mean everything to me, really."

Before I know it, my focus has slipped from Mr. Balducci to Nico. But I can't hold on to his smiling grin. If he knew what I was thinking behind my smile, he'd know he means way more to me than I'm letting on. And I snap my focus away.

Nico reaches under the table, and I feel the coolness of the gap now created between our legs. He places a gift bag on the table. "From us." Nico looks directly at me. "For all your awesomeness." Then he returns his leg to where it was, resting it against mine.

Reaching into the bag, I pull out a book wrapped in white tissue paper covered in black, hand-drawn cartoon plants. There's a cactus labeled *Izzy, Plant Extraordinaire* with the cutest googly eyes, long hair, and the pockets of her cargo pants overflowing with Pinkie Pie chocolate bars.

Mr. Balducci, Mrs. Wilson, Nico—everyone is there. Nico cactus rides a bike into a bush wearing a t-shirt that says *Plants are cool.*

Nico grins. "If the bike-tour business, lawyering, and landscape design don't work out, we'd make millions selling plant-themed wrapping paper and greeting cards with our planty puns."

It's impossible not to laugh. "Because you so need another job, you know, in your spare time."

I gently peel the tissue paper off. There's a signed copy of Audrey Eagle's illustrated gardening guide. On the first page, it reads:

Izzy, follow your heart, and you will reach your dreams. Audrey.

I re-read the note over and over; it's from someone I admire deeply, and I can't believe Nico would do this for me, and all the other sweet things. I'm bursting with a building urge to hug him.

"Thank you." It's all I can muster. There's too much I want to say, too much wanting. It paralyzes me in a state of indecision, and I end up not saying or doing enough, leaving me regretful.

"Aw, you're getting a bit misty there." Nico's eyes crease at the corners as he grins and swings his arm around my shoulders, pulling me into his side.

"Thank you," I whisper, and he leans his head against mine.

"Welcome," he says, his grip tightening before letting go.

A waitress arrives with another tray of drinks, tapas, and brightly colored dipping sauces. I finish my drink and start on the next.

Mrs. Wilson stands, unhooking her bag from her seat. "I'm sorry I have to dash. I'm off to collect a karaoke machine for Anna. She'll lose her mind if it's not delivered before her guests arrive." She hugs me.

"Thank you for everything," I say.

She squeezes tighter. "See you later." She disappears into the noisy bar.

Nico downs the dregs of his drink. "How are we going to get there?"

"I can drop you all off in the van," Mr. Balducci says, jingling his keys.

Penny squeals. "Perfection. Bring on a dance karaoke challenge; we are gonna slay."

I down the last of my drink, thinking I'm gonna need like ten of these. I don't dance, let alone sing.

Mr. Balducci is distracted by someone he knows in the next booth and leaves to sit at their table. The band in the main part of the bar calls people to the dance floor.

Penny tugs at Eli's arm. "Come on, one dance. I love this song."

They leave Nico and me alone as the waitress returns with six margaritas. Nico and I each take a glass, sipping.

"Thank you so much for the book, notes, and … everything." I pause, stuck on how to put what I'm actually feeling into words without giving too much away. "It's incredibly sweet of you, and I won't forget it." I nervously sip my margarita, officially at the tipsy stage.

"It's nothing. Glad you like them."

I collect the wrapping paper and fold it neatly.

"There's a bin in the kitchen."

"I'm keeping it. I couldn't throw it away. They're adorable and mean heaps to me," I say, pointing at the cute Izzy cactus.

"Yeah, definitely." Nico's focus catches mine, and then darts to the dance floor.

Nico grabs his phone from his pocket. "Ya gotta see this; it's hilarious." And he leans close, holding up his phone. His shoulder rests against mine. He grins as the video plays. It's Nico hurtling down the mountain-bike track just up from where I found him when he crashed. The downhill mountain view captures the sweeping track, with the view of the lake in the distance. A pig and three piglets stop in the middle of the path, and he swerves. "Oh shit. Fuck, sorry, Momma." He falls, and rolls like a ball through the trees, over the drop-off until he stops in a heap on the ground, screeching in pain.

We crack up laughing.

"I'm so sorry, it's not funny. You were hurt.

"It's hilarious."

The giggles take over, and as I place my hand over my mouth, I snort-laugh, which only adds to his hysterics.

"That's the same sound the pigs were making."

And we're in stitches, gasping for breath.

"I couldn't hurt the piglets. I mean, those babies' snorts were adorable."

And somehow, our focus gets stuck. Nico searches my face, and all the noise and commotion of people around us fades. "Thanks again for looking after me," he says, raking his hand through his hair, and it's like time has stopped, and we're stuck grinning at each other. The promise I made myself that I would tell Nico about my new job comes barreling back.

"There's something I need to …" I begin to say, when Mr. Balducci appears at the end of the table, breaking our connection and killing my confidence to say the words that need to be said.

"You lot ready?" Mr. B. says, jingling his keys.

Nico and I follow him through the bar until we find Eli and Penny on the dance floor. Nico rests his hand on my shoulder gently pulling me close. He leans his face to my ear speaking over the music. "You were saying?"

I pause for a beat. Then twist my head to face him, our faces only a centimeter from touching. Our gazes lock and I'm struck with a rush of nervousness. It's the wrong moment and the wrong place to tell him.

"Just work stuff, I'll bore you later."

Me, Eli, and Penny pile into Mr. Balducci's work van and wind our way through a new subdivision, a rabbit warren of streets where all the houses look identical. We pass a park with large overhanging trees and a pond with bench seats. And finally, we pull up next to a white two-story house with fairy lights strung through the trees. Music booms through the windows while people carrying booze walk into the house.

I sink into the seat. Eli slides the van door open and hops out. Nico follows. Penny swings from the seat in front and twists the top off a raspberry vodka, passing me the bottle. The margaritas have gone to my head and legs. Getting out of the van and walking in these shoes could be embarrassing.

Nico puts his head into the van. "Come on, you two. Karaoke it up."

We head inside. I clutch my drink as we walk down the hall. Music vibrates through my chest. In the lounge, the couches are pushed against the wall, and people crowd a makeshift stage, watching two guys sing karaoke. Penny stops to talk to a couple of friends, and Eli and Nico disappear into the kitchen with a bunch of guys giving Nico grief about falling off his bike.

I rest on the edge of the couch and sip my drink as I watch Anna write my name on a piece of paper, then drop it in a hat.

"Happy Birthday," I say.

Her focus is on Nico as he makes his way toward us.

"Thanks, so nice of you to come." She smells nice, her smile is nice, and she's wearing a dress that perfectly and elegantly shows off her boobs.

"Your turn won't be long," she says brightly.

After finishing my drink, I place the empty bottle back in the carton and open another, wondering if there's any casual, non-obvious way I can weave into the conversation the question if she and Nico are a thing, or if she's hoping for a thing between them.

We watch three terrible karaoke songs as more people arrive, and the packed house gets louder and louder. Anna pulls a name from the hat. Nerves eat my stomach, fearing it will be me next. I've slipped past the optimal boozed point of misbelieving I can sing. I'm worried about navigating the one step up to the stage, falling on my ass and making a complete fool of myself.

Nico stands next to me and takes a drink from my stash. "Raspberry vodka, eh?" He takes a sip, then scrunches up his face. "Not sure how you and Penny drink this stuff."

"It's going down easy."

He glances at two remaining drinks in the six-pack. "I can see, Izz. Do you need any food? There are snacks in the kitchen if you want some."

"Aw, I'm all good, but thank you," I say, holding up my bottle and clinking it with his.

Anna digs her hand in the hat and pulls out a name. "Penny and Eli." She digs in again. "And then Izzy and Adam."

Chuckling to myself, I shake my head. "Oh hell to the no."

Nico smirks. "I'll get ya some food. Wait here."

Penny squeals as she passes me, dragging Eli by the arm. "Film this!" And they step up onto the makeshift stage.

I get up. The room, the music, and the noise merge into one. I steal Penny's pack of drinks, steadying myself on my heels, and head out the front door. I am way too far gone to sing karaoke and embarrass myself in front of Nico. The night is clear, and stars are popping as I aimlessly wander the streets until I reach a cut-through with a sign that says *Park*. The dark alley winds between houses until it ends at an open field by a pond surrounded by giant sycamore trees.

I rest on a bench under an overhanging willow. Moonlight dapples light across the still water. I wish Nico were here.

Voices up the track break my peace. I set off again, pushing my way through the forest, the thick undergrowth tricky in my heels. I rip my shoes off and thread the straps over a low-hanging branch. "I'll come get you later. Shhh." On my hands and knees, I crawl through the forest, dragging my drinks until my arms ache.

I sink to the ground and stare through the canopy of trees at the stars in my head, ranking my favorite plants from one to ten. Top on the list is the hanging hearts plant Nico gave me.

Nico: *Where are you?*

Me: *n forest hiding. there r voices.*

Nico: *Wait, what? Where are you?*

Penny: *We are looking for you! Where you at?*

Me: *Lost. P.S. I wanna hug him n wrap my arms round his neck*

Nico: *Think that message was for someone else???? No more vodka, okay?*

Me: *I pumice nothin.*

Nico: *We're on our way.*

The trees go in and out of focus. It's peaceful, like floating under water at night, my thoughts and body weightless. And then I fall asleep.

There's a tug on my arm. I bolt up and cover my face with one hand, and with my other I punch the air, hoping to hurt my attacker. "Leave me alone! I have pipp … per spray." My heart pounds, blood racing through my ears.

"Izz, it's me, Nico."

Relief floods my mind.

Nico pulls me up, wrapping his arms around me. "You're safe."

I relax into him, my head against his chest. "I thought you were someone scary."

"I can tell, your heart is going crazy, and you were about to use your pipp … per spray on me," he says, laughing.

"Yep."

When I pull away, my eyes find his, and a nervous grin spreads across his face. His arms are still wrapped around my waist. "You're adorable and hilarious," he says.

"That's funny. You're like the only person on the solar system that would agree with you."

He chuckles. "People on the solar system."

"Yep."

He turns around so his back is facing me. "Jump on."

I scramble onto his back and rest my head on his shoulder. His arms link under my legs. He's warm and smells good. As he walks, ducking under low-hanging trees, I recite the Latin names of all the plants we pass.

When I spot a small cluster of flowers, I shout, "Stoooop! *Olearia fragrantissima*! Ooh, ooh." I point my phone's flashlight at the plant with thin, elongated green leaves in sets of three and delicate yellow flowers.

Nico bends down, gripping my legs tighter, taking a closer look. "You are not wrong."

He sets me down on the ground then gently pulls on the stem, inspecting the leaves. At the same time, I hold the flashlight over the flowers. Our faces are inches apart.

I look up at him. "It's beautiful," I say, breathing in the jasmine floral scent.

"Very." He lets go of the stem, and pulls leaf litter from my hair. And I forget everything—my words, what I was doing—dropping my hand to my side.

His hand slides down my arm to my hand; linking his fingers with mine, he gently pulls me into him. My hand rests on his shoulder and glides down the top of his chest.

And then Eli comes bursting through the forest, shouting my name, sounding frantic. "Izzy!"

Nico and I snap apart.

Eli and Penny appear. "Oh, thank fucking god. You found her," Eli says, glaring at me, giving me the evils. "Don't fucking do that again." He launches at me with a hug. "It's so unlike you."

"I'll call a taxi," Penny says. "Let's get you home, girl."

Eli guides me through the forest, moving branches out of my way before they fling in my face. By the time we reach the road, the taxi is waiting.

Eli slides the door open. Before I get in, I turn back to Nico. "Thanks for getting me and everything."

Eli and Penny are standing there watching us.

Nico, his hands in his jeans pockets, says, "No problem. Anytime."

I take the back seat. The car moves forward. I watch in the rear-view mirror as Nico waves. Resting my head against the window, I close my eyes as Eli and Penny debate the different dimensions of the multiverse.

If a multiverse existed, I'd be simultaneously stargazing with Nico as we lie on the forest floor, and at the lake hut with Dad sipping Pinkie Pie hot chocolate.

Twelve

Mom bangs on the door. "Get up, Izz. You don't want to be late for your first day of work, right?"

I pull the blankets over my head; it's stuffy and suffocating but better than what the rest of the day is about to bring. The upside of working for Mom is the sleep-in. The downside of working for Mom is that I'm working for Mom.

Think of the money for law tuition.

Mom pushes the door into my room. "Right, hear me out." She pulls back the blanket and holds up the same clothes I took back to the shop. "They're a size up. They *should* fit," she says, pulling the pants from the hanger. "Warm material too. Wool, I think."

Oh joy. I'll be sweaty and itchy while working a job I don't want to be doing.

Mom slides open the door to my closet. "Don't wear these," she says, pointing to my steel-cap work boots. "Wear these." She dangles the strappy black heels I borrowed from Penny for Anna's party. "But clean the mud off first."

The moment Nico found me drunk and pulled me close has replayed over and over in my mind. My hazy, drunken, pink-vodka-induced memory has me questioning if I remember correctly that we nearly kissed. And if he felt the same rush.

A pang of guilt grips me. It's not just the forest and lake hut that will be destroyed if the apartment complex gets final approval from the council—his mountain-bike business will suffer too. I hate that, although he doesn't know it, it will be partly my fault.

The shower water flows down my back. Nico will already be at Mrs. Wilson's by now, working on the new plan I made for her garden. I make a mental note to send him my "Landscape Garden Ideas" file.

Wrapped in a towel on the edge of my bed, I email Nico the documents.

Me: *Morning. Sorry, that was a huge info dump. Just some garden plans I came up with for some of Mr. Balducci's clients, ideas, really.*

Nico: *Everything is next level. You know you've just planned about a month's worth of gardens for me right there, right?*

Me: *Welcome, but I know you'll add your awesomeness and they'll be even better.*

Nico: *so, question. You sure you wanna leave for law? Just saying you slay the landscape thing.*

Me: *Sure sure.*

Nico: *Shame, but I get it. P.S. Happy first day at your new job. You'll be awesome.*

We pull into the parking lot outside Mike and Mom's work. The office occupies the top story, and Suits Café sits underneath—aptly named, given that through the windows, everyone is predictably wearing monochrome business getup like it's an entry requirement. I follow Mom out of the car and up the steep steps to the top level. On the oversized black doors, the lettering reads:

Housing Co.
Sustainable Housing Development

I roll my eyes. Sustainable for the environment? No. For the council's pockets? Most definitely.

Deb, Mom's receptionist, sits behind the desk, phone to her ear. Deb waves hi. "Yes, as part of the council process to approve housing developments, an environmental plan must be submitted." Her tone is a calm monotone, like she's bored out of her mind.

"This is where you'll be sitting," Mom says, resting her hand on the chair next to Deb. I take a seat and Mom places a document in front of me: *Rockridge City Council Housing Development Proposal in Conjunction with Housing Co.* "Familiarize yourself with this. I've marked the most important sections with sticky notes."

The first page reads: *Housing Co. will deliver environmentally ethical housing for the Rockridge community.*

I flick to the map of the proposed development. It's much bigger than I expected. The lake hut, and the forest surrounding it—the forest Dad planted—will all go, replaced with a subdivision of lakefront apartments that extend up the hillside.

I look up at Mom. "You mean to say the council has already bought the private land by the lake for housing?" My tone is tight. "So, destroy all the forest Dad and Mr. Balducci have spent years regenerating to build environmentally ecological apartments." The irony is not lost on me.

Mom ignores my tone, which is etched with sarcasm.

While I'm ranting, there's another voice bashing around my mind: *Quit your ranting. You need the law tuition.*

"Yes, the council bought the private land, and it's looking good that our proposal to subdivide will be accepted. The city council had already identified the land for development."

I can't hold Mom's focus; my insides are twisted, because she's smiling, but I don't believe her eyes. To be fair, they're brighter than they used to be. "Where the lake hut is?" I'm repeating myself, hoping she might hear how messed up this plan sounds.

"Yes." Her face is blank. Like she's heard my words, but their meaning's lost, or she's choosing to gloss over the hole in their shady, environmentally unfriendly plan.

I turn to Deb. She looks down, avoiding eye contact.

"Then why am I here if it's a done deal?"

Mom glares. "Izz, we must complete two proposals. The first, for subdivision consent, has already been submitted. The second is a record of consultation with the community affected, encouraging their support—that's your job."

My throat constricts with frustration, swallowing my words. If she cared about Dad, she wouldn't do this, but I know that's not entirely true. I wish I could figure her out.

"Locals will not be convinced." Despite my best efforts to keep my tone calm, my words come out bitchier than I intended.

"It's your job to convince them otherwise. We have an environmental plan to mitigate any concerns."

It's bullshit. For the businesses that rely on the forest, like Nico's bike-touring company, without the forest, there *is* no business, and no amount of sweet-talking will change their minds.

"Izzy, as a lawyer, your job is to be neutral and leave all emotion out of it. And I'd like to remind you to appreciate this job; you wouldn't have the means to pay your law fees without it."

I know she's right. She is right. "True, thank you." I hate the way she looks at me, disappointed. Like I'm being unappreciative. And I guess in a way, I have been.

Guilt is a bitch. All-consuming, no matter what you're fighting for. So I shut up, creating a weird moment of silence between Mom and me, the air thick with unspoken words. What if we said what we really wanted to say?

Mom heads into her office and shuts the door without saying another word. I know she's trying to help me. So why does it feel like she's just trying to help protect herself? Like removing the forest will wash away the pain of losing Dad.

Listening to Deb on the phone, I tap the proposal with my pencil to the beat of death-metal drums while dreaming of yeeting the sucker into the waste bin.

Deb rolls her eyes as she continues her phone conversation. "Yes, there is an environmental action plan that will mitigate any loss to flora and fauna." She speeds the words out.

I flip to the impact report for the apartment complex. At the back of the document, it reads: *No risks to ecological, historical or cultural aspects of the land were found.*

There must be historical value in the hut, but flipping through the document, there's no mention of it at all. And I remember Dad saying Rockridge's early settlers probably built it. And he never shut up about the threatened flora and fauna. I have the list he would rattle off memorized.

"This is bullshit," I say to Deb as soon as she finishes her call.

"Yup, but the council is keen. Probably easier not to fight it. It's more or less a done deal." She sighs as the phone rings again, before taking the call.

I get an idea, and scribble a message on a sticky note.

Getting us coffee. Be back soon.

And I stick the note in front of Deb. She picks it up while still speaking on the phone, but before she has a chance to comment, I grab my bag and head out of the office toward the botanical garden.

The path meanders along the river. A family picnics under a willow tree, its tendrils drooping into the water's edge.

A kayaker glides past. Ducks nosedive into the water, rushing to an elderly couple with a bag of bird food. Up ahead is the Rockridge

Botanical Garden—a giant greenhouse with a man-made stream running through the middle, and my favorite café.

Inside, I follow the cobbled path through the lush, re-created forest to the café entrance. The Rockridge Botanical Society's map on the wall shows the region's ecologically significant plants and historical structures. I cross-check the area for development identified in Mom's plan with the map; no plant species listed in that area are labeled as endangered. Nor is there any mention of the hut having any kind of historical significance.

There's a poster tacked to the map.

The Rockridge Botanical Society, in collaboration with Nico's Mountain Bike Tours, invites you to our next meeting to discuss our petition against the council's housing development plan.

And there's Nico's address. Under the text, two signatures, Jan's in tidy handwriting and Nico's in messy print. Below that is a photo taken at the picnic table with the lake and forest in the distance.

My insides sting. Then there's a tap on my shoulder. "Hey, this couldn't be more perfect timing."

And there's Nico with an older woman holding a stack of posters.

"Don't you start your new job today?" Nico asks.

My mind scrambles, searching for the right thing to say.

"Just grabbed a quick coffee," I say, trying to act casual.

"This is Jan from the botanical society. Jan, this is Izzy, who I've been telling you about. Izz, we're putting up posters along the river path and uptown. Come with. If you have a spare ten mins of course."

I nod. "Yeah, for sure." My mind crowds with competing thoughts. *You shouldn't do this* versus *you should definitely do this.*

Nico's smile widens. He passes me a wad of posters. There's something so heart-flipping about him, it makes it hard not to look a little too long.

We wander through the café seating outside, the coffee tables overlooking the river. Nico digs his hand in his pocket and retrieves a packet of Blu-Tack, lays a poster on the table, and attaches a small ball of tack to each corner. He flips the poster over, pressing his finger firmly down on each corner.

I attach a poster to each spare table. My phone beeps.

Mom: *Where are you? You can't just disappear when you feel like it.*

Me: *I'll be ten.*

I shouldn't be doing this. A pang of guilt claws my insides.

Walking along the river path, Jan and Nico paste posters to the lampposts.

Nico stops at the children's playground and pins a poster to the restroom entrance. "We've put some up around town and we'll head back this afternoon," he says, facing me as we walk, then he moves his focus to the path. "Thought I'd hit the bars and restaurants when everyone's finished work and chilling." He rakes his hand through his hair. "I could pick you up after work if you want to come along? If you're not busy, of course. We could have a drink after?"

I'm swooning. I can feel my body wanting to inch closer to his, grab his hand. "Oh, I would have loved that, but I'll be working late." A big fat lie that sounds like I'm brushing him off, and I hate that. I stop walking and face him. "But another time, definitely?" I'm hoping it comes across as genuine, but it's hard when my nerves are stitched up from covering a secret. And I'm rattled by what a terrible daughter I'm being right now.

My phone rings. It's Mom. I ignore the call.

"Shoot. I have to get back to work."

"No worries. We'll see you at the Wednesday botanical society meeting."

Say no, say no.

"Yeah, for sure."

"Here, take more posters. We're picking up extra copies uptown."

I hold out my arms, and his hands brush mine as he drops the pile on my stack, and sunshine spreads through my core. "Oh, yeah … I'll put these up." I awkwardly pat the pile.

My phone rings again. Mom.

Nico glances at me. "I should let you go, but we'll be seeing ya."

I watch as Nico and Jan meander down the river track.

Taking the call, I speak before Mom does. "I'm so sorry. I'm on my way."

"This is not good enough, Izzy."

"I know."

Believe me, I know.

I roll the posters, place a hair tie around the middle, and hide them in my bag before taking the cut-through path that veers away from the river and into town. I reach the office front door. Mom is on her knees. She dips her hand in a bucket, lifts out a dripping sponge, and presses it against the poster Nico has pasted to the front door.

She glares at me. "Look at this bullshit. You're late. I had to let Deb go; she has a doctor's appointment." Her tone is snappy. "You're it." She drops the sponge in the bucket and passes me a scraper. "I'll be contacting this botanical society," Mom says before bursting through the office door.

If I could just be honest with her about the tightrope I'm walking. But I dread not knowing what she'd do with that information. Plus, she's been through so much. And I can't upset her and go back to Mom hibernating in bed with the covers over her head.

When I return to the office, I spend the rest of the day searching the city council website for anything about reclassifying council-owned land into a protected reserve. There's little definitive information.

When everyone has left the office for the day, Mom and Mike emerge from her office. I shut down my computer before she arrives.

"We want to take you and Eli out for dinner. We've got something we would like to chat about." Mom's gaze dips away from mine. She fiddles with the strap of her bag.

Mike rests his hand on the small of Mom's back. Then Eli bursts through the door, breaking the awkward tension.

"Sup, where we eating? I'm starving." He sits on the seat next to me, spinning around. "Nailed that drop-off up Gabby Track. It was sweeeeet." Literal sunbeams could shoot from his smile. "Gotta do it while we can, hey." He darts a look at Mom, using humor to gloss over what he really means.

We all know what he's getting at. Mom ignores him, rolling her eyes.

Mike raises his hand, ready to high-five. "Nice work, man. Respect."

Eli slaps Mike's hand. "Thanks, man. It's one of the most beautiful riding tracks. There were heaps of people out enjoying the trails."

I smirk, enjoying Eli's not-so-subtle hint while maintaining the peace.

Mike pulls his hand away and darts a worried look at Mom. He clears his throat. "Izz, where would you like to eat? We could go to Elma's. It's quiet there with those little booths." A gentle, genuine smile spreads across his face. "Up to you."

He's grown on me more than I expected. Even if I wholeheartedly disagree with his plan to massacre the forest and lake hut. When Eli and I couldn't get Mom out of her darkness, he did. And I think I will like him forever for that.

"Yeah, Elma's." I grab my gear, and we head outside.

As we walk down Main Street, traffic is gridlocked. Lines of people queue up outside restaurants and bars, waiting for a table. It's getting darker earlier now; the sun has dipped, the sky glowing pink and purply blues on the horizon.

Mike and Mom walk up ahead. Eli matches my pace.

He whispers, "So what do ya think their goss is all about?"

"More land that they're developing? Maybe we're moving into one of the fancy apartments they're building. Oh god, better not be."

"Bumped into Nico." He shifts his focus to people standing at a table laughing, at a bar we pass.

Waiting for him to finish his sentence, I crack. "And?"

"He's pretty stoked you're helping him with the forest thing. You might want to tell him the truth before things get out of control." He stops, points to the lamppost up ahead. "Case in point."

Then there's a curdled "What the hell?" from Mom as she inspects Nico's poster plastered on not just one lamppost, but all of them up the street. My heart drops into my stomach.

Eli gives me a scrunched, pained look. "It's only a matter of time before they both connect the dots and find out."

Mom rants at Mike as we continue up the street, passing lamppost after lamppost. "For fuck's sake, I've had enough of this lot."

I slow my pace and keep my focus on the footpath.

Eli says, looking ahead, "You like Nico, right, Izz?"

My stomach tingles up into my chest. "He's a friend, I guess," I say, watching Mom farther ahead taking photos of each lamppost like every poster is different.

Eli tugs me on the arm, bringing us to a stop, then digs his hands in his pockets. "Tell them. It's better than them finding out through the grapevine, from a random person or whatever. If you don't, it will hurt her, Izz. She's been through enough. And it might save your friendship with Nico."

"Yeah, I know." My eyes sting.

As we catch up to Mom and Mike inside Elma's, they're at the counter discussing pizza toppings. Eli and I take our seats overlooking the street, the sliding windows in front of us open. Down the street, I spot Jan and Nico. I duck below the window.

Eli laughs. "What the hell?"

And then I hear Jan's voice. "I'm sure it was your friend Izzy."

I look up, and Nico and Eli fist-bump. "Hey, man. We still gotta catch up for that ride when my leg is better." His focus shifts to me. "Hey, Izz."

I glance over at Mom and Mike, who are next in line to order, internally screaming, *Please say nothing about the posters!*

Nico says to Eli, "We've put up a ton of posters. Stellar effort by the amazing Jan."

Jan laughs. "This old girl can't keep up with this one."

Nico jingles car keys. "I'm about to take Jan home." He faces Jan. "You did amazing."

Jan grabs Nico's elbow. "I'm sorry, Nico. I'm not as fit as I used to be." She genuinely looks sad.

"Jan, you're legendary. No worries about the time. I'll finish the rest tomorrow. Izzy might be free to help?"

I gulp air and glance again at Mom and Mike, who are paying for the order. I can feel Eli's eyes on me. "Yeah, absolutely," I say, trying to sound upbeat.

I'm digging myself a pit. I need the conversation to end.

Nico sticks a key in the car parked in front of the pizza place.

Jan reaches through the window and rests one hand on my forearm, her eyes weathered and sleepy. "Thank you, lovely. I look forward to seeing you at the meeting on Wednesday."

I hear Mom still ranting to Mike as they edge closer.

"Bye." It comes out weird, too fast. Like I'm brushing them off, because I am, but they have to get gone.

"Yeah, see ya," Nico says. The way his smile fades like he knows something is off makes me want to jump in the car, drive away with them, and make everything okay.

As Mom sits down next to me, Nico opens the passenger door of Jan's car and patiently waits as she gets in, before going around to the driver's side. Once in, I wait for the window to roll down and for him to wave, but as the car pulls away and disappears, he doesn't.

"Who was that?" Mom says.

I freeze.

Eli clears his throat. "An old uni friend," he says, giving me the stink eye.

I suck in air and bend down to place my bag on the ground. Eli leans behind and mouths, "*What the actual fuck?*"

"So, we have some news," Mom says. "And we want to put it on the table for discussion." Mom glances at me and then at Eli. Tension spreads across her face as Mike speaks over the noise of the restaurant.

"Don't feel you can't be honest. All feelings are valid," Mike says. His focus is solely on me. I glance outside to where Jan's car was.

Mom taps my arm. "Earth to Izzy."

"Sorry." I shift my focus back to Mom.

"Mike's apartment is being renovated next month, and we wondered how you guys would feel if Mike moved in …" she pauses, watching my face, then Eli's, "… while his apartment is being renovated, and if things go okay … permanently."

Eli bumps my leg with his. Like a reminder, that we need to do whatever it takes to keep Mom from falling apart again. Keep her happy.

I glance at Mike. "It would be nice to have you around more." I know Dad would approve. Mom smiles more since Mike's been around. Fact is, we all do.

Eli holds up his hand, and Mike high-fives him, beaming. "More epic riding trips, bro," says Eli.

"I'm going to look after you guys, okay?" Mike's voice cracks a little mid-sentence as he hugs Mom. She sinks into him, and I watch her face shift into a dream-state smile.

Since Dad died, it feels like I've been carrying the weight of living in two worlds—law, and keeping Mom from falling apart again.

Thirteen

Last week Mom and I worked on an action plan to consult the community about their feelings toward the lakeside apartments. This included writing a survey. I removed all emotion, pretended it was not real, not happening, and the apartments wouldn't get council consent. We completed the action plan and a phone transcript for the survey. Mom actually looked pleased. And when we met with the lawyers to check over our plan, it was exciting. One of them told me I was a natural and have a genuine talent for law policy. I could have hugged him. And when Mom's smile screamed proud, I felt proud too.

But today, at seven forty-five on a Monday morning, I'm sitting at my desk at home, with the phone transcript for the survey resting in front of me because Mom thinks it's best to call people before they get to work. I can't bring myself to pick up the phone. Reality has set in that I have to actually action the survey, talk to people and convince them tearing down the lake hut and Dad's forest is in their best interest.

The irony—tonight is the botanical society meeting. I both want to save the forest, and don't want to save the forest. Simultaneously, I risk ruining my chances of going to law, destroying the forest, and hurting the people that matter the most.

Nico: *Morning. The diggers have dug up the paddock.*

Attached is a photo of the newly excavated area by the river at Mrs. Wilson's, ready for planting and seating to go in.

Me: *Yay! Exciting. Wish I could be there.*

Nico: *Me too. Don't forget the botanical society at mine tonight.*

I agonize over what to do, whether I should go. I stare at the phone transcript I should be using.

Me: *I'll be there.*

Nico: *P.S. I found this on the council website. It's BS.*

And he's attached the council's policy document on mitigating historical, environmental, and cultural impacts when developing new subdivisions.

I don't need to open it. Little does he know I'm more than familiar with that document and its many loopholes. Land cannot be subdivided if it poses a threat to historically, environmentally, or culturally significant customs, biodiversity, and/or structures. The problem is, their classification system of what is considered significant is laughable.

But it gives me an idea.

I retrieve my backpack from the depths of my closet and rest it on my bedroom floor. As I gather my coat, Rex nudges his way inside the pack and curls in circles until his face pops out, and he playfully bats the toggle that pulls the top of the bag closed. It reminds me of the day Dad and I rescued him from the forest hut. Dad restrained him in his bag so he couldn't escape, and with his head poking out the top, Dad walked as Rex growled and hissed, batting Dad's head the entire way home.

I pull Rex out of my pack and lift him into my chest; he nudges his face into my neck before biting my hand. He's chilled out a little, but is still his unapologetic self.

Gliding my water bottle into the side of my bag, I wish I could remember the tangents Dad would go on about the hut's history. At the time, I'd roll my eyes and tune out, but I'd do anything for those conversations now.

I leave a note on the kitchen table: *Going for a drive. I'll be back in time for work.*

I drive to the lake and park outside the hut. The water is choppy, and low-hanging mist obscures the deep, forested valleys. The trees surrounding the hut sway in the breeze, and the cool air blowing off the lake whips my cheeks.

I peer through the missing plank in the step that leads up to the hut. It's always been there, always stepped over and avoided. Dad had been meaning to fix it.

Vague memories of Dad on his hands and knees, peering into the hole with a flashlight flood back. Maybe there's something still under the hut, left behind by early settlers, that would make it culturally significant. I try to remember the half-forgotten conversations with Dad about how early settlers possibly stored things under the hut. The memory prompts a sadness that I'm forgetting our conversations, but worse, the sound of his voice.

I grab the shovel from inside the hut and jam it into the hole, lifting two planks of wood, leaving a gap big enough for me to fit in. On my hands and knees, I poke my head through the hole. I crawl into the pitch black and wait for my eyes to adjust. After fumbling around in my bag and sticking my headlamp on, my heart pounding, I turn on the light, dimly illuminating the low-hanging space. I crawl forward. The air, musty and stale, makes it hard to breathe.

With every movement forward, dust releases in plumes, catching my eyes. I make it to the center, where there's a stacked rectangular pile covered in canvas. Pulling the cover off, a plume of dust wafts into the air before settling, revealing a stack of planks. Stamped on the ends of the neatly packed wood is *Packham Woodmill 1861*.

I slide my phone out of my pocket and write the details using my notes feature. I'm not sure how old the place would have to be, to be considered for heritage classification, but it's a start, something to research.

I move past the pile of wood to a smaller rectangular shape and lift the corner of the canvas, revealing a long metal box with a rusted locked padlock. I grab the rock that once held the canvas down and smash it into the lock. Flecks of rust and metal float into the light. Without a key, there's no chance I'm going to get it open.

Along the back wall, I find metal buckets of glass bottles of varying shapes and sizes.

Gripping a dusty jug around the broadest part, I run my hand along the raised letters. *Ramsy Farming Co.* My headlamp flickers. I'm now regretting not replacing the batteries before I left—a rookie mistake. I wrap my jacket around the jug and slip it into my bag as the light from my headlamp fades and then dies, leaving me in darkness. The only light left is from the cracks in the steps.

Backing up the way I came, I push my head through the gap in the steps, gasping for clean mountain air.

I pull up into the drive as Mom is getting in her car. I'm relieved she hasn't left yet.

As soon as I get out, she barks, "Where have you been? Actually, I don't care, I had to do a Zoom meeting from home because you weren't here, and I waited around for you. Jeepers, what's going on with you?"

I race inside, get clothes to change into, and slump in the passenger seat of Mom's car.

She immediately answers a call and talks to some guy from the council as she drives.

I google Ramsy Farming Co. and reach a page about the history of milk production in the area, with a black-and-white photo showing crates of milk bottles on the back of a horse-drawn cart up the forest track. Ramsy Farming Co. delivered milk to militia stationed at the lake throughout the 1800s.

Mom stares at me. And I navigate away from the page.

"Is starting law getting to you? Your orientation day is coming up." Her eyes dart from me to the road. "You've got law in your blood, kid." She imitates Dad's voice like he used to say it. I know she's trying to lighten the mood, but it's me who should be apologizing.

"Yeah, you know, just worried about lots of change," I lie.

"That's understandable. Change is …" she pauses, "hard."

This makes me feel more guilty because she fully understands what it's like to feel like life is hard. Her husband died, his business went bankrupt; money troubles, leaving her job, living in a house haunted by memories of Dad; being a single mother, Eli ditching law wasting thousands of dollars, nearly losing our house.

She smiles, but her eyes are lying. I know she's not okay.

"I'm sorry for being late."

"It's okay. But don't do it again." A smile sweeps her face, more genuine this time. "You know, Mike said an interesting thing, that you won't struggle to find work after you graduate. There's a shortage of environmental lawyers. He's trying to find one now, with the same core values as Housing Co., and it's not easy."

"Right." I focus out the passenger window. Maybe Mike's having problems because environmental lawyers are environment-loving creatures that don't want the forest cut down. If anything, they'd fight hard to save it. But I say nothing. Mom is smiling, and I don't want to change that.

Mom turns off from Main Street toward Mr. Balducci's.

I dart my focus to her. "Where are we going?"

"I'm trying to convince Mr. Balducci to take on the landscape design for the apartment complex."

Tingles etch up my back. He'll never go for it. It's ten twenty-seven, and at ten thirty Mr. Balducci holds his weekly staff meeting, which Nico will be attending.

Mom parks outside and opens her door. "You coming?"

I sink low in my seat and pretend to wade through my bag, looking for something. "I was going to call Highmont and check the dates for everything." A lie—like, why would the uni get them wrong? The risk of bumping into Nico with Mom is too great. He's bound to recognize her from the billboards we saw at the mall. I'm stalling and need a good enough reason she shouldn't drag me in there too.

"Perfect. Better to be prepared." From the back seat, she picks up a roll of plans, tucks them under her arm, and lifts her handbag over her shoulder. A line of Nico's posters are stuck to the front window of Mr. Balducci's shop. Mom stops and stares. The posters give her the answer to her question, but she's not one to give up and carries on inside. What if Nico is inside and it becomes clear I am the daughter of the property developer destroying the forest Nico is trying to save?

I'm about to get out and walk to work when Mom pushes through the shop door, her face tight, frown lines etched on her forehead. She slumps into her seat.

"He said it doesn't align with his business values." Mom looks at me directly. "He turned down a massive amount of money and a career-changing contract with the council. Not a smart business decision." She snaps the words.

She's frozen, gazing out the windshield. Her eyes crinkle at the sides. I hate that she's disappointed. "Of all people, I thought he would have supported us. We've sent so much work his way. It was me who recommended him for the community college redevelopment."

"I'm sorry, Mom." Sorry that she's upset, not that Mr. Balducci declined her offer.

She starts the car, and we make our way to work in silence. She keeps glancing over at me like she's about to say something.

The car comes to a stop at the café outside work.

"Izz, do you agree with Mr. Balducci that the forest shouldn't be cut?"

I'm reminded of Eli's comment. I fiddle with the strap of my bag. It'll hurt Mom less if I'm honest. "Yes."

"You know that saving the hut and forest won't bring Dad back. If anything, it's the thing that's holding you back." She spits the words out and grabs her bag.

My tone is meek. "Mom. It's the thing that's keeping me together."

The only way *she* knows how to move forward is to destroy the forest.

"I see." The disappointment spreads on her face. She gets out of the car and heads up to the office.

When I get to my computer, Mom is in a meeting with the door shut. Stuck on my laptop is a note: *Focus on completing as many surveys as possible.*

I slump in my seat and read through the transcript. *I can't do this. I can't.*

Deb leans over. "Warning, your Mom is not happy." She rolls her eyes.

"Don't I know it."

After work, Penny picks Eli and me up. We wind down Nico's drive. There are way more cars than I expected—from my count, thirty. Let's say two people per car, that's sixty people, possibly more. When the car lurches to a stop, I lean back in my seat as Eli and Penny unlock their seat belts and get out. They're at the steps to the veranda when they both turn around. Eli jogs back and opens the door.

"It's bad enough I'm doing this behind Mom's back, worse if you bail now."

"You know you don't have to go along with any of this," I say.

"I want to be here. And I'm waiting for you to be ready, to tell the truth." Facing me intently, he says, "I don't want to lie to Nico or Mom any longer. It's awkward AF. So I'll give you till after your birthday, then we tell them, together."

"You're right." Eli is only ever serious like that when it means a lot to him. And he is right. It needs to be done.

Nico waves from the veranda as he welcomes an elderly group of people and escorts them inside. We follow a group of others into the lounge. Garden chairs in neat rows sit facing the largest wall, where a projector casts images of the lake, forest, and hut on the wall. We stand with the others at the back, and my focus shifts around the room to Nico, guiding Jan to a seat next to Mr. Balducci.

Penny taps my arm. "Where'd Eli get to?" She stands on her tippy toes, looking around the room. When Eli returns with another person, Penny looks her up and down.

"Guys, this is Margot. We were in the same law class."

Penny puts on her fake polite smile. "Hey."

Nico, standing at the front, clears his throat. The room hushes as his gaze searches the room, meeting mine. He smiles gently. "Thank you so much for coming."

On the wall behind him, photos of the lake hut and forest flick past. Nico pauses on an image of the city council and Housing Co. logos. My insides twist. I feel Penny's and Eli's eyes on me.

"So I'm going to get to the point real quick. The city council has received a proposal from Housing Co. to build luxury apartments where the lake hut and re-planted forest currently sit."

A map of the lake and forested areas flicks on the screen. Land protected under the Conservation Act is shaded in green, and it doesn't include Dad's forest and the lake hut.

"The only option is to convince the council that all the land should be protected under the Conservation Act. And we do this by showing overwhelming community support and proving the negative impacts outweigh the benefits."

Mr. Balducci peers back at me, and I worry about what, or if, he's told Nico.

Nico continues, "So here's what we're going to do. We'll split into groups." And he holds up a stack of large sheets of paper, divided into four sections. "At the top of each section, I've added a heading: *Ecological impact, Community impact, Historical, Other.* Plus *Question ideas for the petition.* We're going to brainstorm ideas under each heading."

He walks down the rows of people and begins handing out the sheets. "Then we'll combine everything into one master document and develop an action plan."

Nico hands me a paper. "Hey, hey, so great to see you all. Thanks heaps for coming."

"Oh, of course." I'm bursting with guilt over what I should tell him but haven't. I take the piece of paper.

"Oh, wait, have you got pens?" he says.

"Yeah, I think." I dig my hand in my bag.

"I have a bucket of 'em. Where is Anna?" Nico says.

And her voice vibrates from the group next to us. "Awesome to see you, Izz," she says, holding out a giant tub of felt-tip markers. "Take heaps. There's plenty to go around." She's so bubbly and clearly cares for Nico. I hate it feels like they'd make the most perfect couple.

I dig my hand in and grab four different hues of green.

Nico laughs. "The exact colors I chose." He flicks through the pile of paper and holds up his sheet, the sections prefilled with text in the same shades of green.

As Nico moves on to the next group, Eli, Penny, Margot, and I sit on the ground around the paper. In the *Historical* column, I write *Check the historical significance of the hut (e.g., Ramsy Farming Co, it might give clues to the hut's age)*. Under *Ecological*, I list plants I've seen up the track that are potentially endangered.

The decibel level of the room increases as the groups discuss and write. Eli and Margot sit and gossip about old times. Penny whispers, "Did they go out or something? She may as well have hearts in her eyes."

"I've never heard about her before," I say.

Nico asks the first group to read out their responses. I thrust the piece of paper into Penny's hands and whisper, "You read it out."

"Sure, sure," she says, rolling her eyes.

On a large whiteboard, Nico adds each new answer under the appropriate column. "And Izzy up the back?" he says.

Just as Penny's about to speak, he adds, "Has anyone checked the historical significance of the forest hut?"

Jan clears her throat. "As far as we know, no one has pinpointed the hut's exact age because it has had many modifications over the years."

Penny grips my notes, ready to read off the page.

I gently bat her arm and whisper, "Actually, I got this."

Penny mouths, "*Yus, go girl.*"

"Ramsy Farming Co. delivered milk to militia stationed at the lake throughout the 1800s." From my bag, I lift the jug, holding it high for everyone to see. "I found a Ramsy farm milk jug under the hut. If it's been there the entire time, it might prove the hut is older than first thought."

Nico's directed smile edges me on. "Structures built before the 1800s may qualify for protection under the Historic Places Act."

Jan says, "That dairy company operated for years."

The room bounces into commotion.

"Thank you, this is epic," Nico says. The way his face lights up with the potential of where this could lead warms me.

"I'll continue to research."

Nico nods in agreement as he writes: Check the historical significance of the hut (Izzy).

An hour later, Nico's whiteboard is jam-packed. "Thanks heaps for coming. I'll type this up and email it to everyone."

Anna wanders over holding a plate with slices of chocolate cake. "Thank you for coming. Would you like a piece?"

"Thank you. It looks amazing, but I'm good."

She moves on to Penny, who happily takes a slice and begins jamming cake in her mouth, moaning like something is wrong with her.

Anna resumes wandering the room, handing out cake like she isn't sweet and perfect enough.

"Oh my god, it's like a mouthgasm," Penny says, her hand over her mouth, her voice muffled from overstuffing. She pauses mid-gasim. "Oh, wait, sorry, it's terrible, and she's totally not lovely."

"No, she is nice." And I sigh.

"Sorry. She really is," Penny says.

As everybody leaves, Mr. Balducci walks over to me. "Nice work, Izzy, on the forest hut finding."

All I can think about is begging him not to tell Nico that Mom and I work for Housing Co.

Margot stands from her seat between Penny and Eli. "I've got to get going, but Eli, we should catch up. What's your number?"

Penny glances at Eli, then at Margot, who takes Eli's phone from his hand.

"Text me," Margot says, and she leaves.

Eli laughs. "I will not be texting her. She was intense at uni."

Penny's face slips into a smile, and she diverts her attention to Nico, who's returning pens to the bucket. "What's up with the abandoned church in the front paddock? I hear it's haunted. Is that right?"

Nico stands next to me. "Er, I wouldn't say that." He grins.

Penny grabs Eli's arm. "Let's go see. It would make great story fodder for the horror screenplay you're working on."

Eli laughs and tilts his head back as he's pulled toward the door. "Wanna come, Izz?"

"No thanks. All good."

As they pass the lounge window, Penny's voice carries in. "Boo, you scared, Eli boy?" And they chuckle together.

An elderly man taps Nico on the shoulder, and they get lost in conversation, debating the moral ethics of Housing Co. "They're only in it for the money," the elderly man says, "demolishing a pristine forest to build luxury eco apartments. Questionable ethics if you ask me."

Nico nods. "Damn straight." And they face me, waiting for me to agree.

"Yeah, absolutely." My ears ring, my heart panic-beats, and I have that out-of-body feeling, like I'm here but watching from a distance. I take that as my cue to leave.

I head outside to Penny's car and wait in the passenger seat. In the paddock, the beam from a flashlight flickers around the dilapidated building. On the veranda, Nico waves off the last lot of people and heads back inside, returning a few minutes later, carrying two cups. He holds the cups up to the driver's side. I push the door open, and he passes me a hot chocolate with a straw and Pinkie Pie floating on top. Then he slips into the driver's seat.

His smile sucks me in, and I get the sense that I'm looking a little longer than I should. A dog bounds through the car door and jumps on Nico's lap. "Gah." He grips the cups, holding them steady until the cutest dog I've ever seen rests on his lap, her ears poking up and an open mouth grinning as if she's waiting patiently for Nico to share.

"Oh my goodness, she's adorable." I can't hold back the laughter. "Here," I say, taking a cup from him.

"Izzy, meet Pickles. Pickles, this is Izzy."

"Hello, Pickles," I say, ruffling the fur on her head.

I bite the top of my chocolate straw. Pickles migrates to my lap and watches intently. "Aww, I'm sorry, Miss Pickles. Chocolate isn't good for you."

I reach into the console between the seats and pull out a strip of beef jerky from the packet. "How about this?" I offer it to Pickles. She gently grips it with her teeth, walks across Nico, jumps out of the car, and carries her treasure onto the porch, where she collapses and gnaws on the jerky gripped between her paws.

"Aww, she's so happy."

"You're next level, Izz. FYI, the Pinkie Pie is expired by ten years," he says, running his sentences together. Nico takes a sip of his hot chocolate through the chocolate straw.

"The best chocolate bars are vintage." And both of us chuckle, our eyes stuck on each other.

He glances at the paddock, smirking at the lights flicking around. "They're ghost hunting, right? I was joking about there being ghosts in the church. It's technically not a church but an old shearers' hut. There's a thick layer of sheep shit on the floor."

Laughter billows out of me. "So right now, they're wading through sheep poo looking for imaginary ghosts?"

Both of us crack up, laughing too hard to speak.

Nico pulls his phone from his pocket. "Check out the promo vid I made to advertise the save-the-forest campaign." He leans close, our shoulders touching, his face inches from mine. He hits play. Starting at the lake hut, Nico walks through Dad's forest with kids holding saplings to plant, then the view from the picnic table and mountain bikers riding the trails.

"It's amazing. Love that you included Dad's forest, thank you, really. It means heaps. I should ride those trails. I haven't ridden since Dad died. And my bike is broken."

"We gotta fix that."

He looks out the driver's window at Penny and Eli heading toward us.

He holds up his wrist, showing me a tattooed date, beautifully set amongst delicate fern fronds. "It took me a while to get back on the bike after Mom and Dad died, but on the year anniversary of their death, I decided from that day onwards I would live my life without being held back. It's not always easy, not gonna lie."

He's still holding out his wrist, and without thinking I run my fingers along the date following the fern. The sensation of touching his skin sends tingles throughout my body, before I snatch my hand back. "Sorry, I should have asked."

"I really don't mind. I know you get it."

He focuses on my face. His smile is the opposite of his sad eyes. And he doesn't have to say anything. I do get it. It's a constant struggle to keep moving forward without looking back and wishing for what was.

"You're easy to talk to, Izzy."

That is the opposite of what 99.9999 percent of people who know me would say.

"You're easy to talk to, too."

He's staring at me. It's unnerving because I want him to kiss me, but he just told me about his parents' horrific death, and my timing couldn't be worse.

Penny opens the driver's door.

"What are you cool cats doing?" Sheep poo wafts into the car. "FYI, no ghosts, but plenty of sheep shit."

Nico and I laugh as Eli jumps in the back.

Penny is standing at the open driver's door. She glares at Nico. "Yo, y'all in my seat." She grins playfully. "Haunted house, my ass."

Nico chuckles as he exits the car, and Penny hops in. The humid sheep-poo aroma is suffocating.

Nico appears at my window. "We could go for a ride. If you're keen, of course." He pauses. "AKA possibly put a few petition questions together as a survey and test 'em out on anyone who's up the track."

"Yeah, for sure."

Penny starts the car while Nico steps back, and we head down the drive.

"Would you actually go for a ride?" Penny asks.

"I'm not sure." But there's something about Nico—every time I'm with him, I feel like anything is possible.

Fourteen

Mom and I barely talk anymore. And when we do, it's a text request for me to pick up milk on my way home. Or some random logistical detail about going to law school. And even then it's mostly through messenger, and rarely face-to-face. Before Dad died, we used to sit on our front porch eating homemade cake, slurping chocolate milk, and gossiping about anything and everything.

On our way to work, Mom's focus remains on the road. "Have you decided if you're going to the law orientation day or not?" The rain batters the windshield, and Mom increases the wipers' speed. They flick back and forth, the rhythm too chaotic for my mind.

"No, not yet. I figured they offer all the same tours and stuff on the day I move in."

Mom darts an eye roll at me before returning her focus to the windshield. Clearly, I'm not meeting her expectations of law preparedness.

"It's a five-hour drive each way, and we'd need to stay over. I figured the cost of gas and a motel would be too much and I'd rather save the money for tuition," I say. "Gutted, though, because we could've stopped at that organic fruit-and-vegetable farm you love so much, the one with the café we used to stop at on road trips."

"Are you sure there's nothing required on the orientation day that you must attend?" Mom says, ignoring my comment about the organic café and my attempt to have a conversation like we used to.

"No, it says on the university website the tours are purely optional. Remember when we visited the café, and a flock of geese chased Eli and he freaked out?" I chuckle at the memory. He's still terrified of geese.

"If you're sure you're not missing out on anything that counts as credit, then I suppose the money is better spent on tuition."

I give up reminiscing and stop hoping it will ignite a spark and bring back the old Mom. Something tells me the version I used to know is long gone. I just wish the new Mom didn't feel like a stranger.

We make it to the office, and I take my seat next to Deb, her phone tucked under her ear as she wipes a coffee stain off her top. I start up my computer and pull out the phone transcript. After weeks of trying to convince people to believe in the apartment development complex, I've learned two things. One: those apartments will only benefit those who can afford to pay the million-dollar price tag. Two: the amount of money Mom and Mike will make is ridiculous.

It's not locals buying the apartments; it's wealthy tourists, and Rockridge locals are not happy despite the money it will pump into the local economy. This gives me hope that there'll be a big enough backlash from locals and the council may come to their senses.

Finishing her call, Deb puts the phone down. "Good luck. Ya won't even need the transcript because they don't let you get a word in with all the ranting. Then they hang up on you."

"Yup," I say beaming.

"Ha, you're loving that fact." Deb smirks.

"Also, yes."

Deb whispers, glancing at Mom's closed office door, "Same, but I can't rock the boat. I've got my kid's braces to pay for. But you go, girl."

My phone rings.

"Hello, Hous—"

The caller cuts me off mid-sentence. "Hello, I'd like to make a complaint about the proposed land development."

And I immediately recognize the voice. Nico. And in the background, the roar of the coffee grinder at Mr. Balducci's. My heart panics, my words freeze.

"Hello?" His tone is agitated.

More silence.

"Hello, can you hear me?"

More silence. If I answer, he'll recognize my voice.

"Ah, this is pointless. I'm coming in," Nico says, and I slam the phone down.

All my nerve endings are firing off simultaneously, and I can't think what to do next. Is he on his way now?

Deb shakes her head. "Couldn't get a word in, could ya?"

My phone beeps.

Nico: *So Housing Co. called and asked me to phone them, and so I do, and ya can't get through to them. I'm going in. Want to come with?*

My heart is panic-beating, my mind is frazzled; I'm desperately wondering what to do.

Nico: *I can swing by work and pick you up if ya like. If you can take the time?*

Me: *Oh hell, I'd have loved that, but I'm off site in meetings with Mom for the rest of the day. So sorry.*

I'm a big fat liar, and I can't handle how shitty it's making me feel going behind both Nico's and Mom's backs.

Nico: *I'll go in anyway.*

Me: *I found some more leads from the stuff I found under the hut. And drafted some survey questions. I'll send them to ya soon. About to go to a meeting.*

What am I doing? My head is telling me to tell him, to come clean, but my heart isn't listening.

I write on a sticky note and leave it on my desk.

Mom, Feeling unwell. Sorry. I'm going to catch a cab home.

It's the lamest excuse and morally wrong on so many levels. If they both knew the truth, they'd be so hurt. And that thought sticks heavily in my chest.

Deb pulls her drawer open and offers me a cookie from her stash. "Sugar helps, and you look freaked out. It gets easier to deal with."

"Er, sorry, I'm really not feeling well, like I've got a tummy bug or something."

"Oh, that sucks. The kids have had one recently; it's going around. Need me to drop you home?" she asks with actual real freaking genuine concern on her face.

I'm a fraud.

"I'm good, but thanks."

"Your mom has a free spot at ten thirty. She could give you a lift then."

I'm already out of my seat and packing my stuff in my bag. "Thanks, but I got to go now." And I don't wait for her to finish. The last thing I need is to bump into Nico here.

I race down the stairs and take a side street until I reach the river path, where I call a cab.

At home, I rest my bag on the kitchen table and stick two slices of toast into the toaster. I glide the knife into the block of cheese. The kitchen fills with fresh bread smells.

Mom: *You okay? Want me to bring home anything from the pharmacy after my meeting … IF you're sick?*

Nico: *I'm going in. Wish me luck.*

And attached is a picture of him outside Housing Co.

I place the cheese on the toast and pop it under the grill.

Me to Nico: *Let me know how it goes.*

This will not end well, and it's all my fault.

I take my toast down to the basement. Hung neatly next to my bike are Dad's tools. I sit on the bed, leaning against the wall, and switch on Dad's old-school TV. I'm not really watching. I can't get out of my head what Mom and Nico are talking about and if he's going to connect the dots.

From the bookshelf, I grab a horror tape; set up the VCR and press play. I like the old-school crackly sound; I sit and eat my food.

The movie isn't hitting. Even the scariest parts wash over me. I grab my laptop and begin drafting survey questions for Nico.

Do you agree or disagree with the proposed development?

Why is the forest important to you?

How often do you use the forest?

In what ways do you utilize the forest? i.e. for recreation or other?

What impact would the housing development have on your business?

I add a list of places we could hand out the survey: community groups, schools, businesses, up the forest track, cafés/restaurants, the botanical gardens, Nico's website.

I google as much as I can about the farm and the last name Ramsy, but little information points to the hut's age. Ramsy Farming Co. bottled and delivered milk to the militia during wartime. The earliest mention of the hut is dated 1836, which wouldn't make the forest hut old enough to be considered for heritage significance.

I lean back against the bed. There has to be something I'm missing. I check the city museum website, and their current exhibition is on early settlers in our region. There's a black-and-white photo of a guy in militia uniform and the caption: *The Ramsy family settled in Rockridge, 1813.*

The hut would have to have been built in the late 1700s to be considered for heritage status.

After grabbing my bag, I walk to the museum. An elderly lady wearing a volunteer badge and thin rectangular glasses takes my pass.

The exhibition begins with a re-created settler's house. A woman in a corseted dress prepares vegetables at a table with a jug similar to the one I found. Resting on a seat by the fire, a man in militia clothing reads a newspaper. The text reads *Militia Prepares for War*.

I wander through the exhibition to a re-created forest dotted with single-room pitched huts with little verandas. I lift the headphones on, and the audio plays—an interview with D. J. Ramsy, recounting the stories his grandfather told him about building huts up at the lake.

I take photos of information that might be helpful. On my way out, I speak to the receptionist.

"I'm trying to find out the exact age of the lake hut. I don't suppose you know?"

"Oh, that's a bit of a mystery. According to old maps, it existed during the time militia occupied the area in the mid-1800s, but there are no records of who built it or when."

"Oh, I see. Thank you."

She passes me a card with the details of the museum's history curator. "He might be able to give you more information."

Once I'm home, I settle back on the bed in the basement and email the curator, attaching photos of the milk jug.

I get an immediate response.

> *... While we have no definitive proof of the hut's age, it's likely it was built by militia in the early 1800s. The milk jug you found was produced by the Ramsy Farm from 1813 onwards.*

I send Nico an overly detailed summary of my findings from the museum and the list of survey questions I've started.

Me: *I'm so sorry. Not what we wanted to hear.*

Upstairs I make another grilled cheese. When I get back, my message to Nico shows as unread.

I restart the VCR and continue to watch the horror film. I can't concentrate. What if Nico hasn't replied because he's found out where I work?

Halfway through the movie, there's a knock at the front door.

Back upstairs, I open the front door and find Nico dressed in his mountain-bike gear, helmet tucked under his arm. "Hey, I'd just finished a ride when I saw your email and thought I'd pop by so we could commiserate together."

I'm relieved he's here. But the disappointment etched in his eyes fills me with guilt. "Come in."

He follows me into the kitchen and continues, "The meeting did not go well. Sounds like it's pretty much a done deal apart from the community liaison report. Which, according to Housing Co. is going well."

"Pinkie Pie?" I offer.

"Of course, thank you."

He rests his helmet on the kitchen table and takes a seat.

"Such a bummer about the milk jug and hut's age thing," he says, his smile fading.

I tip milk and chocolate powder into two cups and place them in the microwave.

"It's so depressing," I huff out. "At least we can get a petition sorted." I try to sound upbeat. But we know it will take a monumental outrage by locals to stop the council's plans.

I'm torn. A huge part of me is also relieved about the news from the curator. News like that would stop the apartment complex from going ahead, and I wouldn't get the money I need for law fees. It's exhausting and confusing simultaneously, fighting for both teams. I wish I didn't care about the forest. Then it would be easy … easy*ish*. If I could ignore Nico too.

After removing the cups from the microwave, I tear the top off two Pinkie Pie chocolate bars and dunk one in each of the cups before adding a chocolate straw.

"We can't give up, though." Nico's tone is downbeat. "That guarantees nothing changes, so thanks for drafting some petition questions."

"My laptop is downstairs. We can come up with more if you have time?"

Nico follows me into the basement. He glances at the old-school TV playing Dad's horror video. "Nice. Rocking it old-school." Sipping his drink, he wanders to where the bikes are hung. "Your bike."

I nod.

He runs his fingers over the derailer, inspecting it closely. "I can fix it for ya." He lifts my bike off the rack, resting it against the wall, and fumbles through the drawer of Dad's tools. None of them has been touched since Dad passed.

Which grips me, stalling my words. They're stuck on whether to tell him to stop, or if this is like removing a Band-Aid—you just gotta do it and move on.

"Nice tool collection. The organizational system, it's next level." Nico looks over at me. He pauses. "Oh, you okay?" A confused, concerned expression covers his face, and he freezes.

"Yeah, totally." Swallowing the tears, I bite the side of my lip till it hurts. This is a good thing.

"Oh shit. Sorry. I'm an idiot. I can stop."

"No." It comes out more direct and louder than I intended. "It's good. Great, actually. Dad would approve." I feel my eyes glass over but manage to halt the waterworks.

Nico comes over and, without warning, wraps his arms around me, holding me close. My body sinks into his chest. And he's warm and tall, and it's perfect and terrifying all at the same time. And my heart is doing some kind of techno rendition.

He grips me tighter. "I get it," he says. Part of me thinks he needs the hug as much as I do.

"I'll get this bike fixed for ya." When he pulls away, the hug does not feel finished.

I rest on the bed and watch as Nico effortlessly fixes my bike, then returns Dad's tools to their exact locations.

"Here, see if I've got the seat height right."

He steadies the bike, standing to one side, gripping the handlebars as I jump on. My hands overlap his, and butterflies fill my chest. My toes dangle, struggling to steady me on the ground. The bike tilts, but before I fall, he grips one arm around my waist, using his other hand to steady the bike.

He laughs. "Too high."

As I hop off, I rest my hand on his shoulder till my feet are steady on the ground.

He reaches for a tool and drops my seat. "Try now."

When I jump back on, the height is perfect, my toes resting just enough off the ground so I can balance my weight.

"Perfect. You're all ready to ride."

"Thanks so much, really." He's got no idea how that one act of using Dad's tools lifts a weight off my chest. I couldn't touch them before, but now they've been used. It feels like the worst is over, and they can finally be used again.

"No problem."

I hop off and rest my bike against Dad's workbench.

We're standing there in awkward silence. I can't wipe the smile off my face. He grins back. Usually, he fills the quiet spaces, but he doesn't this time, and no matter how hard I try, I can't think of something to say.

Then my phone rings. Mom.

Before I can say anything, she asks, "We're on our way home. Want any takeout?"

"No, thanks. I'm good."

Nico rests on the bed, watching the horror film.

"So you'll be home soon?"

"Yes, on our way."

"Oh, actually, I changed my mind. Yes, takeout would be good, thanks." I need more time. "Pizza from Stephano's and a milkshake from Grimps."

"Oh my goodness. You couldn't have made it easy, could you?"

"Sorry."

And she hangs up. That should give me twenty minutes, half an hour tops.

The music from the horror film increases to a freakish crescendo.

Nico laughs. "I've not seen this one."

"It's one of my faves." I sit next to him on the bed, leaning back against the wall with my legs out. Nico rests back next to me; our legs are inches apart. I glance at him, wishing he would go, but also wanting that hug all over again.

He grins. "The blood looks like jam."

Laughing, I say, "It's awesome, and it gets better. There's pus that looks like mustard."

"Right then. Mustard pus is the thing to look for."

The mattress is old and uber-soft. The weight of both of us pushes our legs till they're touching.

He belly-laughs at the chainsaw scene. "The mustard pus is so unnecessary. I mean, the jam blood would have been enough. The mustard doesn't make sense. It's a fresh wound." The credits roll, and Nico faces me. "Well, that ending was random."

"There are four in the series. All with terribly executed cliff-hangers." I glance at the time on my phone. Fifteen minutes have passed, and Mom will be home any second.

"So I was going to write up that survey tonight," he says, "print a bunch, and put some up the track, talk to some people—a test run, kinda."

"Yeah, that would be great." I stand, not because I want him to go, but because he has to go. Mom cannot find him here.

"I should get going," he says, standing in front of me.

My focus runs across the tattoos up his arm to his lips; I push away the urge to lean into him.

"Thanks for the drink and all your help with the forest stuff," he says. It's like we're frozen in time, stuck awkwardly grinning at each other. Maybe we could go for a ride sometime?"

"Yeah, I'd like that." I break the trance and walk upstairs toward the front door, Nico following behind. I open the front door for him.

"Thanks, Izz. See ya." He slips his helmet on and grabs his bike, walking it down the veranda steps. In the distance, I spot Mom's car heading toward us. "Bye!" he shouts as he rides down the street.

Thirty seconds later, Mom and Mike pull up into the drive.

That was close—too close.

Fifteen

For the past two weeks, on our lunch breaks and after work, Nico and I visit every business, school, and community group we think would value the forest, and pitch our petition. Support has been overwhelmingly on our side. Today is the last day complaints against the apartment development can be submitted to the council. And we've only got my work lunch break today to get it done.

Mom appears at my work desk. "How about we have lunch today? We'll run through a list of things that need to be sorted for the dorms." Before I have time to answer she's distracted greeting clients as they arrive in the waiting room. She's been working mammoth days on the apartment development, and I've managed to slip out unnoticed, sometimes going over my allocated time for my lunch break.

Nico: *Twelve work for you? We are under the pump to get this thing submitted. Talk about living on the edge.*

Mom directs her clients to her office and shuts the door. Most meetings run overtime. And I figure if I just leave, I'll be late for lunch, but not by much.

Me to Nico: *Don't suppose now would work?*

Nico: *Yeah, for sure. I'll pop home.*

Me: *Leaving now.*

I pull up into Nico's drive. As I wind toward the house and reach the front paddock, Nico waves, dressed in his Balducci Landscape Design uniform. He throws a tennis ball over the field. The waist-high grass swishes in a line, and Pickles launches into the air and catches the ball.

I step out of the car, and Pickles bounces up to my feet, one ear up, the other flopped down, and drops the ball at my feet.

Nico grins. "Mind giving us a lift?"

"Of course."

Nico rests in the passenger seat with Pickles on his lap.

Inside the house, Pickles trails behind us as we go into Nico's room. On the back wall behind his bed are framed black-and-white photographs of a lady and man who are spitting images of him. Varying sizes of potted plants cram his bay window, overflowing in green, most in brushed concrete pots.

"Take a seat." He pulls out the spare chair in front of his desk. On one of his monitors, he brings up the back end of his website. "Wow, more petitions have been completed since I last checked this morning. Total, four thousand and thirty-six."

"If you check the shared Google Doc, you can see the graphs I created. I'll have to update them with the new data," I say.

Nico brings up my document on one screen. "These graphs are amazing."

"Seventy-eight percent of locals and sixty percent of domestic tourists aren't in favor of the apartment complex," I say. "But get this. People who voted in favor of the apartments commented there needs to be more accommodation options at the lake, camper vans for hire, cabins, and/or a campsite being the most popular."

Nico's face looks puzzled.

"Woo, sorry," I say. "Am I boring you with stats and numbers? I kinda like that stuff and forget other people don't."

"Not at all. I'm just really grateful for the effort you've gone to. How did you get the data?"

"From the surveys, digging around the council website. And I contacted the Rockridge tourism board."

I don't mention that eighty-nine percent of international tourists want the apartments, and Mom's been overwhelmed with offers to buy.

"You're next level, Izz."

I update the graphs using the new data taken from the most recent surveys.

"All we need is one last read-through," I say, scrolling back to the beginning of the document.

"Iced chocolate?" Nico asks.

"Yeah, please."

Nico leaves with Pickles following behind. From the kitchen I overhear him say, "You're the most adorable canine vacuum cleaner."

The cuteness is impossible.

Nico returns with iced chocolates, chocolate straws, and a Pinkie Pie floating on the top of each. Resting back in his seat, he takes a slurp, frothy milk oozing down the sides of his cup as Pickles races back into the room, bounds up on my knee mid-sip, and knocks the cup from my grip. Iced chocolate spills down my top, over my work skirt, and on the carpet.

"Oh my god, I'm so sorry about your carpet."

Nico grabs the towel hanging on the back of his door, lays it on the ground, and stands on top.

"I'm so freaking sorry. Where's another towel? I'll clean it up," I say, embarrassed.

"Bathroom, and no dramas. Hang on, I'll get it. You're … covered." He disappears into the bathroom, returning with another towel, and we both stomp on the carpet to soak up the iced chocolate.

"God, I'm such a klutz. I'll pay for any damage."

Nico peels up the corner of the mat under his desk. "It's garage carpet, nothing that can't be hosed down. And it isn't your fault. Pickles is a menace." He smirks, unfazed. Calm and collected.

His *don't sweat the small stuff* vibe is oddly homely. And it makes it too easy to be around him, like every part of you is welcome, weirdness and all.

I laugh, noting the milk foam on Nico's and Pickle's noses. "Adorable."

"She's tiny. She gets by."

He thinks I'm talking about Pickles. "I was talking about you." The words speed out before I realize I've said them out loud. "Look in the mirror."

Nico darts to the mirror hanging on his door and laughs. He holds out his hand. I grip his fingers, and he pulls me next to him. And when I look in the mirror, a milk mustache rests above my lip.

"I mean, I'm totally pulling it off," I say.

"You really do," Nico says, bursting with laughter like he's been holding it in.

We're left facing each other, smiling, with zero words like it doesn't matter. Instead, the conversation's playing out between our eyes.

Then Pickles jumps up onto the desk and begins lapping up the last of the spilled chocolate milk and chunks of Pinkie Pie.

"Argh, that's not good for you." Nico's tone rises three octaves, and he scoops her up in one hand. "My sweet little menace." He gently sticks her out of the room and shuts the door.

"I'll get you some spare clothes. They'll be enormous on you, but at least they'll be clean." He rummages through his drawer and pulls out track pants and a t-shirt, passing them to me. Nico leaves, closing the door.

I slip on the gray track pants and black t-shirt with *Nico's Mountain Bike Tours* on the front. They're easily two sizes too big, but they're warm and cozy and smell like Nico. I tie the t-shirt in a knot in the middle, leaving my tummy exposed a little, but not too much.

Using the last dry corner of the towel I wipe away the last of the spilled milk from Nico's desk. Scratches and whimpers come from behind Nico's door. I swing it open, and Pickles jumps up at my legs. "Can't keep you locked out."

"You decent?" Nico says, standing to the side of the door with his eyes closed, which makes me laugh.

"All good."

His focus darts up and down, and a gentle smile spreads across his face. "Suits you," he says, passing me a plastic bag for my wet clothes.

"Oh, er, should we get back to it, then?" I say.

Back in our seats, Pickles jumps on my lap. While Nico rereads the submission, checking for errors, I double-check the graphs and stats.

"Oh my god," I say, beaming at Nico. "It's done." Glancing at him, I point at the submit button. "Can I press it?" The adrenaline is peaking.

"Do it," he says, smiling.

I press the button. "We did it! This is so freaking cool. We actually did it."

"Your excitement is cute. I freaking adore you." The words rush out like he hasn't given them any thought, like they slipped out unnoticed.

I'm stuck on the word adore when he darts his focus away.

"Er, I … I mean …" He's backtracking, fiddling with the pen. "I mean …" He raises his hands in the air. "Whoop, whoop, we got the submission in. It's freaking amazing!" He holds his hand up for me to high-five.

I slap his hand, wanting to link my fingers with his. He wraps his arms around me, and I sink into him.

When my phone beeps.

Mom: *Meet at Suits café in ten.*

I snap away from him. "Oh my god, I'm crazy late. I better get back to work."

"Yeah, of course, shit, sorry, time kinda disappeared, didn't it?" he says as I gather my bag.

It always does with him.

I leave faster than I hoped. I pass by home to get changed, and when I pull up outside Suits café, I'm twenty minutes late.

"Where have you been?" Mom snaps as I take a seat.

"Sorry, I spilled coffee down my blouse and popped home to get changed."

She rolls her eyes; it cuts that she believes my lie.

Mom is actually trying to spend time together, and here's me purposefully going behind her back in the absolute worst of ways. I'm officially the worst daughter, ever. Reading off the notes app on her phone, Mom recites a list of things she believes I need to take with me to the dorms. Guilt has got me stitched up so bad I ignore her patronizing suggestions of removing things I've already packed, like my Balducci work boots.

Sixteen

Six a.m. Saturday.

Nico: *Have an unbe leaf able birthday.*

Nico: *Check this out.*

Nico sends a video of Mrs. Wilson's river garden that I planned. He walks the stone path leading to a wooden platform surrounded by garden beds overlooking the river and sprawling green valley. Pickles sits on the newly built wooden seating, one ear up, one ear down.

Me: *It's amazing. And how cute is Pickles ;)*

I've got a serious case of FOMO. I wish I'd dug in the plants, positioning them perfectly so that when they're grown, they'll provide a shady spot for Mrs. Wilson when she's writing.

A list of things to add comes to mind. A pipe from the rain tank to make watering the plants easier. A storage compartment under the boxed seating for the cushions to keep them dry, and a trellis planted with honeysuckle to act as a windshield when the weather is chilly.

I spend five minutes tapping out my list in a message to Nico when it hits me. It's not my job anymore. It's his. And it would annoy me if someone who wasn't working with me anymore micro-managed from the sidelines.

Downstairs, I head straight for the coffee machine when Mom grips me in a hug. I know she's trying, but it's like there's one too many arms and it feels forced and awkward. There's been too much distance between us for it to feel welcoming.

"Happy birthday. I can't believe you're all grown up and off to law," she says.

She pulls away and avoids facing me. It's a hard day without Dad. She rests at the table with Eli and Mike, where there's a box wrapped in green paper with a black bow.

Mike clears his throat while placing one arm around Mom's shoulders.

"I thought this might come in handy," Mom says, finally making eye contact.

Inside is a makeup caddy filled with all my favorites. I fake a smile, not because I don't appreciate it—I do. It's just that the version of her two years ago was morally against makeup, believing people are beautiful without it.

"Thank you. Really, it's great." There's a glum edge to my voice that I didn't quite mean to leak out.

Eli bats my leg gently under the table.

"It's so sweet of you. I'm sure the student dorms will be short on storage space." I sound way more upbeat and excited this time.

Eli slides a small box in front of me, wrapped in floral paper, a print of Audrey Eagle's hand-drawn daisies on the front. "Happy birthday, I hope you like it." He smiles nervously, like he's not sure he wants me to open it.

Carefully peeling the tape off the sides of the box, I flip it open.

I lift out two earrings, a cluster of yellow kowhai seeds set in a rectangular block of beautifully polished black resin. And I immediately know where he got the seeds from—Dad's collection in the basement.

Mom's eyes widen while Mike watches on, clueless.

The backs of my eyes sting, but I hold back the tears, somehow forcing them away.

"They match the resin kowhai pendant that Dad gave you," Eli says.

Pulling him into a hug, I whisper, "Thank you, this means so much. And they're perfect."

Mike laughs. "Never knew earrings could have that effect on people."

Mom says nothing. But I feel it's fair to fill him in.

"They're made from seeds that Dad collected."

"Wow, that's such a cool idea," Mike says, upbeat—excited even.

"It is cool!" I say, returning Mike's excitement. He has a way of shifting the air from somber to happy, injecting brightness into an otherwise sad situation. It's something I appreciate more than he knows.

I put the earrings on and wrap my arms around Mom. "Thank you for the makeup—they're all my absolute faves."

"So, what are your birthday plans?" Mike questions.

Eli grins and thrusts a card at me. On it is a picture of him and me as kids, our faces side by side, sitting on the jetty at the lake. It was the moment before he pushed me into the lake full of terrifying eels.

Eli laughs. "I still crack up thinking about that."

He's hilarious.

"Just so you know, I'm still terrified of them and no, you're not forgiven."

I open the card, and all it says is: *Meet me at the lake hut at three, Love Eli.*

"This better not have anything to do with eels," I say.

Eli smirks. "I'm saying nothing, except they're looking forward to seeing you."

Mom and Mike laugh, and by the looks on their faces, they're in on whatever is going on here.

"You two be safe and have a great—"

Eli cuts Mom off. "Woo, woo, woo—no spoilers, people."

It's nice to see Mom laugh. She rests her head on Mike's shoulder. I am glad he's here.

A flustered Penny bursts into the kitchen. Still dressed in her cool-storage assistant uniform and clutching a bag, she launches a hug on me. "Happy birthday, love you, on my break, got three minutes." And she races out of the kitchen, up the stairs, and returns a minute later. Chucks a now full bag at Eli. "Here. Got to go; running late. Love you, happy birthday and bye." Launches another hug on me.

"Love you too."

And she runs out the front door.

"That was awfully suspicious," I say to Eli.

"I don't know what you're talking about. That's perfectly normal Penny behavior."

"Ha ha, it's one hundred percent on point for her, yes. But the bag?"

"I'll meet you at the lake hut at three. It's when we're swimming with the eels—oh whoops, I've said too much." Eli's trying to act all serious, but he's failing, and he cracks up laughing.

"Before we go, though, we're taking you out for brunch."

After brunch, parked outside Nicola's Mexican Cantina, Eli starts the car as Mike and Mom wave us goodbye from the footpath.

"Are you totally sure your car can handle the road to the lake?" I ask.

"Of course." Eli slides one of Dad's old cassettes into the player. His car is practically prehistoric and possibly the only vehicle that accepts vintage music software.

On the way to the lake, we belt out Dad's songs from a cassette labeled *Family Road Trip*.

Eli parks in front of the lake. The water is calm and steely blue, the tree-clad valleys Kermit green. And the sky is clear, the sun blazing.

Eli turns the music down. "So, you're not to go into the hut or Dad's forest just yet. Stay in the car until Nico gets ya. 'Kay."

"Wait, what?"

Nico's van pulls into the park next to us. He immediately gets out and pulls my bike from the roof of his van, resting it against his door. A second later Penny, Eli, and Nico huddle together, speaking in hushed voices. All very shady but cute behavior.

"Ready?" Penny asks the boys. They nod in unison, like using some unspoken language only they understand. Penny and Eli grab bags from the back of Nico's van and head off toward the lake hut. Leaving me alone with Nico.

"Happy birthday," he says, opening the car door.

"I thought you had to work today?"

"I took a half day." And he grins. He lifts his bike off the van roof, placing it next to mine.

He took a half day to take me for a ride. I've not been riding since Dad died, and the thought of it now catches me off guard a little.

"I've got something to show you," he says. "Totally cool if you don't want to ride; we can walk. No pressure, totally up to you."

He grips the straps of a pack and struggles to lift it onto his back. I'm not sure what's in there, but whatever it is, it's heavy. He's gone to an effort to celebrate my birthday, and it's sweet.

"Actually, riding sounds like fun." An exaggeration of the truth—I'm worried all the memories of riding with Dad will flood back, and I'll be in a ball of tears in five minutes. Though at least I'll be with someone who will get it.

"Awesome, I'm stoked," he says. "Let's go." And Nico holds out his hand. I don't need help to get out of the car, but I'm not about to turn him down, and there's something comforting about the way he gently grips my fingers and guides me to the bikes.

"Like I said, totally no pressure if you want to walk instead."

My hand is still tucked inside his, and he gives me the most reassuring smile, like no matter what happens, it will be okay.

"Er, one slight problem." I glance down at my jeans and silk blouse I'm still wearing from brunch.

"Oh, that's right, nearly forgot." From the back seat of his van, he passes me the bag Penny packed this morning. "Penny stole your riding gear."

"I'll be back."

I pop to the public bathroom and change. When I return, Nico is riding around the parking lot with the bag on his back.

We begin on the flat trail that winds around the edge of the lake. It's wide and even—this is where Dad taught me to ride.

After a while, the path narrows, and we reach the far reaches of the lake. I haven't biked beyond here for years. The foliage on the side of the track swishes against our bikes until Nico stops by the lake's edge. Nesting birds sit amongst the tall rushes; ducks call, drowning the hum of the cicadas.

"We'll stop here," Nico says, hiding his bike in the bushes.

"Please tell me we are not going for a swim with giant eels and Eli put you up to this."

Nico laughs, and looks confused. "No, promise, no eels."

I stash my bike next to his.

"I promise, you'll like it."

He leads me off the trail and up the steep side of the track, holding back vines and twigs so they don't flick in my face. At the top of the bank, the land levels out, and we walk through the forest until we pop out onto a flat expanse of tall grass filled with wildflowers.

From his bag, Nico pulls out a rolled-up piece of paper and passes it to me.

"I hope this is okay. I nearly didn't do it, but I checked first with Eli, so … you know."

I unfurl the paper; it's a map of the lake and forest. Colored in green are patches labeled *planted*, and colored in gray are areas labeled *left to plant*. I pinpoint where we are, and at our precise location, it says *to plant*. At the bottom, in dad's handwriting, are the words *Reuben Rivers*. This was Dad's plan. The location we are at now was next on his list to plant. It would connect two surrounding forest fragments. It was Dad's dream to connect all the fragments together.

And when I look up, dotted through the entire expanse of wild-flowers are newly dug-in baby trees, almost hidden by the tall grass.

I'm holding it together the best I can, but tears threaten to leak down my cheeks. I'm not sure if it's more from how much Dad would love this, the ache from missing him, or how overwhelmingly sweet and thoughtful Nico is.

Nico and I wander through the long grass and wildflowers, stopping at each of the trees Nico has dug in. When I'm done, we sit in the middle of the grove and soak in the sun warming our faces.

"I can't believe you've done this." My throat catches. "Thank you."

"You're welcome. I'm relieved you like it."

There's a faded scar just above Nico's eye that I'd never noticed before, and in this light, his eyes are greener than hazel. His smile widens.

"Like it? I *love* it," I whisper. Our focus holds, not shifting. I'm never going to forget this moment, sitting amongst Dad's trees and wildflowers—the moment when I realized my feelings for Nico have most definitely crossed the friendship line. I wish he'd bridge the gap between our lips, but Anna's face pops into my mind, and I turn my head to face the bushes.

Eli, followed by Penny, pushes through the forest into the grassy area. Penny's bent over, catching her breath.

"Thank … god … we … made … it … they're … here," she says, collapsing next to me in the grass.

Eli rests his hand on my back. "Okay?" His eyes are concerned.

"Definitely."

Eli shakes Nico's hand. "Thanks, man."

From his bag, Nico pulls two saplings, their roots wrapped in newspaper covered in a plastic bag. He rests them on the ground, along with a mini spade.

Nico passes Eli the spade, and he chuckles. "It's not much bigger than a spoon."

Eli and I wander the grassy field, and eventually I stop in the center. "Here," I say, and I dig a hole using the ridiculously tiny spade, and plant Dad's tree. On the other side of the field, Eli digs a hole and plants his tree. When it grows, it will have a view over the lake.

Nico and Eli climb the largest trees bordering the field.

Penny and I lie in the grass, watching the wisps of clouds pass by.

"You know, Izz, Nico's great, hey?" She tilts her head to face me. "Kinda sucks you're moving away."

"Yeah," I say, turning my focus back to the clouds.

She rests her head on my shoulder. "It's so peaceful here, like I get why you need it so much—well not fully, obviously, but at least a bit. He'd be so happy, Izz, watching over."

"Yeah, Dad would be. I can't believe Nico did this. Dad would like him."

Penny laughs. "Your dad would have recruited him to his forest-planting ways within five seconds of meeting him." It's funny because it's true—Dad never shut up about protecting this place, and rightly so.

The wind picks up, and with the sun lowering in the sky, we bike back, reaching the lake hut as the sun is setting.

Inside the hut, a chocolate birthday cake rests on the table split in the middle with white frosting. The top layer is lopsided, as if at any moment it might slide off.

"You made cake," I say to Penny, my voice rising with excitement.

Penny laughs. "Look, girl, I'm no baker, but the recipe said, and I quote, 'the best chocolate cake ever,' so there's that."

"It's perfect, I love it." The table is set, a large mason jar filled with wildflowers sits in the middle, and in separate bowls are all the ingredients to make burritos: lettuce, ground beef with beans and peppers, salsa, guacamole, and cheese. Also a pitcher of chocolate milk, and an entire box of Pinkie Pie chocolate bars.

"You guys are the best. I can't believe you've done all this. Thank you."

"Happy birthday, amazing you. Who's hungry? Coz I'm starving," Penny says.

We all make a plate, and I'm about to sit at the table to eat when Nico playfully nudges me and says, "Have a look outside."

Fairy lights are strung through the canopy of the forest Dad planted. Folding chairs are grouped around a low wooden table.

I take my plate and sit at the table. Penny places the pitcher of chocolate milk on the table and tips in a boatload of chocolate liqueur. "For added pizazz," she says, laughing. And pours four glasses. Then rests next to me with her plate of food.

Nico has moved his van as close to the forest as possible. Chill summer beats play from his car stereo.

Nico rests in the seat next to me … and then Anna appears. "So sorry I'm late, Nico. I got held up at work. I hope it's not too late for this." She rests an enormous tent bag on the ground.

My insides shatter, falling to the ground. But I fake a smile. She's done nothing wrong.

"Happy birthday, Izz. It's beautiful what you've done, guys."

Eli inspects the tent. "Thank you. I'll put it up if we need more sleeping space. I wasn't sure if there would be other people already using the hut."

Another woman wearing vintage dungarees appears, carrying a bag of tent pegs. She has the most beautiful wavy auburn hair. "Should I put them here?" She rests the bag next to the tent.

"Hey, guys, sorry to interrupt. I'm Nella, Anna's more-organized other half. I mean, we would have been here before it got dark, but ya know what my girl is like, can't pull herself away from work."

Anna laughs. "Like you can talk, Miss Emergency Nurse who worked two back-to-back shifts this week alone." Her tone is playfully mocking.

Wait—*other half?*

I catch Penny's grinning gaze, as she also picks up on that new piece of information. All this time I was worried about Anna and didn't need to be.

Nella playfully grabs Anna's hand and kisses her cheek. "Ya know I love ya for it."

My phone beeps.

Penny: *Now you can suck his face off, no holding back.*

Me to Penny: *Smooth lol.*

Penny: *That's me.*

"We should leave these guys to it," says Anna.

"Stay," I say. "There's plenty of food and space to sleep now we have the tent. It will be fun."

Anna swings her arm around Nella's waist. "I'm keen if you are?"

Nico and Eli pitch the tent on the lake's edge and build a bonfire. And Nico moves his van again, so we can keep listening to music.

Nico sits next to me on the largest log, with more gap than I would like between us.

Eli places branches on the fire; flames flick lit ash into the air like mini fireworks, and the heat radiates onto my face. We gossip about old times at the lake, and the night soon turns inky black, lit with the brightest of stars.

Anna tells a funny story about how she and Nella got together. "I thought Nella was annoying and a hard-core micro manager at first." She laughs.

Nella leans on her shoulder, and with one hand pulls a blanket up over their knees. "I was just making excuses to talk to her."

"Aww, that's adorable," Penny says, sitting next to Eli on the smallest log, their bodies sandwiched next to each other.

A cool wind gently blows off the lake, sending goosebumps down my arms. I hug my knees into my chest and wrap my arms around my legs. I feel Nico's eyes on me, when he gets up and walks to the lake hut, coming back with a cooler filled with beer and raspberry vodka, a stack of blankets balanced on top. He hands around drinks to everyone else before stopping at me.

"Drink?"

"Yeah, thanks, taking a beer."

"Whaaat?" Penny screeches. "You mean you're not drinking raspberry vodka?"

"Safe to say I will never touch a raspberry vodka again."

Nico laughs, grabs his own beer and a blanket. He sits next to me, this time much closer.

He pulls the blanket over his legs, gripping the corner. "Blanket?"

"Yeah, thanks." And he pulls it up over both of our knees.

Penny and Eli argue over whether eels are carnivores or herbivores.

"Clearly carnivores." I laugh. "One tried to eat me for lunch when I was twelve. I'm lucky to be here still." My comment makes Nico erupt in laughter.

"They're really not going to go near you," Nico says, tipping his head back and laughing. "I mean, if you really get deep and mess up the water, sure."

"I can confirm Eli pushed his little sister off the jetty and eels bit my toes."

Penny bats Eli in the chest. "Dude, you pushed her in?" she says in her mean voice, which suddenly switches to a laugh. "Ha ha, she's been terrified of them ever since."

Eli holds up his phone, showing the page he's just googled. "Eels are predatory carnivores. Their diet consists primarily of fish." He laughs. "Remember, I did jump in and rescue you after all the hand flailing and crying made me realize you were actually terrified and did not find it funny. Which, for the record, I thought you would."

"Terrified is a strong word. I was mildly concerned."

"All right then, Miss, should we recreate the photo?"

Not one to be proved wrong by my big brother, I say, "You're on," and regret it immediately.

Nico faces me with a concerned smile. "Err, you sure?" he whispers.

I whisper back, secretly terrified, "I can't let Eli win. He's very annoying."

"Gotcha," Nico says as everyone ambles to the edge of the jetty. Eli and I stand in the exact pose to recreate the photo.

"I'm nice. I'll give you a countdown," Eli says. "Five, four, three ..."

But before he gets to two, Penny laughs and says, "You're mean," and pushes him. He side-flops off the jetty into the water. She rips off her t-shirt and jeans and in her underwear, launches herself into the lake. When her face bursts through the surface she screeches, "Holy shit, that's cold," and grips Eli, her arms around his waist.

Anna, Nella, Nico, and I are in hysterics. Nico pulls off his t-shirt. Bare-chested, he leans close to me. "Okay if I push you in?"

I pull off my mountain-bike t-shirt and stand there in my sports bra and shorts, already freezing. "Yes."

Nico wraps his arm around my waist and launches us off the jetty.

We sink under as our bodies break apart. For a moment I'm free-falling, the rush of water tossing against my ears. The black silence makes my heartbeat rapid; panic gets the better of me, and I flail my arms, maniacally searching for the surface.

Nico's arm wraps around my waist, pulling me into his chest as he thrusts us upward; our faces break through the surface and I gulp panicked breaths. He hugs me close, our faces nearly touching. "I got ya," he says, and he kicks his legs, gripping me close with one arm, swimming us toward the jetty.

A slippery smooth something gently slides past my leg. I flinch. "Eels definitely down there," I say, taking a shivered breath between each word.

"At most, you'll feel them glide past, but for the most part, they'll stay out of your way."

"For the most part." I grin nervously.

"Yeah, unless they're starving," he jokes.

"Oh, lovely. Well you've got bigger feet, sooo …"

My lips chatter with cold. He holds me closer to him; our bare chests are pressed together, and his arm is gripped around my waist as he floats us to a wooden piling. I glance at the stars hanging in a thick electric mass over the lake. When I glance back at him, he's watching me intently.

"Thank you for this," I say, "it's the sweetest and best birthday."

"I'm happy to be a part of it," he says. Nothing—nothing at all—could have made this night any more perfect. My teeth step up into a new level of chattering. It's impossible to stop my body from shaking with cold.

"Do you want to get out?" he asks.

"Yes, and really, really, no."

"Same."

Penny and Eli duck-dive in the water, and thrust their legs straight up in the air; their attempts at handstands look more like an uncoordinated synchronized dance. Anna and Nella haul themselves out and onto the jetty.

"Fark, it's cold," says Penny as her face emerges from the water. "I'm getting out."

My body shudders. "We should get you warm," Nico says. Water droplets coat his eye lashes.

"Yeah, although if we go numb, we won't even feel the eel; problem solved. Hypothermia aside."

Nico grips my hips, gently lifting me up as I haul myself out of the water and climb on to the jetty. When Nico is out, he grabs my hand. My fingers link with his, and we run back to the lake hut. We change into dry clothes. It takes every part of me not to look over into his corner where he's in his boxers slipping on a dry t-shirt.

When I'm fully dressed in jeans, t-shirt, and a hoodie, we return to our spot by the fire with the others.

Resting on a log, Anna yawns. "Sorry, guys, I gotta sleep. I've been up nearly twenty-four hours."

Nella stands holding out her hand toward Anna and takes her into the tent, the front open, overlooking the moonlit lake.

Like yawns are spreading, Penny gets up. "Woo, ditto, four a.m. starts are killer. I'm calling it a night. Night, guys."

Eli follows Penny. "I'm checking you don't steal all the space and blankets."

"Calm down, Eli boy, I'm willing to share," trails from inside the tent.

Nico laughs. "Is it just me, or is it obvious to everyone that they like each other and would be the cutest couple and they're the only ones that don't know?"

The fire pops and crackles, shooting smoke into the sky.

"They are kinda perfect together."

Nico's eyes search my face. "Warm enough?"

Before I answer, he grabs Penny's blanket, left on the log, wraps it around my shoulders, and sits close. Our legs are jammed together, and we shift our original blanket over our knees. I rest my hand by my side, accidentally bumping Nico's. Before I move it away, he links his fingers with mine. When our eyes catch, he releases his hand, glides it around my back and pulls me into him. I rest my hand on his shoulder, run it down his chest, gently grip a handful of his t-shirt, and pull him toward me. I'm not sure if time disappears, speeds up, or stands still, or who kisses first, but our lips meet. Soft and gentle.

From the tent: "Eli, you're going to have to deal with the fact I'm wearing socks to bed. It's freezing."

Eli: "It's a bit weird, and it's not that cold."

I can't contain the laughter, and Nico and I pull apart, our faces still close.

Penny: "That's because you keep stealing all the blankets. It's farking freezing."

Eli: "Well … come … closer then."

And then there's silence.

"Aww, that's a bit cute," Nico says, pulling me back into him and kissing me all over again. When the log becomes too uncomfortable, we lie on the lakeshore, huddled under the blankets, watching the stars and listening to the lake's water gently lap against the jetty. My face is pressed into his chest, our arms are wrapped around each other, and I'm struggling to keep my eyes open when Nico kisses my forehead and says, "Night."

Seventeen

Nico closes the back of his van and hooks his arm around my waist, pulling me close. The sun is just rising, peeking over the valley, illuminating the lake.

"Moving to uni tomorrow, huh?" His tone sounds disappointed.

"Yeah, but I'm back next month for planting."

"That's way too far away. How 'bout I come to visit after you're settled in?" He grips me closer, kissing my forehead.

"I'd love that, like, any time." I lean into his chest, and his head rests on mine.

"Come on, Izz, I gotta get to work," Penny says, sitting with Eli in his car, pretending they're not eavesdropping on us.

Nico's phone rings. He ignores it.

"I'll see you soon, okay?" He leans down and kisses me while his phone continues to ring. And we don't stop kissing, basking in the morning sunlight, the birds in full morning song.

Eli starts the car.

We pull apart. "Bye, I better go," I say.

"Bye. Can't wait to see you soon."

Nico's phone rings again. I get in Eli's back seat.

"Sorry," Nico says, phone pressed to his ear while watching me, "a burst pipe. I'll be there ASAP." And he waves as we pull out and begin the drive home.

I lean my head against the window, and the winding, forested highway zooms by in a blur.

From the front seat, Penny bats my leg. "So freaking happy for you."

"Yeah, he's so great," I say, grinning.

Penny laughs. "I was referring to you beginning law tomorrow." Her face turns serious.

"Of course," I say, horrified law wasn't the first thing that came to mind. "I'm excited, like, can't wait to begin." It's one hundred percent true.

Penny laughs, and I realize I've been had.

"I'm just messing with ya, ha ha. You two are cute, and so perfect together."

"You're a mean, mean girl."

"Yeah, I'm a bitch, but ya love me for it."

"I really do." It grips me how much I'll miss Penny, Eli, and Nico when I move.

We pass Mrs. Wilson's drive, the red mailbox repainted, shiny and bright. I tip my head back as we pass. Today Nico will be working on the river garden I planned. And I'd do anything to kiss him by that river with no one watching.

My phone beeps.

Mom: *I hope you had a lovely birthday. I wanted to let you know the apartment complex has just received official confirmation from the council that they have approved it.*

"Nooo," I groan.

My chest tingles like I'm sinking through the floor of the car, and my heart is being dragged along as we drive.

"You okay in the back there?" Eli says, glancing in the rear-view mirror.

"The apartment complex just got official approval from the council."

"Fuck," Eli says.

"What the actual fuck," Penny says. "I'm so sorry. Can anything be done?"

"No," I say in a hush, glancing out at the cars speeding by in the opposite direction. Tears seep down my cheeks.

Dad's forest and Nico's mountain-bike touring business will be destroyed. I should have listened to Eli when he warned me about keeping news like this from Nico. At least he would have time to prepare, rather than being shocked.

Mom: *We will easily be able to cover your fees. P.S. There's a meeting at the council chambers tonight, your last time working for me.*

The relief of knowing I can pay my law fees is immense. But as we drive further away from the forest and Mrs. Wilson's, it also feels like I'm leaving a giant part of me behind.

We pull up at Penny's, and I walk her to her front door and launch into her with a hug. "I'm going to miss you," I huff out, my voice catching.

She squeezes me tight. "Go chase those dreams, lawyer girl. It's not goodbye forever, so don't you dare cry on me, okay?" She pulls away. "We'll Zoom, when you're settled, have a virtual raspberry vodka or somethin'." Her eyes are teary but she's smiling.

I scrunch up my face. "Ugh, they're awful. I'll add some chocolate liqueur to my cup of chocolate milk or something."

"How lawyerly and sophisticated of you." She laughs, looking me up and down. I'm wearing jeans ripped at the knee and an oversized t-shirt.

"Yeah, I'm gonna be the odd one out, hey? I forgot to pack my pressed blouses and pencil skirts."

"You're perfect, don't change." And we hug one last time before Penny tells me to go away so she can bawl her eyes out alone.

"Eli, boy," I say when I get in the car. It makes him laugh because I'm mimicking Penny. "Would you hurry up already and tell Penny you want to be her boyfriend?"

He grins, dips his head, and rests it on the steering wheel. "She's so scary, though," he says, laughing. "What if she says no and then it's awkward?"

"Isn't it worth the risk that you'll both be happy?"

He contemplates for a second.

"Or she might think you're not into her and end up with Chad from the frozen foods section—ya know, the tall, overly handsome dude she works with."

"No, not him. Point taken … as much as I hate taking dating advice from my little sister. You make a valid point."

We pull up in the drive at home. Mom's lying on the porch couch, her legs resting on the veranda fence. She smiles in a way I haven't seen in a while. Relaxed looks good on her. But it knots my insides. Can she really be happy to see Dad's forest go?

She meets me on the steps and wraps her arms around me. "I hope you had the best time, sweetheart." She says the words just like she used to. It hasn't hit her yet that when the forest is gone, it will feel like Dad has died all over again. I've seen it before, when Mom closed the door to Dad's law practice for the last time. This is her calm before her next storm.

"Thanks, Mom, it was fun," I say, as Eli walks past without a word. When it comes to Eli, his silence is more hurtful than his words could ever be.

Mom follows me to my room, seemingly oblivious to the fact that Eli just shut his door and didn't acknowledge her existence.

"We will easily be able to pay for your fees." Her excitement is palpable.

"Yeah, it's a relief." I place my bags on my bed.

Mom reads off a list on her phone as she wades through the packed boxes in my room. "Do you have to take your work boots?" She lifts them from the box, pulling a playful face like I'm crazy.

"Yes! They're coming. Highmont has one of the best botanical gardens."

"Have you packed your bedding?"

"Er, no, Mom. I got it." Her energy is freaking me out, and I wish she'd just quit it with the lists.

She picks up the hanging hearts plant Nico gave me. "Really, Izzy," she says. "Do you think you'll have time for obsessing over plants? Honestly, where is your brain? Sweets, law is intensive. You'll have little time to fluff about with plants."

"I'll pack," I say firmly.

"Okay, okay. I'm immensely proud of you for getting into law. You did it." The way she looks at me, full of pride. "You should be proud and excited."

For a second I put the forest, landscape design, and what I've done to Nico and Mom aside. I swipe it away, all of it. Just for a second, I let myself be excited. It's been buried under a layer of guilt that follows me around.

"I'll leave you to it, then. Don't forget about the council meeting this afternoon."

The city council meeting room is filled with people. Mom takes the stage, and I sit down in the front row.

When the crowd hushes, a council representative introduces himself and welcomes Mom, congratulating Housing Co. and the council's efforts on a conjoint project.

As Mom introduces herself, a map of the proposed site flicks onto the screen behind her, showing the location of each new apartment building. Before Mom can speak, the crowd gets rowdy, and hands raise. Glancing behind me, I spot Nico and Mr. Balducci in the back row, by the only exit. My mind twists into panic mode. The room's walls feel as if they're closing in, and the words and commotion of voices challenging Mom blend into a static that rings in my ears.

One by one, Mom answers questions, the people asking getting more heated with her responses, or lack thereof, as to how she will mitigate the environmental impacts of the housing development. Last night races through my mind, Nico kissing me; the two of us feels like it's meant to be. If he sees me here, we will be over before we even began, and I'll lose the first guy I've loved over something that's my fault.

"Yes, the person in the back," Mom says.

Nico's voice resonates through the room. "You claim that your way to mitigate the environmental impacts of the forest being cut is your commitment to building sustainable eco-friendly structures. This cannot replace the virgin forest and subsequent loss of biodiversity. So my question is, what is your plan to prevent any loss to flora and fauna?"

I'm sinking in my seat, too afraid to look back, unsure if Nico has noticed me here or not.

Mom replies with assertive confidence. "There are no threatened species in the area to be developed." She flicks to a slide, showing an ecological report summary carried out by the council; those exact words are highlighted.

I can't handle seeing his expression, or the precise moment when whatever he feels for me dies.

Nico's voice again: "How will you address job losses for those that make a living from the forest? Tourism, for example, will be greatly impacted."

Mom continues unflustered. "Once the subdivision is complete, we expect an increase in tourist numbers and a subsequent increase in jobs in this sector."

The crowd groans and boos as Mom flicks to another slide with a graph showing the number of potential employment opportunities, categorized by industry.

She continues, voice raised, speaking over the commotion. "Luxury eco-holidays are one of the fastest-growing and financially profitable ventures, increasing job availability in cafés, bars, helicopter tours, and retail, for example."

My insides stitch at the mention of helicopter tours, knowing Nico will feel it hard.

"With respect," Mr. Balducci says, his voice rising above the crowd, "once the forest is cut, it is gone forever. And all these so-called mitigation methods support luxury tourists, not the community that lives and works here and deserves to have the forest remain."

His business could be affected too. He'll lose the contract with the council to grow plants to regenerate the forest.

Mom answers more questions; the crowd becomes increasingly agitated. "That will be my last question," she says. "We can assure you, we'll continue to answer any questions you may have. Our contact details are here."

She flicks to the last slide, which shows her staff—including me. Beneath my photo it says: *Community Liaison.*

Tears well and a deep sinking feeling rushes through my core. I'm desperate to hit rewind and make Nico unsee that photo. The commotion in the room turns deafening, suffocating. My thoughts race a million miles, trying to figure out what to do. I'm too scared to look back at Nico.

My phone vibrates in my pocket.

Nico: *You were working for Housing Co this whole time?*

The back of my throat burns tight, tears stream down my cheeks. I don't care who sees. I don't bat them away. I just sit there defeated, sunken in my seat, and stare at my stupid photo still on the screen. Getting up, I yank the cord connected to Mom's computer, killing the image. Every part of me wants to run over to Nico and explain. I look back through the crowd; he's standing next to Mr. Balducci by the door. For a split second, our eyes meet, and his emotionless expression says it all. Any feelings he had for me have died.

Mom's ranting at me. "What did you do that for?" And she says something else, which I block out.

As the crowd quickly disperses, Nico and Mr. Balducci disappear through the door. Mom slumps in the seat next to me, oblivious to how lost and broken I am right now.

"I think that went terribly," she says. "I'm relieved it's over. People don't like change. They'll see the benefits once the apartments are—"

I cut her off before she can finish. "Who's it benefitting, Mom?" My tone is meek.

"You are. I'm doing this for you."

I gulp air. I think she needs the change because it distracts her from Dad. Erasing all memories of him will make it easier for her to deal with the fact that she'll never see the love of her life again.

"Izz, what's the matter?" She's avoiding Dad just like I'm avoiding facing Nico.

I stand and rush through the door, gliding and weaving past everyone. Out in the car park, I reach Nico getting into his van.

Tears stream. "Everything I said about the forest, everything I did, I meant it." Each word catches as I push them out.

There's hatred in his eyes. "Yeah? I'm finding that hard to believe."

Mom appears next to me. "What's going on?" she snaps at Nico.

"I think you were helping me so you could get inside info for *her*," Nico says, pointing at Mom.

"You were helping him?" Mom says. "*Him?*" She spits the word out with too much force.

Nico gets in the truck, slams the door, and drives off, leaving me gulping air.

"I'm sorry," I say, facing Mom. "I never wanted the forest cut; I only took the job because I needed the money."

Mom glances around at people getting in their cars, and she falsely smiles as they pass, pretending there's no emotional outburst involving her.

"Let's go," she says, walking ahead to her car.

On the way home, she says nothing. She's cold and distant, and rightly so.

When we get home, I lie on my bed curled around Rex, my room packed away in boxes.

Me to Nico: *I'm so sorry, I 100% meant everything I said and did to try to save the forest. I should have told you about my job.*

And I hit send even though I know I'm the last person he wants to hear from.

Eighteen

I survey my room; everything that matters is packed in boxes on my bed-room floor. The plant Nico gave me, Audrey Eagle posters, and my plant ID books, in case I get time to visit the botanical gardens. I can't believe today I move to Highmont University and start life as a law student.

Resting on my bed, I check my phone for messages from Nico. There are none.

The message I sent him last night sits unread. Although … there's a green dot by his name. My heart somersaults—he's online. It's taking all of me not to message him again. My mind is reeling, replaying fragments of yesterday. The moment I saw in Nico's eyes that his feelings for me had died. The thought that there's no possibility of there ever being an us catches my breath like it's trapped in my chest, and I can't breathe out.

Penny: *You'll be awesome. Sending ya luck and love xx.*

I head downstairs. Eli is at the kitchen table, inspecting a box wrapped in silver paper with a black bow. "Woo, Izz, big day. You'll nail it, sis." And he slides the box across the table to my usual spot.

Mom pours coffee into Mike's cup, avoiding my attempts to make eye contact. She's barely spoken to me since the council meeting, even when I broke down crying and apologized profusely. All she said was thank you for saying sorry, and that my focus needs to be one hundred percent on making it through law school. I totally deserve it. But the coolness of how she said it made it clear I met her limit of tolerance, a boundary I thought I could never cross.

Mike taps the present. "Thought this would come in handy. I have a buddy who helped us get a great deal."

I open the card stuck to the front. In Mike's handwriting: *You will make the best lawyer. We are proud of you.* In Mom's handwriting: *Love, Mom, Eli, and Mike.* And a note from Eli: *You rock. Love you.*

"Thank you."

"Well …" And Mike taps the present.

I unwrap the box and lift out a laptop, the top covered in a botanical print skin, and place it on the table.

"Is it cool? Yay or nay?" Mike looks worried, his smile scrunching like when you're pulling off a Band-Aid "Penny helped. I did my research. The street-art-style flowers in popping colors rimmed in black—we thought you'd like it." His face is still scrunched.

My insides catch. "Really, it's cool. Like, *really*. Thank you." The flowers remind me of Nico and working at Mrs. Wilson's.

"What a relief," Mike says, pouring me a coffee and topping off everyone else's cups.

"Make sure you look after it," Mom says with zero emotion, "okay, Izz? It wasn't cheap." Mom's coolness is killing me.

"Oh, course she will," Eli says. "It's not her style to not be careful. It's your thing, right Izz?"

It's a five-hour drive to Highmont. As soon as Mike sets off, Mom and Mike argue over the fastest route. "Take Interstate 13. It's faster," Mom insists.

Mike keeps his eyes on the road. "If we go I-12, we bypass the city and drive through the forest. It's more scenic." He glances in the rear-view mirror, catching my gaze.

Mom, her tone terse, says, "I think I've had enough of forest-related things."

I lean into the seat and doze. When we stop for gas, Mike goes into the shop to pay, leaving me alone with Mom. I look up the Highmont website and click on the schedule of events. Orientation mixer and guided tours on the hour.

"There's a campus tour at four we might make," I say, "and a student orientation lecture tonight." I hold up my phone.

Mom stares out her window. "They'd be good for you to go to, Izzy." She faces me and smiles. I know she's forcing it to keep the peace or whatever. She's trying, and considering what I did, I'm lucky to get that.

Mike returns with bags of Doritos, chucking one at me through the window.

"Anything healthy?" Mom says.

"Road trips aren't for keeping to your macros. On the road, the macros don't count." Mike and I exchange smirks in the rear-view mirror.

Penny: *How goes it? Bet that car ride is intense. Peace, sending you peace.*

Me: *Could be worse. Kinda glad Mike is here. Who knew?*

Penny: *Yeah, he's all right.*

Penny: *Saw Nico uptown.*

Just someone mentioning him makes me feel like I'm free-falling. On Messenger, the three dots dance to show Penny's replying, and I can't hack it. It's like the words won't appear fast enough. And then the reception drops—zero bars—as we wind our way into a valley.

I jam my ear buds in and listen to a podcast from *Bloom and Grow Radio* on how to bring wildlife back to urban spaces, and eventually I fall asleep.

I wake as we reach Highmont City. The tree-clad highways are replaced with a towering concrete cityscape and gridlocked traffic. While we wait at a light, a swarm of people crosses the intersection. Resting on the hill ahead are the three iconic towers of Highmont State University.

I check my phone.

The last message I sent to Nico is still unread. Every single part of me is internally begging that he reads it and knows I mean every word.

Me to Nico: *I don't expect you to forgive me, and I totally understand if you never want to talk to me again. I am so sorry. Just wanted you to know that. Please stay friends with Eli and Penny. I don't want them to lose you too.*

Nothing I write conveys the regret and depth of how sorry I am. Or that I lost someone that made my world feel hopeful and sunshine filled.

Penny: *Nico looked somber. Said he has to cancel a lot of his bike tours.*

We reach the university's tall concrete towers with zero green space. *Highmont University School of Law* is stamped on the top of the building in metallic letters. Those words and this place—everything I've worked hard all these years to get to. I hold my camera out the window and snap a picture, for Dad.

Me to Dad: *I can't believe I made it.*

It should feel weird to send messages to my dead dad, but it's a comfort despite the hundreds of unread messages I've sent him that will sit on delivered but will never be opened.

Mike pulls into a parking spot outside the entrance.

Mom, already out of the car, opens the trunk, and Mike unloads my bags onto the sidewalk. Each of us carrying boxes, we take the path past the law building, following the signs to *Student Accommodations House B.*

As we pile into the elevator and it rises, Mom says, "Oooh, you'll get a view over the city."

Something about the words *city* and *view* doesn't hit the same for me as it does for her.

The elevator stops at floor sixteen, and we follow the hallway until we reach room eleven. I knock, Mom and Mike behind me, and the door swings open.

A girl with waist-length dark hair and thick, black winged eyeliner greets us. "Izzy?" she asks, her tone friendly and upbeat.

"Yeah. Amelia, right?"

"That's me. Come in." Her false eyelashes are perfection, making her brown eyes pop. I adore her jeans, ripped at the knee, and fitted tee that reads *Equality for Everyone*. "I haven't chosen a bed yet. Thought I'd wait for you."

I set my boxes on a bed that's pushed up against the window with a view over the city. I spot the only green space, where the world-renowned Highmont Botanic Gardens are.

Pinned to the largest wall are posters that say *Love is Love* and *Human Rights Matter.*

Amelia glances at my box filled with plants. "Nice. They'd love the window ledge."

"Yeah. Would you mind if I took this bed, then?"

"Not at all," she says.

Mom and Mike set their boxes on my bed. "We'll grab the rest. You unpack."

"Law, right?" I ask, facing Amelia.

"Yeah, human rights lawyer is the dream! You? Wait, let me guess, environmental law?"

"Yup, also the dream."

I'm relieved she seems friendly and easy-going and is pro plants.

Music plays through four speakers she's rigged around the room. "Feel free to play your own if you don't like the vibe." Chill summer beats drift around the room as we unpack. I place the plant Nico gave me on the windowsill. The hanging chains of heart-shaped leaves nearly reach my bed. Cramming the rest of my plants around Nico's, I run out of room and line the rest on the back wall of the desk that sits next to my bed.

On the wall above my desk, I hang the Audrey Eagle posters Dad got me, and set up my laptop.

"There's that orientation meet and greet tonight. Want to go together? I can't wait to start," Amelia says, upbeat. She lifts a stack of folded t-shirts from the open suitcase on her bed and places them in her drawers. "It's going to be four years of intense slog practically living in the library, I hear," she says, her voice drenched in excitement like she's a kid on Christmas morning seeing her presents under the tree for the first time.

Her excitement about spending years inside at a desk doesn't grip me the same. I just assumed everyone accepted it's a necessary and unfortunate fact that you put up with. A *do what ya gotta do* situation so you can get to the end, eventually.

"We've just got to get through it, I guess, one day at a time."

She unzips an art folder. "I can't fuck anything up. I'm on a scholarship. One fail, and I'm out of here." Amelia slides out detailed sketches of Martin Luther King Jr. and the Dalai Lama, placing them on her desk. The lifelikeness is blowing my mind; they could almost pass as black-and-white photos.

"You drew these?" I ask, my voice rising. "They're incredible. You could sell these."

"Yeah, won't be much time for drawing now, but who cares? I'm living the dream."

Mom and Mike return. "Izz, the room looks more comfy and cheerful already," says Mom.

The words *comfy and cheerful* catch me off guard, and why does it remind me of Nico? It's four o'clock, and he'll have just finished work at Mrs. Wilson's. Usually, he sends me a daily progress photo and even though I know he won't today, I check my phone anyway.

Mike looks out my window. "You can see the botanical gardens from here. Couldn't be more perfect for you, right?"

"The guided orientation walk starts in ten. Ya wanna come with? It says all are welcome," Amelia says, glancing at Mike and Mom.

"We'll leave you to it," Mom says, actually smiling. "Looks like you're settling in nicely already, and we've got a long drive home." She hugs me. It's awkward and robotic. "Proud of you," she says.

My throat catches, but I keep it together. "Thanks, Mom."

Mike wraps his arms around me and grips me close. "Anything you need, we're only a phone call away, okay?" That's what Dad used to say and look how that ended. But I appreciate the sentiment.

And then they disappear. I rest on my bed. I'm alone, starting law. Breathe. I did it. Put all the shitty stuff I did at home aside and focus on law. I say it to myself like a mantra, but no matter how hard I try to swipe away what I did, it flicks Nico's face to the forefront of my mind.

Amelia watches me. "It's hard to say goodbye, right? But we'll see them on university break."

I probably won't see Nico ever again. "Yeah, of course," I say. I swallow back the sting in my eyes, threatening to leak tears. I don't want to be the weird or annoying roommate that cries on her first day.

Amelia and I take the elevator and follow the path until we're outside the front of the law facility. Amelia sucks on her vape, releasing a billow of smoke into the smoggy, gray sky. "Selfie?" she says excitedly. She stands under the *Law Faculty* sign with her phone held high. Her other hand motions for me to stand next to her. "Well, this is a bit F-ing exciting, isn't it?" she says, pressing her head next to mine with a wide smile, and she snaps a picture. Her upbeat, enthusiastic energy is contagious, reminding me that it *is* exciting.

"Yeah, it is amazing," I say.

Everything that's happened between Mom, Nico, and the forest has clouded the fact that it's a miracle I'm here.

I send the picture to Penny with the caption: *I made it!! FYI, my roommate is cool AF.*

A clean-cut guy in jeans and a tailored jacket introduces himself as the student rep for law. We all follow like sheep into the law administration building—a dull, gray, open space with a high-pitched roof and an admin desk at the back. The only redeeming feature is the floor-to-ceiling windows, making it a great greenhouse. But with not one plant in the entire space, it's a wasted opportunity.

The tour guide speaks in a bored, monotonous tone. "This is where you come for any admin queries: accounts, changing papers, complaints, switching majors, disenrollment, that kind of thing."

Amelia leans in. "Woo, this room would be a great space to study in."

I smile to be polite, but seriously, I think I must be missing something.

We follow the guy through a bunch of dingy lecture theaters where the only natural light is from narrow rectangular windows close to the roof. We stand in the middle of the largest. It's like a mini sports arena; rows of seats rise steeply, looking down over the stage at the bottom like a soulless underground bunker. The upside is, with nothing interesting to steal my attention, it will make it easier to focus on studying.

We visit the cafeteria and health center, and library. The guy stands by the law books, whispering, "Most of your time will be spent here."

Every desk is occupied with students furiously typing on their laptops. It gives me an idea for Mrs. Wilson's garden. A stone path leads from her home library to a lush garden reading nook. I remember her saying she wanted one.

The tour ends back where we started. "Tonight, there is a meet and greet. Lexus Band will play, and there's a free barbecue, so see you guys then," the tour guide says.

We make it back to our room.

"Oh my god, that was awesome," Amelia says.

I pull my linen out of the box and make my bed, stretching the fitted sheet onto the mattress.

I glance out the window at the sun setting across the botanical gardens. It will already be dark up at the lake hut. I check my phone. Nico's read my message, and a wave of nervous butterflies engulfs my chest. I rest on my bed, staring at the message, and I wait, desperately hoping he'll reply.

Scrolling through Facebook, there's not one post from Nico— no photos of views, gardens, or mountain-bike-related memes, not one. Checking his profile, the blue button by his name says *Add Friend*. He's unfriended me.

I dump my phone on my bed. Amelia breaks my trance, as I stare out of the window.

"Hey, you want to go see the band?" She pulls a top from her drawer and holds it up, looking at herself in the mirror.

"Thanks, but I think I'll stay in," I say.

"Oh, okay, no worries." Sitting cross-legged on the floor in front of the mirror, she applies her eyeliner, tipping her focus up toward me. "If you change your mind, text me, and I'll come get ya and drag ya through the mosh pit."

Amelia leaves. I change into my cactus-themed pajamas and sit on my bed watching the band playing in the courtyard below. After a while, I bury myself under the covers and try to block out the noise, but it seeps through the open window. I reach up to tug the latch, but accidentally knock Nico's plant off the windowsill. I hear it smash on impact, six stories below.

I get out of bed, grab one of the empty boxes, and race down the hall in my pajamas. While I wait for the elevator, two other girls arrive, their makeup done, plastic beer cups in hand. They look me up and down and smirk. I don't care if they're judging my clothes, or that I'm repeatedly pressing the elevator button. I care if I can't hold it together and fall apart in front of them. Fighting tears until I can't take waiting for the elevator any longer, I open the door to the stairwell and race to the bottom.

Outside, the bass of the band vibrates through my chest. Weaving through the dancing crowd, I push my way around the side of the building. Below my window, the shattered pieces of Nico's pot lie scattered across the concrete being blindly stood on by people. I pick up any shoots that might be salvageable. But the leaves are badly bruised and torn, and the roots are snapped off, the rest squished into the concrete. The hanging hearts plant he gave me is unsalvageable.

Back in my room, I bury myself under the covers in bed again.

Mom: *How are you?*

Me: *Went on the tour and am about to go to see a band.*

I don't have the energy to disappoint her with the truth. Once I get over Nico, I'm sure this place will feel like home.

Nineteen

Amelia is cool, and we share most of the first-year law classes. We walk into our first lecture of Law and Ethics. Amelia paws my arm like an overly excited Labrador.

"O-M-G, this is iiiiiit," she says, dragging me to the front row, where we take our seats.

Our lecturer, nicknamed Madman Max after his reputation for taking no shit when it comes to late assignments or attendance, steps up to the lectern behind a microphone. Seated behind me are more people than the population of my high school.

The class goes silent.

"To survive law, you must be focused and dedicated. Those that can't keep up won't make it."

He introduces himself as Max Chester and outlines the law program, showing us overly detailed slides with print too small to read.

"Look to the person on your left, then to the person on your right," he says. "By the time you finish law, only one of you will graduate."

Amelia gives me a look of horror and whispers, "Not us, though. We got this."

"I haven't spent five years dedicated to getting in to fail," I whisper back.

"Exactly," Amelia says, her focus not on me but on Madman Max, who glares at us in a way that confirms there is some truth behind the rumor behind his name.

My phone vibrates in my pocket.

Penny: *Yo, home gurl, how goes it? Just a heads up, I spoke to Nico, and he told me he's heading to the Highmont Botanical Gardens in a few weeks with Mr. Balducci for a conference. Just want you to know in case you wanted to avoid the gardens then.*

Seeing his name and knowing he will be in town makes my stomach woozy, like when you drive down a bumpy road too fast. His face, and when he kissed me on the lake, flash through my mind, followed by the last time I saw him when he found out I betrayed him, and the look I'd never seen from him before. The one that said there was no chance he would want to see me, now or ever again.

My phone resting on my lap so as not to draw attention to myself, I keep glancing at Madman Max, so he thinks I'm paying attention. He's rattling on about maintaining grades and attendance, but his droning voice fades into the background as I read and re-read Penny's message.

Amelia glances at me and grimaces like I'm crazy for being on my phone.

I google the conference, *How to Create Sustainable Urban Landscapes*. It's not a public event; it's only open to landscape designers, regional council employees, and related businesses. If I were still working at Mr. Balducci's, I would be going. And if I hadn't lied to Nico, I'd be going with him, possibly as his girlfriend. And those things make me swallow back tears.

How long does it take to get over a guy you're in love with? Because it's seriously stealing my focus. Failing law is not an option. Even if I can't see how to move on, I have to.

The lecture ends, and Amelia and I run to the next, taking our seats.

Penny: *How's the lectures going? Killing it, no doubt.*

Me: *Law is okay. I'm lucky to be here. Finding it hard to focus tho.*

And then Eli messages me with the same message as Penny, about Nico and the botanical conference.

Penny: *Thought this might make you feel better.*

She's attached a video of her and Eli standing on the lakefront, moving from the view of the water to the lake hut and Dad's trees behind. Just in view, parked to the side of the hut, is Nico's black van.

Amelia bats my arm as the lecturer begins her introduction. Her grimace says it all. *What the hell are you doing?* I look up to see the room full of faces, with their focus on me. The video still plays the sound of Penny's voice: "We miss you, girl," with ducks and cicadas chirping in the background. The noise rings through the lecture theatre, until I turn off my phone and the lecture theatre goes silent.

My cheeks overheat with embarrassment. "Sorry," I whisper, glancing at the lecturer, a woman elegantly dressed in a blouse and pencil skirt, and she says, "Welcome to Environmental Law. Hands up if you are passionate about making a difference in saving and protecting our environment." I thrust my hand in the air faster than anyone. "Well, you're in the right place, then. Welcome." And the lecturer gives me a warm smile.

And it's enough for me to swipe away all the distractions and remember why I am here.

Twenty

Each night I sleep with my window open. There's something rejuvenating about waking to cool, crisp morning air sweeping your face. After having a shower and getting changed I water the plants on my windowsill. Low-hanging clouds weave amongst the treetops of the botanical gardens and the city's high-rises. I'm reminded of the morning after my birthday. Waking up on the lake with Nico's arms wrapped around me, watching the mist lift from the lake, and the sunrise.

Amelia, fresh out of the shower, wrapped in a towel, runs a comb through her hair. "You planning on going to Madman Max's optional study group thang?"

"Yeah, for sure," I say.

"I'ma defs going to go." A grimace paints her face. "I need aaaalllllll the help I can get."

Not one person has said law is easy, but everyone says it takes superhuman dedication to make it through. And I want to do more than just scrape by.

Waiting for Amelia to finish getting ready, I check my emails. There are three messages from Balducci Landscape Design. I can't open them, they're too distracting, a painful reminder of what I did and who I've left behind.

I set up my emails so any messages from Mr. B. go directly into a folder, so I won't see them, like they won't exist.

Rain hammers my window, and dark gray clouds now completely obscure the trees in the botanical gardens. I look down at the pavement where the plant Nico gave me fell, and the space where it once sat on my windowsill. After what I did, he will never look at me the same way again, as much as I deeply want him to. I have to let him go.

Ignore the way Nico sets my heart on fire. Bury it, deep. Even better, learn to forget.

Amelia and I walk to our lecture and sit in the front row.

Halfway through class, Madman Max is mid spiel: "… the following exam questions are taken from previous years Ethics and Law tests," when the door to the lecture theatre creaks as it opens. He stops mid-sentence, his eagle eye on the guy entering the classroom.

"Sorry," the towering guy whispers. He has a soulful smile and dark-brown eyes. He takes his baseball cap off, rests it on the desk, and sits down next to me. He opens his laptop, and Madman Max continues talking.

"Did I miss much?" Late Guy whispers, directing his attention to me.

"Not really," I whisper back. I turn my open laptop toward him. "Just this, you're welcome to copy," I say, diverting my attention to Madman Max, who's glaring at us as he continues to speak.

"Just so you know, thirty percent of people fail the test." He scribbles an exam question on the board. And he spends the next hour decoding each important word and explaining how to properly structure an essay.

He's not exactly the lecturer that fills you with confidence. But his optional study class has been super helpful. The lecture ends and I slide my laptop into my bag.

"Woo, that test sounds impossible already," Amelia says, packing up her stuff.

"Err, trust me," Late Guy says. "Take it from someone who flunked this paper last year."

Amelia lets out a groan. "Noooo."

"I'm Amelia, nice to meet you," she says, reaching her hand past me, holding it out to Late Guy.

"Jack," he says, shaking Amelia's hand. "And you are?" he asks, facing me as he stands, ready to leave.

"Izzy," I say.

Jack's smile is broad and friendly. "Nice to meet you both." He rests his bag on the desk, pulls out a black hoodie, slips it on. I notice the white Conservation Corps logo in the top right corner. It's the organization Dad volunteered for, sending him to far-flung places around the world, saving forests.

Jack rakes his hand through his hair and puts his cap on. We follow behind him as we squeeze through the narrow row of seats and make our way outside.

"Catch ya next time," Jack says, his tone calm and relaxed, and he strolls on ahead to his next class.

"Aww, Jack seems nice," Amelia says.

"Yeah, I guess." I'm sure he's cool, but what's not cool is now I'm wondering about his involvement in the Conservation Corps. But worse, Jack reminds me of Nico.

Huddled under Amelia's umbrella, we walk through to the other side of the campus. Rain catches in the puddles on the pavement. We've got ten minutes until our next class. Amelia makes a beeline for the coffee cart that sits outside the library.

"But coffee first," Amelia says.

"For sure." We order and wait under the eaves of the library. Rain drifts in sheets across the courtyard. Mini torrents of water flow into the tiny clumps of garden cut into the concrete. Whoever did the landscape design favored fitting in wildlife like it was an afterthought. I force away the thoughts of landscape design, because I know where it will lead—to Nico and the missing and what work he's doing at Mrs. Wilson's.

Amelia returns, clutching our coffees.

"Izzy," she says, holding out my to-go cup, "you all right? Ya zoned out."

"Yeah, totally fine. We're lucky to be here, hey?" I reply, more as a reminder to myself. A way to snap my focus back to where it needs to be.

"I know, right!" Amelia says, taking a sip of her coffee as we head toward our next lecture. "Gotta admit, feeling the pressure, ya know. After so long planning and working my ass off to get in, I don't want to fuck it up."

"Totally get that."

Twenty-One

Amelia and I walk into Madman Max's optional study group and sit in the back. While we wait, I flick through photos on my phone, stopping at a selfie of Nico and me. He's holding the phone up while planting a kiss on my cheek. I'm stung with sadness.

Jack meanders into class and takes a seat two rows in front of us.

"He's nice, right?" Amelia whispers. Her direct question catches me off guard, and I dart my attention to her, unsure I want to answer. Nico is more than nice. He's wild and honest and loves the things he's passionate about to the fullest. "He's one of a kind," I say.

Amelia glances at Jack. "Ohhh," I whisper. I mean, why would she ask about Nico? I've barely mentioned him to her.

Amelia tilts her head. "Um, who did ya think I was talking about?"

"Err, no one, not important."

Her focus is now on Jack and the empty seats either side of him.

Amelia stands, packs up her stuff and takes a seat next to Jack, waving me to follow. I wish she wouldn't. I could purposely sit away from them, but how bitchy would that look? I take a seat next to Jack.

The botanical skin sticker stuck to the front of my laptop captures his attention. And so, too, does the screen-lock photo of Dad and me, in full backpacking gear, the view from the picnic table up the forest track in the background.

"Ahh, the top of the Wilburn Trail. I've been there. That view is something else, eh?"

No, I don't want his commentary on it. Or worse, questions about anything to do with that track. Please, no.

"Let me guess," he says, "enviro law."

"Yeah." I smile politely, and open a blank Word doc to kill the image and, hopefully, further questions.

"Same—enviro law for me too," he says. "Ya know, I once worked on some planting in that area up the Wilburn Mountain Bike Trail, with the amazing Reuben Rivers. It was wild. His work is referenced a bit in the course, actually."

The mention of Dad's name sends my brain into shutdown mode; rapid-fire memories sting my mind. What can I say to bring this conversation to a close?

"Amelia wants to major in human rights law." The words speed out too fast, but his focus shifts from me to her and, thank god, Amelia, obviously smitten with him, heads the conversation in another direction.

"What halls of residence are you in?" she asks.

"Humanities—it's more a bunch of small flats than a dorm." His answer is directed at me. "You?" The way he smiles, there's an easygoing kindness in his eyes.

"Amelia and I share a room, literally, in the dorm across from here."

Madman Max walks in, and the room quiets. Before long he's droning on, putting another practice exam question on the board, and as a class we attempt to answer it. It becomes clear very quickly that we have no clue what we're doing.

I force myself to listen to each word Madman Max is saying, anything to help me re-shift my focus from the forest, from Nico and Dad. The way Jack's hair flips out a little under his cap in the same way Nico's did under his bike helmet. At least he's taken his hoodie off, but the way his shoulders perfectly fill his gray t-shirt … It's stupid how the littlest things can spark big hurtful reminders of people. I'm filled with a gush of emptiness. It's too distracting, too overwhelming.

After an hour, Madman Max leaves with a stern reminder: "Three weeks until your Law and Ethics test. Not all of you will pass, let that be your motivation to study hard."

He's such an ass. But his logic is strangely motivating, igniting the competitive part of me. I will not be one of those who fail the test. I can't handle messing up anything else.

Amelia scrolls through the notes she's taken on her laptop and lets out a frustrated sigh. "Just when I think I'm starting to get all the jargon sorted in my head, he introduces more terms that contradict the previous ones."

"He's insufferable," Jack says, "but if you're serious about making it through, he will help you. Mess around, and he won't give you the time of day, and if you fail, trust me, you'll have to fight to be accepted back in." Something about the way Jack's smile dips as he watches Madman Max pack up his things, and the way his smile returns when he leaves the room, tells me Madman Max does not take any bullshit.

Jack stands and glides his hand in the side of his bag, and rests his phone on the desk. I can't help but notice the image of him and an older-looking woman, his arm wrapped around her shoulder as they stand on a cliff overlooking a stunning view. I dart my eyes away and stare at the wall. I hate how everything is a reminder of home, how it's taking every part of me to forget.

He passes me an advertisement for a community basketball game three weeks from now. "All proceeds from the tickets go to an at-risk youth forest camp—an outdoor adventure of sorts. The kids have had a rough start. Some have never been out of the state, let alone climbed a mountain. Anyway, it's a big deal for them," Jack continues. "Woo, sorry, I'm being real salesey. But if you want to come, any donation for the tickets is totally cool."

"We'll come," Amelia blurts out before I've had time to think.

Jack directs his focus to me. "So, you'll come? Sorry to sound desperate." He pauses. "Ha ha, I'll be straight. Please come."

"Yeah, we'll be there," Amelia repeats, more enthusiastically than I'd like.

Jack looks directly at me. "Well then, I'll see you there. And thanks heaps." He leaves.

Amelia and I pack up our stuff. If she were Penny, who I know almost as well as myself, I'd ask her what the fuck was that all about, but I don't, and seeing as I barely know Amelia, I settle on, "We got cornered into that one."

"He's doing a nice thing for those kids. We should go. Study hard and a basketball game to celebrate."

I know she's right. And a forest adventure for at-risk youth. If wilderness can do anything, restoring wounded souls is its specialty.

Twenty-Two

It doesn't take long for the duo, i.e., me and Amelia, to turn into a trio, including Jack. We share most classes, and he now joins Amelia and me in study sessions at the library. He keeps to himself, and away from friends he clearly knows from his first year at law, and I can't help but feel there's something more there, something he's staying away from. All he's mentioned is he wanted to restart law with no distractions. I felt that.

Amelia and I are on a bus on our way to Jack's basketball fundraiser. The bus weaves through the center of the city toward the far side of town. Half an hour later, we reach a suburb of older weatherboard houses with chipped and peeling paint, broken windows, some with boards covering the doors.

Jack left uni to travel on a Conservation Corps mission, something he'd almost given up on being accepted into, but when he finally was, mid–first term last year, he jumped at the chance and flew to Papua New Guinea to help re-establish a forest there.

Leaving law, much to his father's horror. But more horrifying is, his dad is Madman Max.

We pull up at the last stop, five minutes from where the game is. I flick to the last message from Jack with the instructions on where to go. We reach the front of the high school pictured in the photo Jack sent me. The parking lot is full and cars line the roadside. Happy cheers boom through the air. We follow the hordes of people to the courts behind the main building and wait in line. We reach the ticket guy, wearing a basketball jersey, not much older than fifteen, with full-sleeve tattoos that ride up his neck and the side of his face. I hand over our money. "Thanks for coming," he says brightly.

"Welcome."

People fill the grandstand; one half are wearing green, and on the other side, blue.

"Jack said to sit on the blue side," I say, and Amelia and I find a seat way up the back.

On the court, two teams, one at each end, huddle around their coaches. The blue team is crowded around Jack. The whistle blows, and the teams ready themselves in position. Then, my phone beeps.

Penny: *Hey stranger, how're things?*

Attached is a picture of her and Eli at Nicola's Cantina, sitting in front of their plates of food. They're at the outside table where I had my farewell dinner that Nico organized. And the memory stings with sweet sadness.

I shouldn't, but I search the photo for any sign of Nico. There's none.

The blue side of the crowd cheers as they get the first point. I glance up, not sure what to reply to Penny.

I haven't been avoiding her, but I haven't been messaging as much as I used to. Not because I don't want to, it's just that every reply I get comes with a photo or a mention of home that grips me and makes the missing worse, and it's always a reminder of the forest and Nico. It's confusing—simultaneously wanting to avoid everything and anything to do with home, and craving it like my soul requires it to feel alive.

The same guy who sold us the tickets weaves through the crowd with a tray of hot dogs. "Three dollars or a very generous donation to our forest trip." He stops in front of Amelia and me. "Ya know ya want to," he says, beaming a cheeky smile.

Amelia hands him ten dollars. "Two, please," she says, as the blue side erupts in cheers again.

"Yeeeya," the guy shouts toward the court, "you got this game goin' on!" He waves his free hand at Jack.

I take a photo of my hot dog covered in sauce, with the basketball game in the background, and send it to Penny.

Me: *Basketball.*

Penny: *You at basketball, whaaaaat?*

Me: *Doing new things.*

Penny: *Out of yo comfort zone. NICE. Miss you.*

Me: *Miss you too.*

Penny: *Random q. Have you been checking your emails? Mr. B was asking. Said you hadn't replied or something.*

My insides stitch. I've been purposefully avoiding them. I figured if it were anything really important, Mr. Balducci would text me.

Me: *Probably lost a landscape file or something.*

I'm sure someone at work, i.e., Nico, has sorted it by now.

Penny: *Lol. Zoom tomoz?*

Me: *Yup.*

At half time, I watch as Jack gathers with his team. He holds up a whiteboard and draws with a board pen until they fist-pump and take to the sideline, slugging water from their bottles. Jack rests on the bench seat, focusing on his phone.

Jack: *Where are you guys?*

I stand; Jack's searching the crowd, when he spots me and waves.

Amelia launches to her feet. "There's Jack!" She waves out.

Me to Jack: *Game is tied, huh? Your team is doing amazing.*

Jack: *technically, they're all my guys, ha-ha. But yeah. Thanks for coming—Sweet of you. Let's hang out after.*

"Jack said to stick around when the game finishes," I say to Amelia. "I've got a ton of study to do, though."

Amelia sighs. "He text you that?" She glances at her phone. "Aww, he didn't message me."

"I'm sure he meant both of us." I am absolutely counting on it.

"Na, it's cool. He's into you," she says, her tone defeated. "No hard feelings, I'm not looking for anything serious, and he seems like the settle-down-forever type, ya know."

He really does.

"Like hotness and kindness but without the player-ness," I say.

Amelia playfully nudges my shoulder. "So, you're keen, eh? I think he likes you."

I feel guilty. I can see in her eyes that she likes him more than she's letting on.

Just the thought of him asking me out makes me want to hide. I really like him as a friend, but my heart is crushed, and there's only one person who can put the pieces back together and, as nice and amazing as Jack is, it's not him.

Amelia nudges me. "Eh, eh?" Like she's run with the fact that I find him hot and assumes that means I want him.

"No, and no." I smile. But I can tell she doesn't believe me.

"Uh ha, hmmm." And she winks at me.

"Still, no."

The game has come down to the wire, tied with three minutes to go in the last quarter.

The crowd's energy is infectious. "I didn't think I would ever like it this much," I say to Amelia; both of us are standing watching as the last few minutes play out.

Ten seconds to go, and the game is still tied. "Oh my god, how do people watch this game all the time?" says Amelia. "It's so stressful."

A player from team blue dribbles the ball, intercepting and passing, and one second before time, he dunks the ball, swishing it through the net. The blue team take the win, and the crowd roars.

Jack high-fives his team, and the boys ram into him, wrapping their arms around his shoulders. The adoration they have for him is obvious, and going by the smiles on both teams' faces, it's clear the feeling is mutual. And I have to admit, the effort Jack is going to, to love on these kids and give them a forest adventure, grips me a little.

Holding the microphone, Jack speaks. His calm voice, pitched with excitement, spreads through the tinny speakers in the corners of the court.

"A massive thank-you to everyone for coming."

The boy who sold us tickets steps toward him, holding a piece of paper.

"The final total is in, and—"

The crowd cheers, and Jack stands there smiling, waiting for the rowdiness to simmer before he continues, "Seven thousand and sixty-eight dollars. It's enough for our teams to go to their forest camp, and we can't thank you enough for your support."

Jack lines up the teams on either side of the footpath, and as people leave, the players thank the crowd as they walk past. It's the sweetest of gestures.

The wilderness has a way of bringing people back to life. I know that for these kids who have landed on hard times, a forest-survival course could be life-changing for two reasons: the forest can heal, and Jack's belief in them could change the trajectory of their lives in a new and unexpected positive direction.

Amelia and I reach the footpath. The red team is lined up on one side and the blue team on the other; their beaming faces and thank-yous get me caught up. Their sheer happiness is the sweetest thing, and I'm happy for them. Their excitement and energy are palpable, their spirits lifted, and Jack is a big part of that.

I reach Jack at the end of the footpath. "Thank you for coming, it means a lot," he says, his smile bordering on bursting.

"Your team won," I say excitedly.

"Blue or red team, we all won!!" His broad, tanned arms and shoulders fill his basketball jersey. Before I know it, he launches a hug at me, one arm around my waist, the other over my shoulder, pulling me into him. My head rests against his chest, barely reaching his neck. "Thanks so much, and for putting up with my constant jibber jabber about organizing the whole thing," he says.

"Welcome," I say, and pull away.

His attention is diverted to the crowd squeezing past me. "Bye, thank you for coming," he says to them, before his attention snaps back to me. "Hang around, for a little bit?" He glances at Amelia, patiently waiting behind me. "We're having a barbecue, just a few humble sausages, if you want to join us, both of you?"

I feel Amelia's energy behind me, her focus boring into me.

"I'm sorry, we'd love to stay," I say, "but I've got way too much study stressing me out at the moment."

"Totally understand. I'll catch you in study class tomorrow?"

"Yeah, for sure."

Amelia and I take the bus back to the university.

Just before we reach our room, I get a text:

Jack: *Thanks for coming to the game. Loved seeing your face in the crowd cheering the team on.*

Twenty-Three

Today is Nico's birthday. Madman Max is droning on. I have no clue about what. I've spent the last six hours in class staring at the wall, wondering if it's a stupid idea to text Nico *Happy Birthday*. It's a dumb idea. He does not want to hear from me. Yet there's a delusional small part of me that's like, what if I'm wrong?

After class, instead of returning to the library, where I'm supposed to meet Amelia and Jack, I sit under the small clump of trees outside the library. The teeny patch of grass is barely wide enough to sit on. It's the only wilderness Highmont Uni has to offer, yet it's still better than being stuck in a lecture.

Smells of freshly brewed espresso waft over from the campus coffee cart. Those waiting for their drinks sit on the benches and soak in the sun and crisp autumn breeze. I rest my hand on the hard-packed earth, disappointed that the soil isn't loose enough to dip my hand in and sift it through my fingers.

I wonder how Nico is celebrating his birthday. Is he at the lake or forest, or Mrs. Wilson's? And after I don't know how long, I conclude he's probably gone for a mountain-bike ride while he can, before the forest is cut. Scrolling Facebook, I wish I could send him a message, but we're no longer friends. I drop my phone on my lap and lean back against the tree, staring at the sky.

Jack walks out of the library and over to the coffee cart and makes his order. He glances up and beams when he sees me. Sometimes the way he looks at me makes me think his feelings have crossed the friendship line. And the thought makes me nervous.

A few minutes later, he strolls toward me, carrying two cups of coffee.

"Hey, thought I might find you here," he says.

A random rush of missing Nico returns with force. I swipe the thoughts away, squeezing my eyes shut for a split second and shaking my head before I realize how awkward that must look.

"You okay?" Jack rests the coffee cups on the concrete before resting his hand on my shoulder, his brown eyes deep with concern. "Were you about to pass out?"

"No, no. Really, I'm fine."

Relief crosses Jack's face.

I force a ridiculously silly smile and shake my head back and forth, which makes him laugh—embarrassing myself in an effort to avoid any hint of sadness that might be seen as an invitation to ask me what's wrong.

"Oh good." He sits beside me, passing me a coffee.

"Thank you so much." I scrounge in my bag for money and gather coins to pay him back.

He rests his hand on my arm. "Put your money away," he says, gently nudging into me.

I quickly drop the coins into his bag.

"Wait, that was a sneaky maneuver."

"I appreciate the energy boost," I say, holding up my coffee. "Thank you."

Jack smirks. "I mean, I'm going to have to pay you back, like with a movie or something. Yeah, I think I'ma have to take you to a movie to say thanks."

His logic is ridiculous. "That feels like a very unfair deal," I say.

He leans back against the tree. "A movie. When works for you?"

"Should we check what's on and see when Amelia is free?" I ask. I can see where this is going, and I don't want to do or say anything that would suggest we're anything more than friends.

"I was thinking just the two of us, if you're okay with that?" Our heads are leaning against the tree. He turns his face to the side, so it's facing mine. His gaze searches my eyes in way that connects people before they're about to kiss.

I dart my focus to my cup, and am relieved when I spot Amelia walking toward us.

"Sorry, I was just about to text you and say come and have a coffee break," I say.

"Thank god," she huffs out. "My brain is fried. I need like a triple shot or something." She faces Jack. "Dang, man, why does your dad have to be so mean? His study questions are hard-core, dammit. Why?" And she groans.

Jack laughs. "Yep, and yep, no answer for that, sorry. He is a nice guy under all of it, just takes his work very seriously."

"Yeah, that's an understatement," Amelia says, heading toward the coffee cart, returning a few minutes later with her drink.

We eventually get to work under the shade of the tree with our laptops on our laps, until the late-afternoon sun dips behind the library, and the wind picks up, covering my arms in goosebumps. But with the clear blue sky and fresh air, I can't move. I've missed being outside too much. I crave being lost in the wilderness at the lake forest and the wholesome feeling after a day's hard work, hauling soil and digging in plants. There's something so soulful about it.

"It's freezing," Amelia says, packing up her stuff. "I'm heading back to our room. Coming with?"

"Actually, I have to head off too," Jack says, sliding his laptop into his bag and glancing at the time on his phone. "Taking the crew for a spin class tonight. We're working on getting our fitness up for the forest camp." He stands and holds his hand out. "Haul up," he says.

I grip his hand, which engulfs mine, and without any effort he pulls me to my feet.

He lets my hand go, removes his hoodie, and offers it to me. "You look freezing."

"No, really, I'm good."

"Just take it. I can see you're cold. I gotta run. I'll catch ya both tomorrow." And he takes off before I can thrust his top back at him.

Amelia and I walk back toward our room. "So, are ya gonna put it on or what?" she says with a smirk.

"No." I try to casually change the subject. "Dorm food for dinner, or is it nasty noodles in a cup in our room?"

But she's not buying it. "What the actual—why not?"

"I just can't," I say, looking ahead, and she doesn't question it further.

When we get back to our room, we opt for cups of noodles for dinner, both exhausted from a week's worth of constant study. And being a Friday, we sit next to each other on Amelia's bed and watch Netflix.

My phone beeps.

Mr. B: *Did you get my emails? Hope all is good. Miss you.*

Just the thought of reading his emails makes everything come barreling back. Dad's forest and how the guy I love feels less than nothing for me.

I'm trying to think how to reply when I get a Facebook notification that Anna has posted a new reel. I know I shouldn't, but I click on the notification. And immediately regret it. The caption, *Happy Birthday Nico*. Nico's arm is draped around Anna, and another girl who's looking at him with loved-up eyes. I know that look; I feel that look and am certain that whoever this girl is, she's into him.

I lean back against the wall. Amelia is engrossed in the movie. I stare at the screen, pretending I'm watching. Tightness builds in my chest as sadness creeps up my throat, until I can't fight the tears any longer.

I nearly text Penny to ask if she was there, and then it occurs to me that I've not heard from Eli or Penny, and on a Friday, I usually do. And neither of them has told me otherwise, probably so as not to hurt me because they will be with Nico celebrating his birthday with the mystery girl.

I don't know what comes over me, why I would choose now to message Nico, but embarrassing desperation gets the better of me, and I text him.

Me to Nico: *Happy Birthday I hope you're having the best day.*

And I hit send. I immediately regret it.

I rest my phone on the bed and try to focus on the movie.

My phone beeps.

Jack: *So, we never finished that conversation about going to the movies? Keen Saturday night?*

Twenty-Four

In the food hall, I take a lunch tray from the stack, Amelia behind me.

"Have you started the Law and Ethics assignment yet?" Amelia picks up an apple from the giant tub of fruit, resting it on her tray.

"Yeah, I finished it last night."

She darts me an eye roll and twisted grimace. "O-M-G, you're a machine. How the hell do you write them so fast?" she says, picking up a packaged box of vegan salad followed by a box with two sausages, adding them to her tray. Amelia and I spend nearly every minute together. And as far as people go, I could do way worse. She's a hilarious mix of contradictions, and I've come to like her a lot.

"Sorry." I shrug. "I've not started studying for the test, though. I've heard it's crazy hard, and weeds out the class numbers. Fail the test and fail the paper."

"It's so stressful," she groans, sounding like a wounded animal.

"Yup." I dump a vanilla pudding cup on my tray with three others. Amelia smirks.

"Library snacks."

"Yup." Anything small and easily hidden in the library saves time finding food.

She copies, neither of us concerned that the lunch lady is glaring at us.

We take the window seat. And a few minutes later, Jack appears. He rests a giant sandwich and an apple juice on the table and then sits next to me. A grin spreads across his face. "My brother is having a birthday party at his this Friday, low-key drinks from eight. You guys should come."

I never responded to his text about going to the movies, and guilt hits me. Not that he's mentioned anything about it since. He's not the kind of guy to be pushy or anything. But I owe him an answer. He's become a great friend. Even if sometimes it's awkward when I get the hint that he possibly wants more.

Amelia's expression is conflicted, and she lets out a groan. "Yeeeeessss. But also, Nooooo. I'm drowning in assignments."

Jack laughs. "I feel ya." His focus shifts to me. "We've been working our asses off, a little break might rejuvenate our studying mojo." His voice is playful, and his corny overdone grin makes me smile.

"Err, maybe …," I say.

Jack's smile flattens. And now I feel worse for ghosting his offer to take me to the movies. "Actually, why not? After a full day's study, it wouldn't hurt to go for a little bit," I say.

"Yus!" Jack grins. And he turns to Amelia, who's still having a moment with her head resting on the table.

"Okay, I'm going. Can't get drunk, though, coz studying hungover is not the one."

"Deal," I say, "we'll see it as a study break. It would be nice to see something other than the library and lecture theatres."

Jack finishes his sandwich. "I gotta gap it, hitting the gym. We're gonna par-tay," he sings as he leaves.

My phone beeps. An email from Mr. Balducci's personal Gmail account. I'd only redirected his work emails to that folder so I could ignore them. But banishing both would be taking it too far. He's been like a dad to me.

The subject line reads: *Hi team. Important updates.*

Even before reading further, the need to ignore this is bursting back to the surface, knowing the email could contain details about what Nico's been working on. Or that it might mention the exact date and time the forest will be slaughtered. I dread it. I'll remember the date like it's tattooed on my face. And when that day and time come, I'll be a wreck. The thought of all of it is too much.

But somehow, I can't draw my eyes away, and I read on.

Nico will be promoted to landscape manager while I am teaching my landscape design course at the community college. Congratulations, Nico.

And for those of you attending the conference at the Highmont Botanical Gardens, we leave Thursday at 5 pm from the office. Please don't be late as it is a long drive. The conference starts at 9 am on Friday.

And lastly, the community college has offered my staff 30% off tuition. Here's a link to check out the program.

Without even thinking, I click the link. What am I doing?

Start your career in landscape design today!

But I swipe away before reading further.

Nico will be in town this weekend.

It's Friday, and Nico is in town.

Amelia is hogging all the mirror space to put her makeup on. "Got to admit, knowing we're going out tonight did make me study harder," she says.

"The party should be a great distraction." I look out over the botanical gardens where Nico's conference is.

I pull out my phone and type a message to Mr. Balducci: *I hear you're in town. It would be so great to see you. If you have time, I could meet you somewhere. No worries if you're too busy, though.*

I hover my finger over the send button. I know I can't and shouldn't hide from him. I hit send anyway. And get an immediate response.

Mr Balducci: *Ah Izz, so nice to hear from you, my girl. I'd love to meet up. How about I meet you at Kizmit bar and grill? I'll be there from eight PM onwards. It would be lovely to see you.*

After everything I did, he still wants to see me. I knew he'd always look out for me—a promise he made Dad. But everyone has a limit. I had wondered if, like Mom and Nico, I'd done him wrong and pushed him away too.

Amelia and I walk through town. The rush-hour traffic is grid-locked both ways.

Jack: *Boom, we are all ready. People are arriving already.*

And he sends a video of a lounge filled with people sipping from red plastic cups. Some are dancing to music playing in the background.

Me: *We are on our way. Need anything?*

Jack: *Just you. Lol. I may have had a few.*

Me: *LOL.*

I brush off his message as drunkenness. I could move on with Jack—I care for him and he's amazing, and I know we would be great together—but my heart is stuck on someone else.

We wait for the lights to change and walk with the mass of others across the busy intersection. Amelia is telling me about her ex-boyfriend back home and how she's sworn off anything serious until she finishes law.

"Law is like five years," I scoff, telling her nothing she doesn't already know. "You mean to tell me if the perfect guy comes along before you finish law, you'll tell him to go away?"

"Yup," she says, smiling proudly as we continue along the footpath, passing packed bars and restaurants. "Because there's no such thing as a perfect guy. But having a bit of fun might be okay." She laughs, tapping my arm playfully.

"Do you know where the Kizmit bar is?" I ask. It comes out randomly and totally out of context.

"You okay? You seem distracted," Amelia says.

"I'm fine, just some stuff on my mind."

"The boy kind of stuff."

"How'd you guess?"

"You spent the entire study time in the library stalking Nico's Facebook photos." She smirks.

"You saw that, huh?"

"Well, I didn't think it would be the guy on the other website you were looking at— some botanical society thing with an elderly gentleman holding a spade."

I laugh. "No point in denying it, then."

We have spoken about Nico, but mostly I've avoided talking about him, quickly changing the topic.

"So, this Nico," Amelia says, her voice pleading for more details.

"I don't really want to talk about it," I reply, looking straight ahead.

"Do you want me to tell you where Kizmit is?" she says, finally answering the question. She tugs on my arm, bringing us to a stop.

"Please. I could probably google it, but yes." I smile at her. "Sorry for being distracted."

"Kizmit is around the corner, next to the botanical gardens. It's like a garden bar of sorts."

Makes sense.

"Would you come with me later? Just for a bit, then we can go right back to Jack's party." I hate how my voice is practically begging her to come. Usually, I wouldn't care about going anywhere alone, but on the off chance I run into Nico, it will be less awkward if someone else is with me.

Amelia wraps her arms around me. "Of course. I don't know what he did to you, but he's not worth it."

That's just it. He *is* worth it, and it's me that wasn't worth it.

We reach the humanities campus. It's dark when we finally find Jack's brother's party. People spill out into the hall, dancing to music that is way too loud for such a confined space.

My phone vibrates in my pocket. I leave Amelia to search for Jack while I duck around the corner into a quiet corridor.

Eli is on the other end. "So, hey," he says in a glum voice.

"You okay?" I ask. I brace myself. The last time he called me sounding like this, it was bad news. Dad had died. My heart's panic-beating, and I'm already trying to slow my breathing.

"The forest will officially be cut on April twenty. Just thought I should let you know."

My chest tightens, and tears immediately fall. "That's only ten days from now," I say, the words catching.

I gulp in a breath. I knew it would come. I knew it would happen, eventually, but now that it will actually be happening, I can picture bulldozers plowing through the lake hut and acres and acres of forest that Dad and Mr. Balducci spent years replanting.

Tears roll down my cheeks and I bat them away, staring at the wall.

"I just thought you'd want to hear it from me first and not Mom. I'm so sorry."

I'm partly to blame, and powerless to do anything about it. "I'm so sorry." My voice wobbles.

"You were in a difficult position, Izz."

We hang up. I sit on the ground, my knees to my chest, resting my head on my knees, batting away the tears from my cheeks.

Amelia sits down next to me and swings her arm around my shoulder. "You want to go back home?"

At first, I think she means back home to Rockridge, and I don't know what I would have said. But then I realize she means back to our room.

"It's no worries for me, really. I'm not bothered either way," she says.

"Thank you, yeah, I want to go."

We leave the crowded hall filled with music and people, students lapping up student life.

Jack: *Where did you guys go? I saw Amelia and now I can't find ya.*

Me: *Sorry. Slight change of plans. Sorry. Family stuff.*

Jack: *Here if you need anyone, always xxx.*

I don't want to lose him as friend or hurt him. I owe him a straight answer about us.

Walking back through town, I tell Amelia about Nico, the forest, and working for Mom and going behind Nico's back.

"You know," she says, "you were in a hard place, torn between family loyalty and saving the forest that connects you to your dad."

"I did it for the money. I wouldn't have the fees for law otherwise."

"I get that. I would have made the same decision."

That's comforting to know, I think.

She pauses at a busy intersection. "The shortcut to the botanical gardens is that way. We could visit Kizmit if you want?"

The light signals for people to cross, but I don't move. I'm at a crossroads. Turn one way to go back to our dorm room. Or turn the other and meet up with Mr. Balducci, with the possibility of running into Nico. Either way, I know they will know the exact date the forest will be gone.

Amelia waits patiently as people cross in all directions.

"Yeah, let's do it," I say. I at least owe them an apology.

We continue to walk, taking a shortcut off the main path signposted *To the Botanical Gardens*. The path winds through a park-like forest, eventually reaching a lake. Moonlight dapples the water, and there are bench seats under weeping willows.

Following the path, we reach the back of Kizmit. Lanterns are strung on the open-air deck with a view over the lake and the botanical gardens. People sit at tables, sipping drinks and chatting. It's a beautiful setting.

My chest sucks in air when I spot Nico sitting with a bunch of others.

"That guy is kinda looking hard out at you. He's hot, but it's creepy."

"It's Nico," I huff out.

As soon as my eyes catch his, we hold our focus for a second. I don't smile or wave or run to him and say sorry; I stand there and stare like an idiot.

"Want to go and talk to him?" Amelia says.

"Yeah," I say.

I take a step toward him. I'm desperate to talk to him, but his face says nothing but *leave me alone*.

He gets out of his seat, and my heart thumps like it's about to explode. Just when I think he's about to walk toward me, he turns around and walks back inside.

The backs of my eyes sting. What was I thinking? No apology is going to fix what I broke. I watch his back as he walks further into the bar and out of sight. How selfish of me. Me being here is like rubbing everything he's lost in his face.

"Let's go," Amelia says, and we begin walking back in the direction we came.

And then I hear Mr. Balducci's voice. He catches up to us, and before I say anything, he wraps me in a hug. I sink into him like a daughter would to a dad, and that's when the tears rush, and I gulp air, sobbing into his shoulder. "The forest and hut will be destroyed."

Mr. Balducci pulls me away from him. I glance over his shoulder in the hope Nico might have followed him, but his seat is still empty, and he's nowhere to be seen.

Mr. Balducci rests his hands on my shoulders. "You did what you had to do. There are no hard feelings. I love you like a daughter." He speaks the words just like Dad would have done. He pulls me in close again.

"I miss Dad," I say into his chest.

"I know, sweetheart, but you can't let the missing hold you back. You must keep moving forward in whatever direction your heart tells you to go. It's all we can do."

I say goodbye to Mr. Balducci, and in silence, Amelia and I walk home. Something about Mr. Balducci's last comment repeats in my mind. Mr. Balducci lost Dad, and then his wife to cancer, in the space of a year, and based on how much his heart fills the world, I think he knows a thing or two about how to keep moving forward, following whatever direction your heart tells you to go.

When we get home, Amelia and I watch a movie. I can't remember the title, and I have no clue what's happening. I'm mindlessly staring at the screen. And when Amelia falls asleep, I text Nico: *I regret everything I did. I wish I had never done it. I'm so sorry.*

Twenty-Five

We're walking out of Madman Max's lecture a week after seeing Nico. The Law and Ethics test is nine a.m. tomorrow and it's safe to say I'm less than prepared.

The week's classes were a blur. Without Amelia reminding me every minute to do this for my dad, I would have skipped classes—so uncharacteristic of me.

"Library?" says Amelia.

"Ugh," I groan. "I've had enough of studying in there." Sitting in a dingy underground lecture theatre for three hours and then studying in the world's most uninspiring monochrome library; I can't handle it.

"Think I'll go to the botanical gardens and study."

Amelia looks at me like I've lost my mind. Her head tilt and eye roll give her away.

I'm hoping studying outside will help me focus on what I should be focused on. AKA, Madman Max's Law and Ethics test.

We walk toward the library.

"Because it won't remind you of a certain someone or forest, that's already stolen your focus and turned you into a house sloth ever since you saw him … at the botanical gardens," says Amelia.

"You make a very valid point. I just need to get out of here for a bit. Really, being outside helps me focus." We arrive at the entrance to the library.

"Rigghhht," she says.

"You want to come?" I ask as she walks up the library steps.

"Na, too distracting." She smirks. "I'll come if you need moral support, while you cry onto your study notes for the test that's worth forty percent."

I laugh. She's reminding me of Penny, and it's kinda nice.

"Can you please stop making very reasonable and valid points? Still gonna go, though." I shrug.

She walks back down the steps, hugs me, then passes me her umbrella. "You'll need it," she says, glancing at the dark and looming clouds heading in the direction of the botanical gardens.

Rain pitter-patters on my umbrella as I walk through the city. Taxis line the road, bumper to bumper; the air is thick and muggy and reeks of gas. I reach Kizmit. I know he's not there. I know I should have avoided the place. All I see is Nico that night and him wanting nothing to do with me.

I continue past to the entrance of the botanical gardens.

There's a tall statue of a girl holding a daisy up to her face. Moss cascades down the stone, streaking her long hair with every color of green.

I reach the information center, where tables are sprawled out over a patio. I run my finger along the plaque with a map showing all the tracks, stopping at the Highmont Sustainable Trail and Seed Bank. Amelia may have been right, the law ethics test is the last thing on my mind and the most important thing I should be focused on.

According to the plaque, the Seed Bank Project is a collaboration between Highmont ecology students and the Highmont Botanic Gardens to collect and preserve local flora.

The weight of my laptop bag digs into my shoulder. The smell of freshly roasted coffee streams from the café. Choosing a table under the cover of the info center, I set up my laptop.

I scroll through Madman Max's lecture notes on the ethics of being a lawyer, but I can't focus on the words or their meaning. I check Nico's Facebook page. I know I shouldn't, but I hit play on his last video. And as soon as I hear his voice, my insides knot.

"Unfortunately, the beginner mountain biking courses run through Nico's Mountain Bike Tours will have to stop until I can find another suitable location. Thank you to the schools, businesses, and community groups who have supported me. Because of the forest being cut, there are limited trails suitable for beginners, and until I find an alternative location, I cannot offer this service."

He doesn't smile once. The thing that matters most to him has gone. And it's my fault.

I'm angry with myself. I'm angry at Mom. I'm angry that I let this happen.

I end up staring into space, imagining bulldozers ramming into the trees and the hut until all that's left is the barren, dead earth.

I call Mom. We've not spoken in two weeks. We're both doing what we do best. I'm avoiding her, and she's emotionally detached, pretending everything is okay when it isn't.

The phone cuts to her answering message.

I text: *Can you please call me back? Just ringing to check you're ok.*

I sip my coffee, trying to focus on work, which feels impossible.

I pack up my laptop and follow the path toward the Highmont Sustainable Trail and Seed Bank.

I wind past the pond that stretches the length of the botanical gardens. Rain scatters the water and drums on the top of my umbrella.

Mom calls, and before I can say anything she says, "There's nothing that can be done." Her tone is distant and vacant, reminding me of how she sounded after Dad died. Cut off and void of emotion.

"I just want to know that you are okay?" I say.

"I wouldn't have worked on the apartment subdivision if I thought I wouldn't be okay," Mom says, but something shifts in the way she says it. Something about the way her voice dips at the end—a stab of uncertainty that makes me think she's regretful.

"Tell me about law," she says.

"It's hard."

"Of course it is. It's law. You knew this."

I pause for a moment, watching the mist float across the lake. There's no point talking to her. There's no point telling her nothing feels as it should, or as I imagined it would, like the Earth is rotating in the wrong direction and I don't know how to make it spin the right way again.

"You've just got to keep studying hard, and think of it this way—one day you will graduate, and I will be so proud."

She says it like the only reason I went into law was to please her. And it dawns on me that's the problem. I used to be one hundred percent sure of why I wanted to be an environmental lawyer, to travel the world saving the environment just like Dad did. But now I'm not so sure at all.

"I've got to go. Better get back to studying for a test."

"Aww, I see. You are stressed over a test. This is what all this emotion is about."

My jaw practically drops into the lake.

"Bye, Mom." And I end the conversation after her lengthy list of tips on how to study for a test.

The back of my throat tightens in frustration. She doesn't get me at all. How can I expect her to? I've been living my life to please her.

And now she's seeing a version of me she doesn't like. The Izzy that wants to, in the words of Mr. Balducci, let my heart decide what's the best path to take.

I veer off the path and take the trail that leads to the seed bank. The planting shifts to tall overhanging trees, underplanted with masses of purple Chatham Island forget-me-nots.

I come to a forest hut—a re-creation of one of the first huts used in this area by the conservation department. *Seed Bank* is written on the front. Inside, I survey the glass jars of seeds lining the walls, categorized by the habitat they belong in. My chest aches, and I grip the pendant of the necklace Dad gave me.

Under the section labeled *Critically Endangered Alpine*, I pause at a jar of hexagonal olive-green seeds with a mustard-yellow stripe down each side. It's labeled *Carmichaelia carmichaeliae*. They're identical to the seeds in the unmarked jar on the fireplace at the forest hut, but I've never heard of this variety before. It was unlike Dad not to label his seeds. He was meticulous with record-keeping, and it makes me think he didn't know the name.

I rest on the bench seat and flick through the city council website, finding the environmental report for the apartment subdivision. There is no mention of this species of plant. In the middle of the room sits an interactive map. I push the button for *Carmichaelia carmichaeliae*, and lights appear where it originally grew, including the site where the forest hut sits. When I google the plant name, I find that it's critically endangered and apparently only found in the Highmont and Rockridge areas.

A couple walks into the hut, and the lady glances around. "Nothing to see. Just seeds," she says.

Just seeds. They could change everything.

I open my emails and enter Nico's address. Butterflies rise in my throat, and my heart races as I type.

I found these seeds at the Highmont Botanic Gardens. I know Dad collected these, but they weren't labeled. They're critically endangered and not mentioned in the environmental report for the housing development. I just wanted to let you know.

If Dad collected seeds of *Carmichaelia carmichaeliae*, and they are sitting in the jar on the mantlepiece in the forest hut, and they're critically endangered, the council, under the Conservation Act, would not be allowed to build there.

I attach photos and screenshots, then hit send. Then email Mr. Balducci and Jan from the Rockridge Botanical Society with the same information I sent to Nico.

I'm buzzing, nervous, and excited, like all my nerve endings are lit. Could this be enough?

Amelia: *How's the study going? I can't believe this stupid test is worth forty percent of our final grade? Like WTF. Stressed to the max.*

Me: *Haven't really started studying, I should get on to that.*

Amelia: *Distracted, huh? Who would have thought?*

Me: *I hate to admit that you are, in fact very, very, right.*

It's going to take a herculean miracle to switch my focus back to studying for the test.

Twenty-Six

I return to my spot in the library and set up my computer at the table in between Amelia and Jack.

Amelia leans over to my side of the desk. "This test, oh my fucking god."

I close the email I'm drafting to Jan. "Yeah, it's intense all right."

She points at Jack, who's deep in concentration with his noise-cancelling headphones on.

"He won't admit it, but he's freaking out."

Jack glances my way, gives me a friendly hand raise and immediately returns his focus back to his laptop. Poor guy does not want to be repeating the Law and Ethics test for a third time.

Amelia peeks at my computer screen, open on the Botanical Society website. "Er, studying hard, huh?" she asks, smirking at me.

"Oh, research for something else."

"How are you not stressing about this test? I'm freaking out. If we flunk, we fail the course."

I flick back to my study notes. "Yeah, you're right. I should get back to it." I should at least try.

I read the sample questions and answers while Amelia goes back to grunting and moaning as she scrolls through her study guides. I dart my focus out the window.

And my phone beeps. It's an email from Jan.

Izzy,

Nice to see your name turn up in my inbox. This plant species is worth pursuing. It was thought to be extinct in this area. It could be enough if we can locate any remaining specimens in the forest hut area. However, the council environment team combed over the area when assessing the application, so I'm not sure of the chances. But it's worth investigating. Nico and Mr. Balducci will go up to the track and take another look using your photos as a guide. In the meantime, I don't suppose your dad has any more of the seeds or proof that he collected them there?

I gasp. "Oh my god." Maybe under the lake hut.

My phone beeps again. Jan has cc'd me on a conversation with Mr. Balducci and Nico. I scroll through to Nico's reply.

Mr. Balducci: *We should all Zoom.*

Nico: *I would rather not talk to her, but I'm keen to take a look and see if we can find any evidence of this plant.*

The screen fogs over, and tears well.

Amelia leans over. "What? Oh shit, Izz. Are you okay?"

I swallow tears and point at the screen where it says *I would rather not talk to her.*

"They're never worth it. Fuck 'em. They just break your heart. You're better off without him."

"That's just it. I'm not."

She rests her hand on my back. "Ya want to go get coffee, take a breather? Trust me, what you're doing now is way more important than some guy back home who clearly has broken your heart."

Actually, I think it was me who did the breaking. But I don't want to unleash any more tears in the library. "Coffee, yes."

Outside the library, we order drinks from the coffee cart. Three little cactus plants sit on the counter. We sit on the concrete steps outside the library with our coffee. I imagine Nico and Mr. Balducci heading to the forest while I sit here, doing nothing, feeling useless.

Amelia tells me a story about the boyfriend who cheated on her before she left for uni, and how it was for the best. She's clearer about her career now. "Focus on the test. It will take your mind off him. And when you ace it, you'll feel better."

No, I won't. And that's just it. I already know I'm doing the right thing by being here, so why does it feel so wrong?

I lean back into the brick wall of the library.

Amelia slips her sunglasses on. "I've dreamed about being a lawyer since forever. I'm not letting anything get in the way. You?"

"Yeah, getting into law was the dream."

Amelia slides her sunglasses up. "Was? You mean *is* the dream, right?"

"Something like that." At least, I thought it was. Now that I'm here, I'm not so sure. Eli told me after leaving law that he'd rather chase a dream as an actor and scriptwriter, and would prefer hustling to get by over wasting his days in a job he hated. Life's too short. I used to think he left law because of Dad dying, but he didn't. That just made him realize our days were numbered and not to waste them. I misunderstood then, but now, I get it.

Sitting in the sun, Amelia chugs the last of her coffee. "We better get back to it. Trust your gut. You know what's right."

It's just that what I thought was right doesn't hit like it used to.

"I might stay here for a bit. I'll be up in a minute," I say.

"Sweet. I'll keep an eye on your stuff." And she heads back into the library.

When I return, Jack hasn't moved and Amelia is in her spot, head down. She smiles before returning her focus to her laptop. I settle back in my seat and flick to the mock test questions, reading the same paragraph repeatedly.

My phone beeps.

Mr. Balducci: *We are here. I don't suppose you have a key for this? We found it under the hut.*

A photo is attached, of a rectangular metal box covered in dust. *Plant Notes and Specimens* is scratched into the metal. Another photo is a close-up of the padlock.

Digging my hand into the front pocket of my bag, I pull out my keys. Only two are mine: one is for home and the other for my room in the residence halls. The rest are Dad's. It's never occurred to me that the three keys I kept for no other reason than they were Dad's, with no clue what locks they were for, could belong to the boxes under the lake hut. I lay the smallest of Dad's keys on the desk, take a picture, and send a close-up shot to Mr. Balducci.

Mr. Balducci: *It could be it. The brand name is the same as on the padlock.*

The possibility of what's in Dad's box could change everything— seeds, maps, notes, collected specimens that could prove *Carmichaelia carmichaeliae* exists up the track. And if we can prove it, the council will be forced to protect the area.

Mr. Balducci: *Think you could send it to us? To make a claim to the council, we would need it ASAP. The forest cutting is starting on Wednesday. It's our last shot.*

Me: *YES.*

If I overnight it first thing tomorrow, there's no guarantee it will get there by Tuesday, and even then, that doesn't leave enough time to make a claim to the council. It's six fifty-two p.m. No post shops will be open. I check my uni schedule. The Law and Ethics test starts at nine a.m. tomorrow and won't finish until lunchtime. If I miss the test, I fail the paper.

I tap my pen on the desk. Amelia glares at me. "You okay?"

"Yeah, actually I am."

"Good, no tappy tapping. Ya girl over here is losing her mind over this test. I don't know how you're so chill about it."

"Sorry," I whisper.

She resumes reading, while I google the train schedule back home. The next train leaves at seven forty-five p.m. Am I freaking crazy? Yup, but it feels right, and that's got to count for something. I pack up my laptop and slide my arms through my jacket sleeves.

Amelia looks me up and down. "You okay, chick?"

"Never been better. I gotta go. I'll text ya."

I give her a very random awkward hug, then tap Jack on the shoulder. He slips his headphones off.

"You are an amazing friend. And we will always be friends." I awkwardly hug him from behind.

"Wait, what?" Jack whispers, as utter confusion spreads across his face.

And I speed walk toward the stairwell.

Amelia whisper-yells, leaning back in her seat: "Where are you going?"

"To do what feels right for me."

"What the hell—" But I don't catch the rest.

I have no time to go to my room and collect my stuff. No time to study for a test that I have no intention of sitting. I run into town. My phone beeps, but I don't stop until I reach the metro station. I try to hail a cab, and each one drives past, not stopping. A bus pulls up, and I hop on. The doors swish shut, and I pay the driver.

"How long does it take to get to the train station?" I ask.

"It's the last stop, forty minutes or so."

The city whizzes past as we trail our way through the center of town. Each time the bus pulls to a stop, the doors swish open, letting in a gust of cool air, and a line of people meanders onto the bus while I internally scream for them to hurry.

I message Mr. Balducci: *I'm on my way home now. I'll go up to the hut at first light tomorrow with the key. If you and Nico want to come, meet me at the hut at 7:00 a.m. If we find anything, we will be ready to rock into the council at nine.*

The bus pulls into another stop. A guy with his arm around a girl kisses her forehead; they're both wearing woolen hats with fuzzy pom-poms. The doors swish open, and they take the back seat.

I message Amelia and Jack: *I won't be coming back to do the test or to finish law. You two were the best thing about being there. You'll both be awesome. Good luck for the test.*

Amelia: *OMG! You go, girl! Gotta fight for those dreams, eh? Because no one else will for ya! So what ya gonna do?*

Me: *Study landscape design because that's my actual dream.*

Amelia: *I love this.*

Jack: *Going to miss your face. Like a lot. But happy for ya, friend. Don't be a stranger xx.*

When the bus pulls up outside the train station, it's pouring and dark. I race to the ticket booth and line up, waiting for the ticket attendant. There's a dad in front of me with two young children. The dad digs through his bag, searching for his wallet as his daughter tugs on his leg, a teddy tucked under her arm.

The dad speaks softly. "You're tired. Everything will be okay, sweets. You can rest on the train."

The love between them makes me smile. Dad would want me to be happy, no matter what career I do. The last thing he'd want is me holding on to something that makes me miserable just because it makes me feel closer to him or because it keeps Mom from breaking apart. I grip the pendant he gave me, dangling around my neck. *Change of plans, Dad, but I got this.*

I hand over my card to the ticket attendant, and he passes me my ticket saying, "Better be quick."

I sprint through the crowd, gripping my laptop bag to stop it from flapping, and make it to platform eleven where the train is waiting. I take the window seat and the doors swish closed. Leaning my knees against the front seat, the world zips by but this time in the right direction.

Mr. Balducci: *Perfect. Thank you, Izzy. I will see you then.*

Me: *Mind if we meet up afterwards for a coffee or something? I want to talk to you about some stuff.*

Mr. Balducci: *Of course, always. See you tomorrow. P.S. Are you on holiday already?*

It definitely feels like it.

Me: *Not on holiday. Great. Thanks heaps.*

I grab my laptop from my bag and find the webpage for the landscape design degree at the community college. On the front page is a photo of Mr. Balducci standing next to his design students, his spade dug into the ground. The heading reads *Study Landscape Design.* Then: *Click here to be sent an information pack.* And that's exactly what I do.

Mom will flip out, but at least I have a plan that's unashamedly and authentically me. My nerves dig deep; telling her will be the hardest part.

It's midnight when the train pulls into the station. As I step onto the platform, a chilly wind whips my cheeks. I hop in a taxi and take a picture of the sign outside the station that reads: *Welcome to Rockridge,* then send the photo to Penny.

Penny: *WTF you're home?*

Penny: *Holiday? Noooo, it's too early.*

Penny: *Oh my god, has something bad happened? No. You would've called me.*

Penny: *So????????????????*

Me: *Ditching law. New plan. Save forest. Enroll in landscape design with Mr. Balducci.*

Penny: *Bout goddamn time. OMG. This is epic. Took you long enough. Exciting!*

And she sends me a picture of her at work stocking shelves.

Penny: *Night fill. Let's talk tomoz. YO A BAD BITCH. Mom know?*

Me: *Nope. Heading home now.*

Penny: *Er, I've loved knowing you. LUCK and LOVE.*

Me: *She'll come around. Eventually.*

The taxi winds through town and, a few minutes later, pulls up outside my house. The light is on in Dad's basement. Which is weird.

"That will be twenty-six dollars," the taxi driver says.

I stay seated. Not because I'm scared, but because disappointing Mom isn't fun. At least my head is straight, and I know she will get used to things.

The taxi driver repeats, "Twenty-six dollars, ma'am."

The curtain in the basement slides open, and Mom's face appears.

"Right, sorry." And I hand over the money.

I step onto the pavement, and the taxi disappears. I stand there staring at Mom, my bag slung over my shoulder. She frowns. Not in an angry way, but like she knows why I'm home. I walk toward the side door of the basement.

Mom swings the door open and stares at me, saying nothing. I say nothing. Her eyes crease at the corners, and they're wet and red. I launch my arms around her. Behind her, spread out on the bed, are boxes with the old family photo albums, loose photos, and Dad's botanical diary and maps.

"Mr. Balducci said you were coming and looking for a key or something."

I pull away, and tears drip down her cheeks. "Mom." And I launch myself back into a hug.

"So I thought there must be a spare key and came searching, and … and I, um …" And she stops, her voice catching.

"I miss him too," I whisper.

Mom collects herself. "At first, I was angry at you." She pulls away from me. "And I still am …" She rests her hands on my shoulders. "But I'm angry at myself more that you didn't feel you could tell me you were leaving uni or what really mattered to you." She releases her grip, and we stand over the bed, looking at our family's life in photos.

I point to one of her outside the forest hut, her face a grimace. "You weren't impressed." And I laugh, pointing out others.

"I'm not a hiker. I always hated the peeing-in-the-bush thing."

And we are both laughing.

"We were pretty cute, though." I pick up a photo of me, Mom, Dad, and Eli in front of the forest hut after camping under the stars for the weekend.

"Not *were*. We *are*."

Eli and Mike burst through the door.

"You're home. Did I miss something?" Eli says, staring at us. Mike is next to him, looking awkward as he holds a plate of homemade cookies.

"Anyone?" he says, offering us the plate of baked goodness. "Nice to have ya home, Izz."

"Nice to be here, Mike." And I grab two biscuits.

Mike walks to the door. "Er, I'll leave you guys to it …"

Before he can get any further, I grab Mike's arm. "No. Sucks for you, but you're one of us now, and besides, you're the best cook of all of us." I stuff a biscuit in my mouth. Out of the corner of my eye, I see Mom smile. And it's worth it for that alone.

A yawn escapes. I sit on the edge of the bed, and Mom sits next to me. Eli and Mike go upstairs to let us talk.

Mom dips her head. "So—no law?"

"No."

"I see." She looks at me. "Are you sure?"

"Never been more sure."

"I see …" She pauses, and I know what she's thinking. There's no going back if I pull out. "So now what?"

"Going to see if I can get my job back with Mr. Balducci and enroll in the landscape design course."

She's silent at first. "You know …" She pauses. "It sounds like a great plan and probably what was right all along." And she smiles meekly.

"Yeah, it feels right. I'm excited." My face slips into a smile.

"Then I'm happy for you." She nudges me. "Even if it is hard to accept." And she brings me into a hug. "Mr. Balducci called. He wanted to inform me what was happening with the seeds you found. He's a good man and wanted to keep me in the loop, not to ruin friendships. I know you're meeting there tomorrow."

I want to say sorry, but I'm not. "Yes, that is the plan."

"We will have to agree to disagree on that topic and not take it personally."

Something about the way her words catch and eyes smile, makes me think we will be okay.

And then she changes the subject. "We should get some sleep. It is lovely to have you back home."

It's one thirty a.m. before I get to bed. As I lie there, the events of the day play over and over, and my mind trips over thoughts about possibly seeing Nico tomorrow.

Twenty-Seven

Eli and I drive the winding forest highway toward the lake. The trees are a mass of orange, yellow, and gold. Fallen leaves are caught in the frosted-over puddles on the road's verge. In one hand, I clutch my keys, and in the other, I grip my coffee.

Eli glances at me before turning into the rural gas station.

"Izz, it's going to be okay. Want anything?" he says, twisting his head in the direction of the tiny shop.

It's six thirty, and time is speeding by while simultaneously having stopped. I both can't wait to see Nico and find out if the key fits, and I also want neither of those things. What if the key doesn't fit? What if Nico won't forgive me? As soon as I see him, I'll know. And seeing his face painted with the fact he'll never speak to me again is what I dread the most.

Eli taps on my window. "Earth to Izz—want anything?" he repeats.

I slip my keys into my pocket, and push my door open. A burst of cool fall air chills my face, and I walk with Eli into the store. We wander up and down the shop's aisles, Eli grabbing breakfast—a piti-ful-looking hot dog with sauce. I'm not hungry, despite my stomach twisting and groaning.

I follow Eli to the counter. "Are you really going to eat that?" I say, as we reach the cashier, who takes our cards in turn to split the cost of the gas. And then I regret asking. It was Dad and Eli's thing. After a ride, they'd religiously stop for gas-station coffee and the finest reheated hot dogs they had to offer.

"Sorry, that was stupid of me to ask. Don't answer that," I say, taking my card from the cashier.

Eli passes me a fake smile. "It's okay." His look says it all—it's not okay, but he says it is, anyway.

I rest my hand on Eli's arm. "I'm sorry," I repeat.

The cashier looks at me like I'm crazy.

"Anything I can help with, ma'am?" His beard occupies most of his face.

"She's just nervous about seeing a boy," Eli says, and smirks.

The cashier laughs. "I'm afraid matters of the heart are not my area of expertise, but good luck with that."

"Thank you, anyway," I say, noticing a box of Pinkie Pie chocolate bars on the back wall.

"Err, how much for the box of Pinkie Pies?"

He laughs. "The whole box?"

"The whole box," I confirm.

"They're dated by like years, sweetheart. Ya don't want to eat these," he jokes. His face turns suddenly serious. "You're not with the health department, are ya?"

"More like the broken-hearted department," Eli jokes, rolling his eyes.

"No, not with any department. I'll take the whole box, please."

He places it on the counter, wiping dust off with his sleeve.

"You can just have them, seeing as you're broken-hearted," he says, pushing the box toward me." Something about the way his eyes are tinted with sadness, makes me think he's all too familiar with the feeling of being broken-hearted.

I launch over the counter and pull him into a hug. "Thank you."

Eli grips my shoulder as I pull away. "Me thinks it's time to go." He pushes me back to the car while I clutch the still-dusty, unopened box of Pinkie Pies.

As I rest in my seat, Nico's van drives past. Nerves grip my chest. It's hard to accept that he sets my heart on fire, but there's no guarantee that he has even a spark left for me. I've made some huge mistakes and I've been wrong about a lot of things. But Nico is not one of them. He lights me up, in a way no one else has, and in a way I never thought was possible.

Eli pulls onto the highway, following behind Nico's van. Nico glances in the rear-view mirror, but we're too far away for me to gauge his expression. I smile back anyway, which is useless because he can't see it. And if he could, would he even want to? After all, he's coming to the lake for the key, not to see me.

For the next five miles, we follow Nico's van. Every time Nico looks in his mirror, I smile, and every time I do, Eli flicks his focus to me before diverting it back to the road.

"You know how you told me to tell Penny how I felt?" he says.

"Yeah," I reply, looking over at him. "Wait—you told her?" My voice rises three octaves. "And you didn't tell me? And Penny didn't tell me."

Eli adjusts his cap, taking one hand off the steering wheel. "Err, no, I haven't told her. But I wish I had." A grimace spreads across his face; it's full of regret, and it cuts me. I can tell he's hurt. "I saw her uptown having coffee with the dreamy cool-storage guy. You know the one, right?"

"He's really not that dreamy, but yes, I know the guy."

"My point is, she looked happy with him, and now I regret not telling her. I lost my shot with her. So tell Nico, Izz. That's all I'll say. Better to get shot down than to not try, and regret it."

We reach the turnoff for the lake and pull up directly behind Nico's van as it waits for oncoming traffic to pass. He's looking back at me in his rear-view mirror, and this time I can see his expression—no smile, no cheerful grin; but a straight-faced guarded glance that reads, *I'm here for the key and the key only.*

"Tell her anyway, Eli. Because you're right, living with regret is worse."

Even if you're ninety-nine point nine percent sure there's no hope they have any feelings left.

"And for the record, I know she loves you. Just saying."

Following Nico, we drive the last stretch of road to the parking lot. The sun casts a morning glow across the lake. The valley's tipped with the colors of fall.

Eli pulls up next to Nico's van. I watch the boats tied to the jetty gently bobbing in the water, and contemplate Eli's advice. It turns out I was good at giving it, but a hypocrite for never following it myself.

"You got this," Eli says, and he gets out of the car, greeting Mr. Balducci. They walk toward the hut, leaving Nico and me still in our vehicles, staring out to the lake. Nerves catch as I think about how and what I will say, and the longer I sit there, the more rattled and long-winded the internal monologue in my head becomes, until I can't hack it any longer and I get out of the car and walk round to his door.

He glances up at me, opens his window. Just the sight of him rattles me, and the semi-coherent list of things I was going to say disappears and instead, words fall out: "Thank you for coming."

Our focus locks, but his eyes are cold. He doesn't want to talk. From my pocket, I grab the key and pass it to him. He inspects it, and that's when it all spills out, figuring this is my one and only shot.

"I'm so sorry for everything. I owe you a massive apology. I regret going behind your back. It was the worst thing to do. I don't expect you ever to forgive me, but I am so sorry and regret working for Mom, and lying to you." I puff out the last few words, stopping to catch my breath. He doesn't look up; instead he grips the car's door handle and pushes the door open, forcing me to move out of his way.

Out of the car he finally faces me, emotionless. "Thank you for apologizing and bringing the key."

I search his face for any sign of the way he used to look at me, but there's no trace. And he walks to the lake hut, where Mr. Balducci and Eli are inspecting the hole in the step, without waiting for me.

I reach the others peering into the hole.

Nico puts his headlamp on. "I'm going in," he says, and burrows his way inside.

"So, what did you want to talk to me about?" Mr. Balducci asks.

"I'm not going to law, and I was wondering if you're looking for a part-timer while I take the landscape design course."

"Of course, Izzy!" His face breaks into a smile, and I feel it. It's nice for someone to share the same excitement. "You officially have your job back."

Before I can thank him, Nico yells, "Bingo! It's the right key." His voice is pitched with excitement.

"Yay!" we all yell at the same time.

Nico climbs out of the hole, dragging the metal box behind him, and pushes it onto the grass in front of us. Using the key, he unlocks the padlock. "Thank you," he says passing me my keys.

"It was the right thing to do," I say. My gaze settles on his, but he doesn't smile.

Mr. Balducci flips the lid of the box. "Let's see if your dad kept any record of *Carmichaelia carmichaeliae*'s existence up here."

I flip to the photo I took at the Highmont Botanic Gardens, of the olive-green, hexagon-shaped seeds, each edge rimmed with yellow. I kneel in front of Dad's collection of documents Nico has lifted out of the box: Dad's notebooks, rolled maps, and loose pages covered in handwritten notes, some with dried plant specimens attached. They bring a smile to my face and simultaneously make tears catch. I clutch the notes to my chest. Something that would have once torn me apart now feels like a discovery of treasure. "I'm so glad we found them before it was too late," I say, looking up at Eli.

I pick up a notebook. On the front is the outline of Dad's hand, traced on by me when I was eight. I flip it over. On the back is my hand, drawn by Dad.

Eli is smiling. "Yeah, he'd be happy too."

I open the box again and pass the stack of notebooks and papers to Eli, revealing neat rows of seeds in mini glass jars.

As I hold up each jar, I compare it with the photo—none match. I glance up at Nico. "None of these are remotely similar."

I watch as Nico's face falls. He kneels on the ground next to me and inspects each jar, comparing them to the photo on my phone, and double-checking. "Nope, none are a match." Him being close sends butterflies rushing around my chest. His arm brushes mine as he reaches for the rolled-up maps, darting me a look before he unravels them, checking each before rolling it back up and moving on to another.

Nico secures the corner of the last map on the ground with a stone. Dad's tracks are color coded with the species of plants he found at each. I run my finger down the list of plant names he identified. In Dad's handwriting: *Refer to ID Book Three.* I find ID BOOK THREE and flick through the pages, each dedicated to one plant. Nico glances over my shoulder.

"There's no page for the species I found at Highmont," I say, "but this one is very similar." I hold the page toward Nico. "Different species, same seed shape."

His face is inches from mine. I feel him watch me for a split second, but when I look at him, he flicks his focus away.

"Oh, wait …," Nico says. He races to the hut door and disappears inside before returning with the jar of seeds from the top of the fireplace. He bends down next to me. Holding out my phone, I show him the photo of the collected seeds at Highmont.

"They're identical, apart from these being much larger," he says, looking through the bottom of the jar. "And there's a thicker line of that mustard color."

"That's the common variety. It's thick up in those unmarked tracks," Mr. Balducci says. He reads aloud from Dad's notes: "*No sign of* Carmichaelia carmichaeliae, *last sighting 1906*." His voice trails off, etched with disappointment. "Your dad didn't find any evidence of its existence up here."

Deep down, I already knew the answer. If Dad had found critically endangered seeds up here, he would have mentioned it, and I would have remembered.

The reality hits—there really is nothing that can be done to save the hut or the forest.

Eli rests his hand on my shoulder. I hug him. "It was a long shot, but we tried," he says gently, letting me go.

Nico walks off into the forest behind the hut and, unseen, I follow him, leaving the others behind. The trees stretch for miles. He sits down on a log and peers up at the sky. He quit law to follow his dream of setting up his mountain-bike business, and I've been partly to blame for destroying that dream.

He still hasn't seen me. Light filters through the treetops. Sparrows and fantails flit from branch to branch.

"I really am sorry." Nico flinches, like he didn't expect me to follow him.

"I'll go if you don't want to see me."

He faces me and shrugs, then resumes staring at the trees.

"It's not that," he says. "Why does it feel like I'm saying goodbye all over again to Mom and Dad?" He pauses, his back still turned. "Their helicopter crashed here. It was supposed to land in the parking lot, but it was windy."

I remember the story. It's why there's a random gap in the forest; it's why Nico wanted to picnic under the trees in this spot on my birthday—because he knew I'd understand. He knew it meant a lot to both of us, and he wanted to share that with someone who got it.

I rest next to him on the log. He finally faces me for longer than a second, grief and sadness etched into his eyes.

"I really do love the mountain-bike tour business," he says. "It makes me happy and excited to get up every morning, but sometimes, this spot makes it hard, you know."

"I know." I've not seen this side of him, and I realize I feel at peace because even though the forest and Dad's legacy will be gone, and I may never accept it, and it will always carry a heavy weight, I can move forward.

"Law sucked, huh?" Concern spreads across his face. The way he's looking at me—it's like he understands how it took my life being turned upside down to finally see the right path, because he's been through the same thing.

Nico stretches his legs out in front of him, crossing one ankle over the other.

"Law like, *really* did suck," I say, wishing there wasn't a person-sized gap wedged between us. "How stupid was I to think I'd like a job that means being stuck inside most of the time?"

His focus catches mine. "Ha, I came to the same conclusion." He smiles, and it's big and beautiful, and even though I've seen it before, it's like the view from the picnic table—it's breathtaking every time, no matter how many times I've seen it. I search his face and smile back.

My shoulders drop, and I huff out, "It's hard to be here, and it's hard to let this place go."

He looks at me, puzzled. "Maybe change isn't a bad thing, even if it appears wrong at the start." He says it like he's not believing his own words, but trying to. "I'm thinking of moving Nico's Bike Tours to Ambleton. There are a ton more flat trails suitable for beginners up there. There's not enough people interested in bike tours for the expert trails, ya know? And they're expensive," he adds. "Most locals don't have the money, or they're able to ride them without help."

I glance at him. I want to beg him not to go. Ambleton is four hours away, and a bigger tourist town, so I understand his reasoning for wanting to move there.

I turn toward him, then face the trees. "I'd miss you so much."

Eli's voice comes from behind. "Hey, sis, ready to go?"

Nico rises from the log. "Yeah, we should get going too." Without looking at me or saying goodbye, he leaves.

Eli rests on the log next to me, looking back at Nico as he walks off. "How'd it go?"

"He's talking to me, at least. I guess that's all I can ask. I can tell he doesn't feel the same, though."

Eli stands up and rests one hand on my shoulder. "Let's go. We can stuff our faces with emotional support—Pinkie Pies in the car."

When Eli and I get back to the car, Nico's van is gone.

I wait for Mr. Balducci in front of the community college. The new purpose-built building sits amongst sustainably planted gardens that

Mr. Balducci designed. He's always taught a few classes for the certificate in landscape design, but when the program was expanded to offer a degree course, Mr. Balducci was offered a permanent part-time lecturing spot.

A Balducci Landscape Design truck pulls up next to me, as I wait in Eli's car. "Izzy," he says, his voice tipped with excitement. "I'm so happy to be showing you around."

He locks his truck and immediately leads me through the main building. It's single-story and open-plan, with a pitched roof, light streaming through floor-to-ceiling windows. There are plants everywhere, hanging from the roof, in giant pots surrounding the administration desk, and in groups by the windows.

"It's stunning," I say to Mr. Balducci, as he watches me admire the plants.

"But wait, there's more." He grins, and leads me through to the administration hub, passing a café that looks over a manmade pond. Tables sprawl onto the newly planted green space, packed with students studying.

We follow a path to three giant greenhouses in the distance.

"So, have you spoken with Nico recently?" Mr. Balducci asks, looking ahead rather than at me. His question comes as a surprise, and is outside the scope of our usual conversation.

I sigh. "Not since giving him the key at the lake hut."

He looks at me with concern. "You know …," he says as we walk through an arch planted with creepers. Their leaves are small now, but soon will overtake the structure, forming a tunnel of greenery. I wait patiently for him to continue. "He's not been the same since things fell apart between you two, and Mrs. Wilson has asked if you and he can be permanently placed working on her garden together. Do you think you two could make it work?"

I suck in air. "Of course. Did Nico say he couldn't? I know I can make it work. I mean, I'm sure, definitely sure I can put aside everything and … sorry, I'm rambling." I pause. My words are flustered. I continue anyway. "But if he'd rather not work together, I'm happy to work on another project." My words are tight. I do my best to force a smile that Mr. Balducci won't see through.

"Are you sure you can work together?" he says.

"Yeah, of course."

"Well, all right then."

We reach the greenhouse, and Mr. Balducci slides open the doors. "Welcome to your classroom."

Inside, waist-high wooden benches sit in groups, and trays of seedlings of every size, color, and shape fill the spaces by the windows. Larger plants—natives and exotics—sit in pots in habitat groups around the room.

A tweeting sound catches my attention and flips my focus to the roof, where there are three hanging birdhouses.

Mr. Balducci laughs. "They were supposed to be decorative. It turns out we have pets, and no one has the heart to evict them."

A starling pops its head out of the hole and then disappears back in.

"And seeing as it will snow soon, and they have fledglings—totally out of season, silly birds—anyway, we will let them stay the winter and then release them."

"Aww, they're adorable."

Mr. Balducci takes me to the back of the classroom and through a door that reads *Ruben Rivers Seed Bank*. I immediately tear up. "Thank you," I say, "for naming it after Dad."

"Welcome," Mr. Balducci says.

Inside, the windows are darkened with curtains, and the walls are lined with drawers with neatly printed labels. Each drawer contains a family of seeds.

"If you approve," Mr. Balducci continues, "your dad's seed collection could be shifted here, and we can categorize, identify, and store them to museum standards."

"Yes." I huff out air. "Dad would love this; I'll double-check with Mom and Eli." I launch a hug on Mr. Balducci. "Thank you. This means everything." The forest may go, and the lake hut, but Dad's legacy will live on teaching the next plant-loving generation.

Mr. Balducci and I wander about the new park-like grounds until we reach the perimeter and the hub for the helicopter pilot course. There's a helipad, and rows of choppers sit in a hangar. A pilot hops in a chopper with storage racks attached to the landing skids; the propellers spin and the air vibrates, taking me right back to the moment Nico was rescued off the bike track.

"What do they store on the racks?" I ask Mr. Balducci.

"Sometimes fertilizer for farmers; medic supplies, bikes, anything really."

And a crazy idea pops into my mind, but I push it aside.

Mr. Balducci and I head back to my car. Then I go home and spend the afternoon filling out my enrollment information for the Landscape Design degree program, followed by a movie marathon, including re-watching *Jaws* with Penny and Eli.

At five a.m. I sneak into Eli's bedroom, gently shaking his arm. "Eli, gotta talk to you about something. It's important."

"WTF?" he grumbles. His eyes pop open. "Are you on something?" He rolls over.

I shake his shoulder. "I need your advice. Please—it's about Mom."

He sits up. "Mom? Is she okay?"

"Sorry to worry you, Mom's fine. I have an idea to run past her, but it kinda involves you too, and won't save the forest or the hut but has something to do with it."

"Would you stop with the lengthy exposition and just get to the point?"

"The apartment subdivision is really for international tourists, right? And half of the apartments have sold, right?"

Eli sits up, raking his hand through his hair, which is at odd angles. "Correct and correct … where are you going with this?"

I sit on the edge of his bed, forcing him to scoot over. "Wait, I'll swing back to that. Mom and Mike have been working with the local tourist board and council to encourage more international tourists to Rockridge, right?"

He rolls his eyes. "Would you get to the point?"

"What if Nico set up his mountain-bike tours in collaboration with Helitours? And had his office and workshop at the apartment complex. Nico could sell his bike tours and collaborate with the helicopter business. It would help Nico out and add another attractive reason to stay at the apartments."

Eli rolls his eyes again. "Does Nico know about this?"

"No." I take a sip of coffee from my cactus cup.

"Do Mom and Mike know about your idea?"

I glug more coffee. "No."

"You're crazy. They'll never go for it."

I shove my open laptop on his lap. "Look—data the council collected shows huge demand for luxury accommodations plus packaged mountain-bike tours and heli flights. See? The survey says it, right here, in the council document." I tap the part on the screen.

"How long have you been up, and how much coffee have you drunk?"

"Two hours' sleep and I'm running off adrenaline and cactus coffee." I hold up my portable cactus tumbler. Its capacity is three pints.

"You're wired, tired, and crazy, but …" He pauses and reads the documents. The wait for his opinion is agonizing.

"Shit, you might be onto something. The stats stack up. You're not wrong. The research is all there. But convincing Mom will be easier than convincing Nico."

"That's why I need your help, with Mom. I'll deal with Nico. Somehow."

"Mike loves mountain biking, right?"

"Yes."

Eli doesn't seem to like where this is heading.

"And he loves Mom, right?" I say.

"It really does appear that way. What are you getting at?"

He pulls my cactus cup from my grip, and slugs back my coffee, screwing his face up. "Gross, it's cold."

"If you leave it long enough, it turns to iced coffee—win, win. Anyway, I'll pitch it to Mom and Mike, and I want you to back me up," I say, snatching my coffee back out of his grip.

"Err, you know this is not guaranteed to make Nico forgive you. It could backfire, big time."

"I know, but I owe it to him to try."

"And, Izz, his parents died in a heli crash. You don't think that's opening up wounds?"

"You got me there, I don't know, I can't help but think it might be the kind of thing that could set him free. I'll talk to him first, then Mom."

Eli pushes me out of bed. "Good plan. Stop with the coffee, you're acting crazy. And close the door behind you, I'm trying to sleep."

"Sure, sure."

Twenty-Eight

Next morning I'm woken by Rex standing on my chest; his chubby, poofy face peers down. Like it's his ultimatum. If I don't feed him ASAP, he'll sink his teeth into my nose and gnaw it right off. I set him down on the windowsill. He squeezes outside and walks along the eaves and onto the roof, then sits facing the view of the forested valley, which is blanketed in a hard frost.

Before mentioning my heli-bike-tour idea to Nico, I thought it was best to sleep on it. It's also given Mom and Mike the chance to digest the concept, after I launched it on them yesterday. And it's given me a chance to think about whether it really is a good idea to mention it to Nico, given his parents died in a helicopter crash.

Later, in the kitchen, Mom and Mike sit at the table glued to their laptops. "Coffee?" I offer, pushing a pod into the espresso machine.

Neither Mike nor Mom answers my question.

I pick up Mom's empty mug from the table, pausing at her laptop, open on the Helitours web page. I switch focus to Mike's screen, and he's on the council website reading health and safety regulations.

"You're considering the idea?" I say, my voice tipped with excitement.

Mike and Mom glance at each other. "To be honest, we had thought of something similar, but we think your idea is better," Mom says. "Research from Rockridge Tourism does clearly show international visitors want more luxury accommodation options—" she leans into Mike and playfully smiles "—tick. And prepackaged tours, mountain biking, and guided forest walks—heli tours, for example." She's grinning at me and it's freaking me out. Is she happy?

A tug of worry catches in my chest that this is not a good idea and Nico will see it as a constant daily reminder of what happened to his parents.

As I stand by the kitchen bench zoned out sipping coffee, Rex weaves between my legs and then sinks his teeth into my ankle. "Gah!"

Mom and Mike jump with fright, snapping their eyes from their gridlock hold on their screens. "Oh my god, Izzy, what was that about?"

Reaching into the pantry, I grab Rex's kibble and tip some into his bowl.

Maybe the mountain-bike heli tours are a way to move forward—a brutal way, I'll admit. I'm reminded of the tattoo on Nico's wrist, marking the anniversary of his parents' death. And how he said it was the date he chose to move forward and no longer be held back. Maybe he might see this as an opportunity.

"You all right, Izz?" Mom says. "You look kinda lost, staring into space." She jumps up and gives me a playful hug.

"Yeah, I'm all good."

Mom is using cutting the forest to move past the hurt of losing Dad. I one thousand percent don't agree with her method. But maybe losing the forest can be both bad and good. Monumental grief over losing what was, and simultaneously a catalyst forcing us to move forward toward healing.

I take my coffee to the front porch and sit on the step. Frost blankets our yard; the rising sun glistens off tiny ice crystals.

I draft a text to Nico. It takes no less than a thousand rewrites before I decide on a version and hit send: *Are you free to meet me at the lake today at four? I have something to ask you.*

And then I stare at my phone for a ridiculously long time, hoping for a reply. Maybe I should follow the advice I preached to Eli, about Penny, about him telling her how he really feels. He's right, it's better to say something and get shot down than do nothing and live with regret.

Nico will be at Mrs. Wilson's, and I dream up a million excuses why he may not have replied. There's a burst pipe situation he's dealing with, he's out of data, or he's in a valley with no reception. But I come back to the most likely—that his feelings for me took such a U-turn when he found out what I did that there's no chance of ever getting him back.

By nine, I'm at Gardening Depot, waiting in line for my coffee from the quaint coffee cart that sits in the parking lot. I have everything I need to start the landscape design course next week, including the engraved pruning shears that Nico gave me.

The barista passes me my drink, and I wander inside, aimlessly strolling up and down the rows of plants.

I love Penny to the ends of the Earth, but my heart literally sinks into the ground when I see her name pop up and not Nico's.

Penny: *Yo, any message from him?*

Me: *No.*

Penny: *So something weird happened.*

Me: *Err, do tell.*

Penny: *These were sent to me at work without a note. From you?*

And she's attached a picture of two tickets to Fanfic Con.

Me to Eli: *So you sent her tickets to fanfic con, cool, but no note to say who they're from. That doesn't count as telling her how you feel.*

Eli: *She'll get it.*

Me: *Not so sure.*

Me to Penny: *Err, not me.*

Penny: *Okay, just double checking it wasn't you before I get my hopes up about who might have sent them.*

Me to Penny: *So you know who it's from, and you're happy?*

Penny: *Yes!!!!!!!!!!!!!!! Times a million.*

Then she sends a screenshot of a message conversation between her and Eli. Eli's text message to Penny reads: *Lol. Those tickets are so expensive. I'd only be buying them for someone I was madly in love with.*

Me to Penny: *Awww, you two are cute.*

Penny: *Next time I see your brother, I'm gonna kiss him and tell him I love him. Damn having to work.*

Me to Penny: *Okay, too much detail ;)*

I aimlessly browse the aisles of plants for ages before choosing nothing to buy, because I can't think straight. I drive to the botanical gardens. I don't go in, but sit under a willow tree by the river and stare into the water. I check my phone, but there's no reply from Nico. And one of those stupid memes that I see floating on Instagram comes to mind.

If he wanted to, he would.

At home, I lie on my bed for the afternoon, listening to a podcast recommended for the landscape design course, on sustainable urban gardens. I flip through the course notes. But I can't focus on the words or what's playing, my mind always skipping back to wanting Nico. On how I can't handle that we ended before we began. And I'd do anything to get what we had back. The way he used to look at me, how my skin tingled when he touched me, the flutters of nerves from just seeing him. And the way it felt when he kissed me and our bare stomachs pressed together.

Me to Penny: *Movie? Nothing romantic.*

Penny: *Has he replied?*

Me: *No. I think he's lost any feelings for me. He would if he wanted to, right?*

Penny: *Yes and no. I'm in for the movies. Meet you there at four.*

Me: *Yup, let's get takeout after and a giant tub of ben and jerry's.*

Penny: *Classic, I'm here for ya.*

I wait outside the movie theatre for Penny. She's fashionably late. Traffic whizzes past and streams of people rush into the cinema.

My phone beeps and I assume it's Penny telling me she's running late.

Nico: *Sorry for the late reply. Meet you in twenty?*

"Yesss." I huff the air out and thrust my phone to my chest.

A group of teens waiting outside the cinema slide me a weird look. I don't care. A rush of nervousness grips my chest. I breathe in and let out another drawn-out breath. Mocking laughter erupts from my watchers.

Me to Nico: *Cool, see you there.*

I'm trying my hardest not to overhype his message. To not add more meaning to it than he intends. He's agreed to meet, that's it. It doesn't mean he wants me back.

But that does nothing to stop my mind from jumping to make-believe situations where it ends with Nico kissing me like it's what he wanted to do all this time.

Me to Eli: *So, here's the thing. I'm waiting for Penny to meet me at the movies. Nico asked if I would meet him up at the lake. Now.*

Eli: *On my way.*

Me to Penny: *I'm so sorry, Nico replied. We're meeting at the lake. But someone else is meeting you at the movies. Please don't hate me.*

Penny: *You're meeting Nico?????*

Penny: *Who's meeting me? Better not be yo Mom, cos I'll be pissed.*

Me: *Trust me, you'll be happy.*

I drive to the lake. By the time I get there, the sun is setting. I park up next to Nico's van and see flames flicking from a bonfire on the shore right next to the jetty. And I spot Nico sitting on a log.

I wander over to Nico. The flames pop and crackle, the heat radiating on my face.

"Hey," I say. I take a seat on the weathered tree trunk opposite him, on the other side of the fire. I hate how it feels impersonal and formal.

"Hey," he says. "It's a beautiful night."

The stars hang low in thick mass over the lake, the hut, and the sprawling forest behind us.

"I can't believe all this will be gone in a few days. It just feels weird," he says.

A pang of guilt grips me. "I'm so sorry. I'm going to miss it too."

He glances out over the lake, and an awkward silence follows. The flames lick into the sky, and I dig the tip of my shoe into the rocks. When he darts his focus back to me, all the words I want to say are right there, desperate to gush out—how much I've missed him, and how much he means to me—but I tug them back, fearful he doesn't feel the same.

"I'm so sorry about Nico's Bike Tours, truly."

He avoids my eyes and looks out across the lake.

"I will forever regret that I was part of ruining that for you."

"You know," he says, finally meeting my gaze, "the Ambleton council have agreed to let me use their forestry plantation until it's felled."

"Oh, that's good." I'm lying. Ambleton is four hours away, and he'd have to move, and once the plantation was cut, he'd have to start all over.

"Yeah, it's an option, I guess," he says. He raises his eyebrows. "You had something you wanted to ask me?"

The way he darts his focus to me and then away, and how I can't pick his expression anymore because it's different. Unreadable. It makes me more nervous.

"Do you want to walk?" I ask.

We wander toward the jetty, side by side. I thought it would feel easier to be actively moving, walking next to him, but as our hands dangle aimlessly beside each other, it feels worse than before. All I want is for him to grab my hand and pull me close.

"So, what did you want to talk about?" he asks. The water laps at our feet; Nico picks up a stone and skims it. Moonlight shimmers, catching just enough of the stone to see three bumps along the water until it sinks.

I pick up a stone and try to skim it. It sinks immediately, with a plop.

Nico searches through the stones in front of us, picks a thinner and flatter gray rock and passes it to me. "Now try," he says, standing behind me.

My heart races with how close he is. Gripping the stone, I swing my arm back when he catches my wrist. His fingers grip it gently. "Release the stone *here*," he says, and he tugs my arm, shifting it into the right position.

"Right, thanks," I say. He releases his grip and the warmth from his fingers vanishes from my wrist.

I try again, this time releasing the rock exactly where he suggested. It glides over the water, skipping once, twice, before it slides in.

"I did it! Oh my god, that was perfect." I don't try to hide my smile.

He grins, and I can't unsee it. It's a tiny spark of what it was like before, and it lights all my nerve endings and leaves me craving more.

We continue to wander along the lakefront. A cool breeze gently blows off the water, swaying my hair in different directions. Nico walks with his hands sunk into the front pocket of his black *Nico's Mountain Bike Tours* hoodie.

"Thank you for meeting me," I say.

"You had something you wanted to talk about?" he repeats.

We reach the jetty and begin slowly edging our way along the wooden planks that lead far out into the lake. The sky is inky blue; the moon has a halo of light and the stars pop, almost like you could reach up and grab them. It's silent, apart from the water gently lapping against the jetty pilings, and the sound of our footsteps.

"So, I had this idea, and it's totally cool if you hate it."

We reach the end of the jetty and stand on the edge, facing each other, nowhere to go apart from back the way we came. I can't leave, not without him knowing I want a chance to be with him. Not without telling him about the Helitours idea.

He's staring at me, patiently waiting for me to get the words out. The way he's smiling, the way his broad shoulders perfectly fill his hoodie, and how much I want him to take his hands out of his pockets and wrap them around my waist, catch me a little off guard.

I tear my eyes away and focus on the water. "What if you joined up with the Helitours company and worked in collaboration with them to offer guided mountain-bike tours, using here as a base?"

I can feel the weight of him looking at me, but I can't look at him before I get all the words out. What I'm asking could be seen as insensitive and uncaring, considering the way his parents died, and I hope he trusts me enough to know that would never be my intention.

"I know it doesn't solve the problem of the learner tracks for kids, but you could use the flat bit of forest you planted for Dad—I know it's not perfect, it's a bit of a ride for young kids to get there, but it could work. I'd help you dig in the trails. I know Eli and Penny would too." I pause. "Gosh, sorry, I'm rambling."

I take in a deep breath of lake air, hoping he'll reply. And now it's silent. We stand side by side saying absolutely nothing.

I try to make out the pontoon in the distance. "You mean so much to me. I feel more alive with you than with anyone, and you're definitely the first guy I ever loved." My voice quivers. I swallow hard to stop the tears from flowing. I don't want him to know how caught up in this moment I am. How hard it will be to walk the length of that jetty, knowing he's watching and doesn't feel the same.

Nico turns and takes a step toward me.

"Loved? Like, past tense?" He takes another step. Now we're face-to-face; any closer and our noses would touch.

"Correction," I say, looking into his eyes, trying to read his expression. "Love. So, present tense."

He's searching my face now, and my heart is running wild, tripping over my nerves.

"Oh, I see," he says. "And FYI, two things." He grins, still standing close. "One: the reason I didn't reply earlier to your message was because I was in a business meeting with Mike and your mom, and they pitched me a proposal that was too good to refuse." He inches closer; the tips of his shoes touch mine. I glance at our feet.

"And the second thing?" I say.

"I love you too."

I flip my focus from our feet to his face.

He grabs my hand, pulls me into him and kisses me, soft and gentle. I glide one arm around his back and rest the other on his shoulder.

"Is it weird I want to swim?" Nico asks, his hands resting on the small of my back, pulling me close.

"Is it weird I thought you'd never ask?"

We rip off our jackets and t-shirts and jeans and dive in. I glide through the pitch black; the freezing water rushes past my skin until my face pops through the surface of the water. Nico slides his arm around me, pressing our bare stomachs together. I hook my legs around his waist, and he kisses me, this time not so softly, but purposefully, under the night sky, drifting in the lake.

Twenty-Nine

One year later

I wait for Nico outside the landscape-design building, clutching my laptop bag. The ground glistens with the season's first snow.

Nico pulls up in his black van and winds his window down. "How was it?"

"Another exam done and I think I nailed it."

An emoticon-like smile spreads across his face. "I knew ya would."

He glances at the stone wall he and Mr. Balducci built. *ROCKRIDGE COMMUNITY COLLEGE LANDSCAPE DESIGN* is etched into the stone. Dotted around the expansive green grass are Dad's trees that we dug up from his forest behind the lake hut and translocated. They will grow to form shaded spots for students to sit under and study, or cuddle with their significant others.

"They're looking awesome. Healthy too."

"It's a perfect day for flying," I say, adjusting my woolly hat and opening the mountain-bike bag I stashed in Nico's work van.

We drive toward the lake; snow dusts the foothills. I pull off my jeans, roll on my tights, and put my mountain-bike shorts on, then layer on warm tops.

We pull up outside Nico's office on the bottom floor of the sprawling apartment complex. The apartments overlook the lake and sit where Dad's forest used to be, stretching to a new tree line far in the distance.

The rotors of a helicopter disturb the air as it appears in the sky and settles on the helipad in the old parking lot.

Penny and Eli wait outside Nico's office, already in their mountain-bike gear.

Nico unloads the bikes, and one by one he runs them to the helicopter, attaching two bikes on each side of the carrier racks.

He returns, beaming a smile. "You lot ready?" He grips my hand and pulls me into him, kissing my forehead.

"Hey, I made you some snacks," Mom yells, running out of her office with a container and flask. "Chocolate brownies."

Through the clear box, in a stack in the corner, are Pinkie Pie chocolate bars.

"Thanks, Mom." I launch a hug at her.

"Be safe, sweetheart—all of you." And she passes each of us a smile, in the way that she used to.

Pickles weaves around Mom's legs, having escaped Nico's office. Mom scoops her up, ruffles the fur on her head. "You little runaway," she says, gripping her into her chest. "You are staying with me, yes you are." And she waves as she goes back into her office.

Penny laughs. "Looks like ya Mom has taken over your boyfriend's dog."

"Ha ha, she's obsessed, gets her treats and bones from the supermarket and everything," I say.

"Ha." Nico laughs. "That's nothing—you should see the Christmas jacket she got her. It has a fuzzy hood. Okay, let's go."

Eli and Penny follow us, arguing about whether the helicopter blades run anticlockwise or clockwise.

We take our places in the helicopter. It rises into the air, the rotor blades whirring as it lifts over the apartment subdivision, rising up and over the lake and the forested valleys below, heading toward the snow-capped peaks.

Nico wraps his arm around me, and I point to the new sections of the forest we've planted, including the one Nico started on my birthday and the sections where we translocated Dad's trees from behind the lake hut.

The helicopter lifts higher as we fly beyond the far reaches of the lake, eventually landing at the highest point in Rockridge. The rotor blades stop and we get out, taking in the view. Snow blankets the ridge; below us is the only snow-free area, where the carved-out mountain-bike trail starts and winds down for miles until it reaches the tree line leading back to the apartment complex.

Nico faces me, his arm still around me. "Ready for some downhill?"

"Yup, I'll race ya." And I kiss him.

When he pulls away, he says, "You know that my bag is basically filled with one giant first aid kit?" He drops his voice to a whisper, and purposefully catches Penny's attention. "She's a clumsy one."

"Oi, I heard that," Penny says, laughing and batting Nico's arm.

"You probably don't want to say that, since she just graduated from your mountain-bike skills course," I say. "Not a good look."

"True, true." He laughs.

Nico unloads the bikes from the chopper, and the four of us ride through new sections of forest, and old. And on our way down, we stop periodically and scatter a small handful of Dad's seeds. When the snow melts, they'll sink their roots into the earth and eventually grow tall until they bloom, setting their seed to start the cycle again.

About the Author

BELLEBIRD JAMES is the author of The Art of Loving Libby Green and Bloom. She lives in Nelson, New Zealand, with her husband, two children, and an excessively hairy dog named Sir Fluffy Pants. Coffee enthusiast, sun chaser, and recovering chocolate fish addict. When Bellebird's not reading or writing, she can be found hurtling down a mountain-bike trail (badly).

bellebirdjames.com
Intstagram: @bellebirdjames
Tiktok: @bellebirdjames

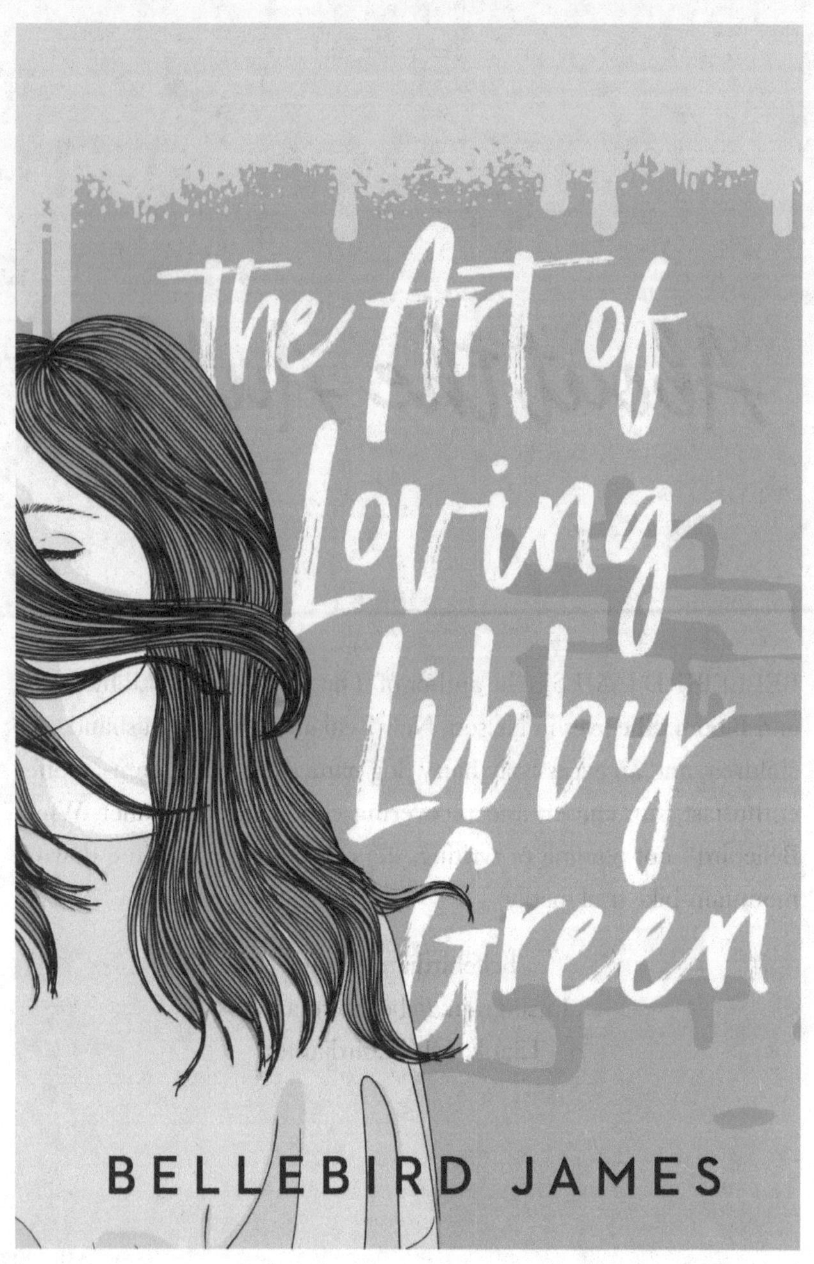

The Art of
Loving
Libby
Green
BELLEBIRD JAMES

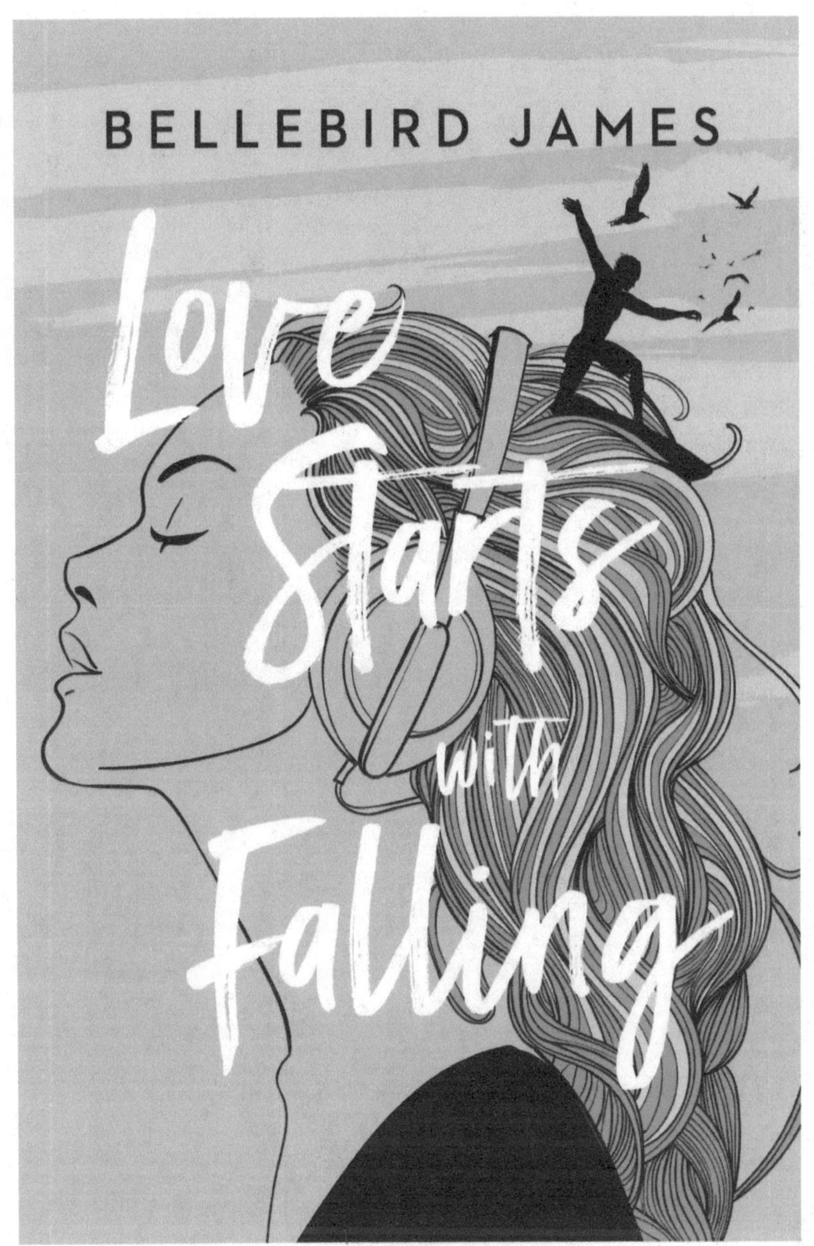

BELLEBIRD JAMES
Love Starts with Falling

www.ingramcontent.com/pod-product-compliance
Lightning Source LLC
Chambersburg PA
CBHW011210190726
48288CB00013B/3395